A WISH FOR JO

AUDREY DAVIS

For my Family

CHAPTER 1

'You have got to be kidding me!' Jo Milligan took another reluctant bite from the slice of still-warm Victoria sponge, then wrinkled her nose in disgust and tossed the piece of cake in the bin. 'Salt instead of sugar!'

Rinsing her mouth with a glass of tap water, Jo paused before picking up a mini quiche she'd removed from the oven minutes before. Taking a deep breath, she nibbled an edge of the pastry, and—

'Give me strength!' The quiche followed the sponge into the bin.

Jo grabbed a piece of kitchen towel to wipe away a smear on her glasses, rubbing vigorously at the greasy spot. A little *too* vigorously, as the frame split and the lens plopped onto the floor.

'This is seriously not my day,' grumbled Jo, bending down to pick up the lens. Her back twinged alarmingly, bringing back memories of the excruciating pain she'd suffered six months ago after wrangling with a fitted bed sheet. Ten physio sessions and some serious drugs later, she needed a repeat episode like the proverbial hole in the head.

The door to A Bit of Crumpet opened, signalling Jo's first customer of the day. An icy blast of air swirled through the café, and she straightened up with a smile. It wasn't a regular, though, but a man she'd never seen before, standing in the doorway and letting the cold lower the temperature of her cosy business.

'Would you mind…?' Jo made a close-the-door gesture. Her customer scowled, pocketed the phone he'd been staring at, and with a sound somewhere between a snort and a groan, slammed the door. Hard. Jo's 'Open/Closed' sign clattered against the glass, and she fixed him with an arctic glare befitting the outside temperature.

Without a word, Mystery Man strode to the counter. For a moment Jo wondered if he was about to whip a stocking over his face, pull a gun, and demand she empty the till. Except that she'd already seen his face — attractive, if craggy and the opposite of happy — and at a little after nine in the morning, the till held a few pound coins and some loose change.

'I'll have a coffee. Black, no sugar. And a slice of that.' He pointed at the remains of the Victoria sponge, which looked appealing but tasted like something that had marinated in the ocean.

'Please wouldn't kill you,' muttered Jo, tipping beans into the machine. Tempted as she was to serve a slice of salted sponge to Mr Obnoxious, she didn't want to alienate him further. Not that *she'd* done anything wrong. He was probably a passing tourist, though Cranley didn't attract hordes of visitors, despite its proximity to Edinburgh.

'Did you say something?' Her customer eyed her suspiciously. Jo noted a silvery scar running down his left cheek, and pock marks that suggested a run-in with acne.

'Just talking to the coffee machine,' she replied. *Which has better manners than you.* 'This cake's not up to standard, but I have a very nice chocolate roulade right here.' Jo uncovered the leftovers from yesterday's successful baking session and prepared to carve a slice.

'I don't do chocolate.'

What kind of weirdo doesn't do chocolate? Jo rubbed her back, her usually upbeat mood taking a downward turn.She needed to head into the back room and get some things off her chest, before…

'Just coffee, then. I'll be over here.' He walked to a table in the corner and lowered himself into a chair. Jo saw him wince and felt a bit of sympathy, which quickly evaporated when he demanded to know how long the coffee would take. 'I haven't got all day,' he huffed, wiping down the spotless table with a napkin.

'Nearly ready,' Jo replied sweetly, fighting the urge to lace his drink with a salt/sugar combo. As the machine signalled the coffee was ready, the door opened again and in strode Janette Cameron, formidable boss of the local post office cum corner shop. Never short of an opinion, solicited or otherwise, she nodded toward the other customer before approaching Jo.

'How are you, hen?' Janette shrugged off her coat, a hideous blue fake-fur creation that brought to mind the Cookie Monster.

'Good, Janette. All good,' said Jo, pouring the coffee and taking it over to the not-so-welcome newcomer. He barely acknowledged her, his attention gripped by his phone.

'Well, I'm fair puggled. Workin' full-time isn't what I imagined I'd be doing when I turned seventy— Sixty-five, I mean. I should be resting my bones at home, not weighing poxy packages and listening to old dears wittering on about their support stockings and incontinence problems.'

Jo stifled a laugh. Until about a year ago, Janette had been a card-carrying member of the Crimplene and sensible footwear brigade. Since discovering the delights of Primark in the city, she'd gone all plunging tops, cleavage-enhancing bras, and shoes Lady Gaga would struggle to walk in.

'What can I get you, lovely?' Jo returned to the counter, knowing Janette's fondness for savoury pastries and tea so dark it needed a hefty scrub to remove the stain from the mug.

'Ooh, one of thae Cornish thingies will do nicely. I know I have them for sale at the shop, but they're tough as old boots. You widnae need a mace spray to fend off a mugger if you had one of those buggers in your hand!' Janette chortled, her ample bosom jiggling like two ferrets slugging it out in a sack.

Jo fixed Janette's order. She glanced over at the stranger, now typing furiously on his phone and muttering under his breath. 'To go, or are you eating here?' she asked Janette.

'Ach, better pop it in a bag. Much as I'd love to stay for a natter, I've put up the *Closed for now* sign. You can bet your life savings someone'll be huffing on the doorstep, needing a stamp or a pound of pick 'n' mix.'

Jo bagged the pastry and accepted a handful of loose change. Janette turned to leave, then hesitated. 'Is the wee lass no' working today?' she asked. 'Not that customers are clamouring for your cakes and cuppas, eh?'

Jo glanced at the door to the back room. 'Erm, she's … busy. Doing a bit of a stocktake.' The faint sound of pop music emanated from within, and Jo suppressed a sigh.

'Well, you take care, hen. If I come across any hungry souls with cash to spare, I'll send them your way.' Janette headed for the door, waggling her fingers at the stranger as she left. He gave her a look usually reserved for the discovery of dog poo on your shoe, then returned to his phone.

'Can I get you anything else?' Jo approached his table, noting the coffee was barely touched.

'How much?' he growled, his cobalt-blue eyes shifting from Jo's face to the threadbare wallet he'd dragged from his equally well-worn coat pocket.

'Two pounds fifty,' Jo replied, stunned at his rudeness. She prayed he was just passing through and hadn't moved to Cranley.

Without so much as a smile, the stranger banged down a five-pound note and got to his feet. 'Keep the change.' Before Jo could respond, he levered himself out of the chair with another grimace of pain.

'Well, bye then. Lovely to meet you,' Jo said to the door he'd just slammed again, stunned at such a blatant display of bad manners. An overly generous tip didn't compensate for being so horrible.

Still reeling, Jo poured herself a generous mug of coffee. Inhaling the comforting aroma, she realised that the music in the back room had grown louder. With a very familiar backing singer...

'Aaliyah!' Jo yelled at the top of her voice, competing with the discordant noise two feet away. 'Get your lazy, useless rear out here right now!'

CHAPTER 2

'Keep your hair on.' Aaliyah emerged, blowing on newly painted fingernails. Or, to be more accurate, lethal talons that could carve up a cake more efficiently than Edward Scissorhands. 'What's all the fuss about?'

Jo regarded her 'assistant' with a combination of frustration and disbelief. The latter still lingered, two weeks after Aaliyah's unorthodox appearance in Jo's life. The former... Well, suffice to say that Aaliyah would never make the grade on the *Great British Bake Off.* Less Mary Berry, more Mary Shelley, with a knack of putting the monstrous into muffins.

'You mixed up salt and sugar, resulting in completely inedible Victoria sponge and quiche,' said Jo. 'It's not blinking rocket science, Aaliyah.' Her simmering anger rose in temperature as she took in the colour of Aaliyah's nails. 'Is that my nail polish?'

'Might be,' replied Aaliyah, flapping her hands around like a demented seal. 'I didn't think you'd mind, seeing as you've got like hundreds of different ones.'

That's a slight exaggeration. Jo liked to treat herself to the odd funky colour when she ventured into the capital. She'd been particularly taken by the ocean blue currently sported by Aaliyah. 'Audaciously Alice' was its name, a quirky title which sat alongside 'Perversely Pink' and 'Defiantly Damson' on her dressing table. The dressing table in Jo's bedroom, which Aaliyah had been told not to enter.

'And I've told you repeatedly that you need to cover your hair with a net when you're baking,' added Jo. 'Customers don't want to be picking strands of it out of their cakes.'

Aaliyah swung her ebony pigtail over her shoulder. 'Alreet, pet, calm your jets. It's bad enough I have to wear *this*' — she swept her hands dismissively down the cotton apron embroidered with the café's logo — 'never mind put that horrible fish-catching thing on my head.'

Jo wondered, not for the first time, how long she could keep this charade going. Why, oh why, had she bought those stupid lamps from Sam Addin? And as for Jinnie Cooper, she'd be having a word with her when she returned from her holiday.

'Aaliyah, you're supposed to be making chocolate-chip cookie dough and the filling for the sausage rolls. This is a café, not a beauty parlour. Come with me.' Jo steered Aaliyah into the back room, ignoring her grumbles. 'Here's the sugar' — Jo pointed at the enormous container with 'sugar' written in bold text — 'and this is the salt. Do *not* mix them up again!' Hearing customers, Jo left Aaliyah to it, praying she wouldn't add a dollop of minced meat to the cookie dough.

'Morning!' She smiled at Ed McCroarty and his girl-friend, Angela, looking as loved-up as ever. 'What can I tempt you with on this chilly day?'

'Ooh, do you have any of that fabulous treacle tart?' asked Angela, tugging off her beanie hat. 'Or carrot cake? I need something super sweet to wake myself up.'

'You mean me bringing you coffee and toast in bed

doesn't do the trick?' teased Ed, smoothing down a ruffled strand of Angela's hair.

'Sorry, lovely, neither is on the menu today, but I have a rather lush chocolate roulade.' Even if it hadn't tempted the rude stranger, who needed more than a piece or two of cake to sweeten *him* up.

Jo served up a slice each for Ed and Angela, with a pot of English Breakfast tea. 'How are your folks doing?' she inquired of Ed. His parents, Ken and Mags, had embarked on a two-month cruise, leaving Ed and Angela in charge of The Jekyll and Hyde pub.

'All good,' said Ed. 'Not that Dad's brilliant at keeping in touch. He looks at my WhatsApp messages, but only gives one-word replies. Mum hasn't a clue how to work her phone these days, so there's no point messaging her.'

Jo touched Ed's arm sympathetically. Since Mags's diagnosis of early onset Alzheimer's, the family had struggled to cope. Jo and Ken had grown close at one point — a little *too* close — but they'd seen sense before anything happened. Ken adored Mags, and Jo hoped that one day she'd find a man who felt the same way about her. Mind you, in her mid-forties, she wasn't holding her breath. Eligible bachelors didn't dangle from the street lamps of Cranley, and Jo had neither the time nor the energy to dive into the Edinburgh or online dating scene.

'How's your friend's daughter getting on?' asked Angela, hopping onto one of the high stools at the counter. 'It's so kind of you to take her under your wing.'

Jo gave an embarrassed shrug. 'She's, erm, adjusting.' She'd hated using Carole, her best friend from school, as a cover story, but she had been at a loss to explain Aaliyah's sudden appearance in the village. She had told anyone who asked that Aaliyah had got mixed up with a bad crowd, and was staying with Jo for some work experience and a quieter way of life.

No one needed to know that Carole had no children and would have been appalled to acknowledge vain, incompetent Aaliyah as her offspring. And no one could *ever* know Aaliyah's true origins. Jo's brain still did a cerebral backward somersault whenever she recalled their first meeting…

'Well, you can't get much quieter than Cranley,' said Ed. 'Not that we're complaining, eh, Angela? Who needs the hustle and bustle of a big city when you've got Peggy's hair salon for all your blue-rinse requirements, and Sam's antiques emporium for all things ancient and needing love?'

Jo shuddered at Ed's remark. OK, she wasn't *ancient*, but for a moment she pictured herself perched on a shelf and being dusted occasionally by Sam's fiancée, Jinnie.

'Cranley's not that bad,' she countered, ladling home-made raspberry jam into individual pots. 'Alison's done a grand job with the boutique, and Janette keeps us stocked up with essentials.'

'Aye, she does. Mind you, she'd run out of con—' Ed received a deathly glare from Angela, whose cheeks were scarlet. 'Conference pears. Because I fancied, erm, a pear tart the other day.' Angela gave Ed a sharp poke in the ribs and Jo turned away to hide her amusement.

At that moment, Aaliyah strode out of the back room, minus her hair net, with all the poise and attitude of a catwalk model. 'I've finished the filling for the sausage rolls, but I couldn't find the mice droppings.' She raised a perfectly plucked eyebrow in Ed and Angela's direction, throwing in a seductive hair flick for good measure.

'She means the chocolate chips,' said Jo, huffing out an exasperated sigh. 'Aaliyah has a dark sense of humour.'

'And such a pretty name,' added Angela, placing a posses-sive hand on Ed's knee. 'Unusual for Newcastle, no?'

Aaliyah shrugged. 'I wasn't born there. My origins are, shall we say, a little more exotic.'

Before she could say more, Jo steered her back towards the kitchen. 'We'll just find the chocolate chips, shall we? Ed, Angela, just leave some cash on the counter. I need to crack on before any more customers arrive.'

Hustling her errant assistant out of sight, Jo wished she could turn back time. Sadly, that was *not* a wish that could be granted…

CHAPTER 3

HARVEY QUINN SWIRLED AN INCH OF AMBER LIQUID AROUND the solitary whisky tumbler he possessed. Packing up and leaving his old life behind with indecent haste meant that little had found its way to his current abode.

Taking a sip, he eyed the newly opened bottle of 12-year-old malt whisky with disdain. At the peak of his 'troubles' — Harvey choked down a bitter laugh at such an inadequate description — he'd downed at least half a bottle a day. Usually after several large glasses of red not of the vintage quality his previous existence demanded. More often than not, the wine came from a cheap three-litre box found on the bottom shelf in the supermarket.

Harvey reflected on the times when he'd been tempted to recline beneath the plastic tap and keep pouring until oblivion kicked in. As it was, he often stripped away the cardboard casing and squeezed the foil bag until it was empty, like a demented bagpipe player.

The plastic container in front of him contained the congealing remnants of his microwave ready meal. Allegedly it had been fish pie, although three insipid prawns and a chunk of cod swimming in a sea of soggy mash hardly earned it that title. Harvey had eaten it straight from the container: it didn't warrant dirtying a dish.

He put down his glass and tugged the ancient picnic rug more tightly round his knees. His current abode, Brae Cottage, possessed central heating, but the radiators gave off less heat than a low-voltage light bulb.

The previous tenant, Jenny or something, had attempted to spruce the place up a little. The rental agent had taken great delight in pointing out the colourful throws draped over the mangy sofas and the fairy lights festooning the unused fireplace. Apparently, she'd moved in with her boyfriend a few months earlier, and left what furniture and knick-knacks she possessed to the next occupant. Harvey wasn't ungrateful. He didn't plan on entertaining in the fore-seeable future, though, so the two folding garden chairs were one too many.

He eyed the chipped mantelpiece, home to two unlit candles (another gift from his predecessor) and a framed photograph. Harvey rubbed his chin, the three-day-old stubble rasping against his fingers. He also traced the scar on his left cheek, the legacy of intervening in a drunken brawl outside a Glasgow pub a long time ago. One of the sparring duo had smashed a pint glass and sliced through Harvey's face with it, then the pair had scarpered into the night, leaving Harvey to find a taxi for a bum-numbing wait at A&E.

So much had happened since then. The scar had faded, but others, much fresher, remained. The biggest and most painful of all stared at him from the mantelpiece. His one true love. His reason for getting up in the mornings and devoting his life to the world of entertainment. Without her by his side, he'd never have attained the success he'd enjoyed:

years of being the bad guy with a nugget of gold tucked inside him. It just needed excavating, that was all.

'Lindsey.' Harvey said her name out loud. He sometimes thought that by saying it she might appear. A glorious apparition, as beautiful as when they'd first met. Thirty years ago, almost to the day.

'You stupid, nostalgic old fool.' Harvey tossed off the blanket, stumbled towards the mantelpiece and picked up the photograph, tracing a finger across the glass. Not a speck of dust, unlike the rest of the cottage. Every day, without fail, he lovingly polished his most treasured possession, making sure the intricate silver frame gleamed and Lindsey's serene countenance shone through.

'Why did you have to leave me?' he murmured. 'Everything's gone to hell, and I don't know how to carry on. My career's in ruins, my so-called friends have deserted me, and now I'm living in a godawful village full of nosy parkers with nothing better to do than waggle their useless tongues.'

Harvey closed his eyes for a second, imagining Lindsey beside him, placing a reassuring hand on his arm — or, more likely, giving him a severe ear-bashing for wallowing in self-pity. *Get a grip, H,* she'd say. *Yesterday's scandal is tomorrow's fish-and-chips wrapper. Things could be worse. They certainly are for me!*

Harvey choked back a sob. Could things really be worse? Unless several body parts spontaneously dropped off, or someone discovered his cold, dead body after several months, he doubted it. The tabloid press had moved on in recent months, but Harvey doubted they'd closed the door completely. One person's word against his was enough to cast a shadow over his reputation.

Opening his eyes, Harvey looked at Lindsey again. That cheeky hint of a smile — never a full one, as she hated showing off the gap where she'd lost a back tooth. In his eyes, it only added to her charm. Practically perfect, with flaws only the forensically inclined would notice. Heck, he was no oil painting himself, unless said painting incorporated pock marks from teenage skin problems and the silvery scar he carried like a badge of honour — or idiocy.

She'd reminded him so much of Lindsey. That woman in the café, A Bit of Crumpet: what kind of daft name was that? She was shorter, her hair darker, but there'd been a feistiness there that punched Harvey in the gut. He regretted his rudeness, but how could he explain? What could he say? *Sorry I'm a miserable bastard, but life's dumped on me from on high and I can't seem to drag myself back into the human race. I'm destined to be a pathetic straggler, watching the rest of the field sprint for the finishing line.*

Moving from his palatial pad in Glasgow's West End to a sleepy Scottish village had been a relief. He was too familiar in those parts — a 'weel-kent face' — and had worn sunglasses and grown a stupid beard as a disguise. He recalled the sideways glances and the glimmer of recognition — the mothers tugging daughters closer to their sides and fathers' lips curling in disgust. *She was young enough to be your daughter.* Words unsaid, but still capable of cutting through Harvey as effectively as that pissed-up lout's makeshift knife all those years ago.

He had been glad to shave off the beard, and he didn't bother with the sunglasses now; nothing said 'pretentious prat' more than wearing shades on a dreich East coast day. He knew someone would recognise him at some point, even in this tiny place, but for now he'd keep a low profile and pray it happened later rather than sooner.

CHAPTER 4

Jo stabbed at a fluffy Parmesan and pine nut dumpling, which nestled in a simmering pesto chicken stew. Normally she'd savour every mouthful of the food served up at The Jekyll and Hyde pub, but her appetite had deserted her ever since the day she'd given an old lamp the once-over with some Brasso and got a lot more than she bargained for.

Waving at Angela, who was drying glasses behind the bar, Jo's thoughts drifted back to that fateful morning. She'd arrived at the café early, determined to get a head start on birthday-tea preparations for a ninety-year-old. For a few months she'd employed Angela as her assistant, grateful for an extra pair of hands as she built up the outside catering element of her business. However, when Ken and Mags took off on their trip, Jo had reluctantly let Angela go and help Ed run the pub, although she still helped Jo from time to time.

With a second strong coffee at hand, Jo had stared at the list provided by the birthday girl's granddaughter:

Nothing with dried fruit or nuts in — they play havoc with Gran's dentures.

No garlic or anything else exotic. She ate some chicken korma once and spent three days solid on the loo.

Sweet stuff is a favourite, but not too chewy (see dentures). Chocolate is good.

A selection of sandwiches would go down well, but use only soft white bread with the crusts cut off. Egg mayonnaise is fine, but no cucumber. It gives her chronic indigestion.

A birthday cake to serve 12 people. Or maybe 10, as her boyfriend (who's 92) has a bad dose of gout and might not make it. And her best friend Elsie's got the flu, although I reckon it's just a head cold.

Jo had settled on a finger-sandwich selection, filled with egg mayonnaise, wafer-thin ham and beef paste, then melt-in-the-mouth (dentures notwithstanding) macarons in an array of pastel hues, and mini vanilla and chocolate éclairs. And the pièce de résistance: a fluffy chocolate cake shaped like a curled-up tabby cat, in homage to the much-missed Mr Moggs. Jo had devoted several hours to creating the cake, slicing and dicing sponges to form the various body parts. She'd worried that it resembled a poo emoji more than a beloved pet, but hoped poor eyesight would work in her favour.

With the food boxed up ready for delivery, Jo had ensured the kitchen area was spotless then turned her attention to front of house. Behind the counter was a long, high shelf which housed a colourful collection of mismatched teapots and jugs and the two lamps she'd bought from Sam Addin's antique shop. Every couple of weeks, Jo gave everything a good wash and experimented with the display. She'd polished the lamps once or twice, a strange sensation sweeping over her each time. As if someone had walked over her grave, as her mother used to say. Jo wasn't sure what had possessed her to buy them, but at a fiver for the pair they hadn't broken the bank.

With an hour to go before opening the café, she picked up the prettier of the two. What exactly made it prettier, Jo couldn't say. In many ways the lamps were identical, although this one had a special lustre that had caught the eye of many a customer. Noticing a tiny dark spot on its surface, Jo grabbed a sheet of kitchen roll and a tin of polish and set to work removing it. Seconds later, she landed on her bottom as the lamp leapt from her hands and clattered into a corner.

Nerves jangling, Jo held her breath as something — someone — materialised before her disbelieving eyes. Her first irrational thought was Kim Kardashian. The person — creature — had a figure that would make hourglasses weep, although how those incredible curves could have emerged from an opening the size of a kettle spout boggled Jo's mind.

The figure took on a solid form, most definitely female, and if Jo wasn't mistaken, frantically chewing gum. Jo blinked rapidly, hoping that whoever (or whatever) it was might be a figment of her imagination. She'd eaten an enormous chunk of truffle-infused Cheddar last night: didn't cheese sometimes induce nightmares? But that was hours ago, and Jo was pretty sure this was no figment of her imagination. Just to be sure, she pinched herself hard on the leg. *Ouch!* Nope, she hadn't drifted off into a daytime, cheese-related slumber.

Struggling to her feet, Jo regarded the figure with trepidation. Any residual wispiness had gone. The woman was as real as the customers who visited A Bit of Crumpet for their daily sugar and caffeine fix — just more glamorous, with her hair done in an intricate chignon that emphasised her angular features. The look was somewhat marred when she blew an enormous bubble which promptly popped all over her perfect face.

'Oops! What a wazzock!' She peeled the pink mass from

her mouth, rolled it into a ball and stuffed it in the pocket of her floaty trousers. 'It's me last piece, so I'm savin' it for later.'

Now on her feet, legs wobblier than a half-set jelly, Jo's sense of disbelief went up a notch. Whatever this creature was, she had an unmistakable Geordie accent, which seemed totally at odds with her exotic appearance. Didn't genies come from— Hang on a minute, had she just said 'genie'? Not out loud, for she wasn't sure her voice would work. Yet it seemed the only logical explanation. *Come off it,* she thought. Genies are fictional beings. They don't just materialise in humble Scottish cafés. And even if genies did exist, surely they didn't hail from Newcastle and chew gum?

Lost in her thoughts, Jo didn't notice her visitor moving closer. When she did, she stood her ground, determined not to faint in the manner of an eighteenth-century lady with a delicate disposition.

'Eeh, you're lookin' a bit peaky, lass. Are you alreet?' She squinted at Jo, who poured herself a glass of water and downed it in one. 'Mind if I have one, too?'

Still unable to utter a word, Jo poured a second glass and handed it to the — the *thing*... Her hand trembled, and some water slopped out. Her companion — Jo was running out of ways to describe her — tutted and knocked it back with very unladylike gulps.

'Ta, love. The name's Aaliyah, by the way. And you are...?' She extended a slender hand, bangles jangling.

'Jo. I'm Jo. This is my café. I really don't know what's going on, but—'

Before she could continue, Aaliyah's gaze fell on the second lamp. With a snort befitting an irritable horse, she reached up and lifted it down. 'Have you rubbed this one?' she demanded. Jo shook her head, then recalled that she'd given both lamps a bit of a buff. She switched to a nod, the change in motion making her feel dizzy.

'Well, don't touch it again — not unless you want two genies in your life.'

CHAPTER 5

Two genies? Jo gawped in horror at Aaliyah, who replaced the second lamp on the shelf. She couldn't wrap her head around one, never mind two.

'Aye, pet. His name's Dhassim. We were an item, once upon a time, but he got too clingy and accused me of flirting with others. And you would not believe how vain he is!' Aaliyah checked her reflection in a glass cabinet and smoothed down a strand of hair, and the phrase *pot and kettle* sprang to Jo's mind.

Jo forced her thoughts away from images of two other-worldly beings jostling in front of a mirror and back to the here and now. 'OK, this is a little difficult for me to understand. You're a genie, I accidentally conjured you up by rubbing your lamp, and now…'

Aaliyah rolled her eyes (immaculately lined with kohl, and with lashes that could fan a small fire) and shook her head, clearly conveying the message that Jo needed to pull up her intellectual socks. 'Look, I know you humans have heard of us through books and films, like. Although Dhassim told me about some stupid blue guy who did our species no favours. Apparently he sang and turned into different creatures. Ridiculous! I'm a WYSIWYG kinda gal.'

What the heck was a whizziwig? Jo felt her grip on reality loosen further. She didn't want to appear any dumber, but she had to ask.

'What you see is what you get,' replied Aaliyah. 'A bona fide wish-giving babe with the very latest technology to get this show on the road.'

She fumbled with her top, producing a glitzy device that emitted a series of buzzes, beeps and jingles. Jo had an iPhone 11 that did a lot of clever things — though, sadly, not the ironing — but she'd witnessed nothing as over-the-top as this.

'This is my Wish Instigating Finder Instrument: WIFI for short. It allows me to check if your wishes are allowed — there are rules, not that Dhassim ever followed them — and grant them. You have three.' Aaliyah held up three fingers.

Jo resisted the urge to hold up two, and not in a Winston Churchill, V for victory kind of way.

'You can actually grant wishes?' Jo realised that was probably a dumb question. What little she knew of genies was all about the wish-granting, Robin Williams's wise-cracking blue guy notwithstanding.

'Of course. Dhassim went a bit OTT with his last mistress, though. I gave him a right bollocking when he told me what he'd done. I mean, giving someone perfect hair, then sorting out a winning scratch card for one of her friends… Not exactly setting the world on fire, eh?'

A winning scratch card? Jo recalled Angela's bubbling excitement when she'd won fifty thousand pounds on a scratch card. Angela had insisted on investing twenty thousand pounds in Jo's fledgling catering business: money Jo fully intended to pay back over time, despite Angela's insistence that she didn't want it. Come to think of it, the hair rang a bell too. Hadn't Jinnie's hair been transformed overnight into an impossibly sleek, super-shiny style that remained impervious to the relentlessly damp and dreary weather?

'Jinnie had a genie?' Jo didn't know whether to laugh or cry. Her friend knew the true nature of the lamps, and had never said a thing. OK, Jo had bought them from Sam, but Jinnie must have spotted them on display in the café. A wee heads-up would have been nice. Such as 'By the way, Jo, these are no ordinary lamps. They contain genies who'll wreak havoc in your life if you unleash them.'

The burning question now was what to do about Aaliyah. Could Jo persuade her that no wishes were required, and she should squeeze her enviable body back into the lamp? Then Jo could offload the lamps somewhere — her wheelie bin sprung to mind — and get back to living a normal if somewhat dull existence.

'Sorry, pet, not happening.' Aaliyah gave Jo the kind of look normally reserved for a naughty child who'd scribbled on the walls. 'I'm here now, and I'm not leaving till I've done my job. No rush, mind. I got hustled back into me lamp last time, so I'm ready to have some fun.'

So her new gal pal read minds, too? Jo vowed to keep all negative thoughts to herself. That might be easier said than done, given that Aaliyah had the knack of pushing her buttons. Speaking of which…

'Reet. This is a food place and I'm clamming, so you can rustle me up something. That'll do nicely.' Aaliyah pointed at one of Jo's legendary home-made sausage rolls. 'Heated up, with a side of those wondrous orange beans you love so much here. They gave Dhassim terrible wind, like, but he always had a delicate constitution. I'm built of sterner stuff!'

Jo watched Aaliyah fiddle with her WIFI. The sound was muted, but the device displayed a sparkling burst of virtual fireworks. *Does my future rely on this gizmo? What do I really want, anyway?* Her needs were simple, if uninspiring: a quiet life, with her business ticking over until she retired. That was still some years away, but—

'Are you going to stand there forever, musing on your existence, or will you fetch me some food?'

Jo snatched up a sausage roll, added a side of beans and slid the plate into the microwave. She pushed the relevant buttons and counted down with the illuminated clock.

CHAPTER 6

HARVEY CURSED AS THE SPINNING WHEEL OF DOOM HALTED HIS writing progress. His laptop was woefully outdated, but he had neither the energy nor the inclination to invest in a new one.

Forcing quit, he was relieved he'd only written a handful of sentences. He doubted his fledgling screenplay would ever see the light of day, but it kept him occupied. Little else did.

Seeking a caffeine fix to fire up his weary brain cells, Harvey went into the tiny kitchen. As he reached towards the cupboard housing his meagre supplies, he remembered he'd run out of his favourite ground coffee. He'd brought a packet with him when he fled his previous life, but had used the last of it the day before.

'Damn it!' Harvey could place an order on the internet, but brilliant as technology was these days, it hadn't reached sci-fi capabilities. That left him with two options. Pop to the corner shop cum post office, which offered an uninspiring selection of cheap instant varieties, or spruce himself up and head to A Bit of Crumpet.

The former he dismissed instantly, a wry smile crossing

his face at the unintentional pun. He had no desire to chat with the busybody who ran the place. Her creased cleavage was always on display and her probing questions brought to mind the Spanish Inquisition. That left the latter. He recalled his curtness on his first visit and cringed. Maybe the owner would lace his drink with laxatives, or refuse to serve him.

'Do I go, Lindsey, or do I settle for a wee dram? The sun's over the yardarm somewhere in the world.' He had wandered back into the living room, his gaze alighting as always on the treasured photo.

Pull yourself together, my darling! Go for a coffee — give your poor old liver a break.

Harvey knew the words came from inside him. He didn't believe in ghosts, and the only thing that haunted him was a past he regretted with every fibre of his being. Not because he'd done anything wrong, but because he'd let the mud stick instead of defending himself.

Ten minutes later, Harvey stood outside the café. He'd combed his hair, put on a half-decent jumper and jeans, and sprayed on some ancient aftershave. He didn't know why — it was unlikely that the owner would get close enough for a sniff, and even more unlikely that she'd give a rat's arse about how he smelled if she did. But at least he didn't pong like the aforementioned rodent's rear end.

'Aaliyah, do I have to ask you again to wipe down the tables? Those school-run mums have left an awful mess: sugar sachets spilled everywhere and sticky fingers all over the condiments.'

Harvey sidled into the café, his heart rate increasing with every step. A young and very attractive woman was stomping around, squirting disinfectant spray with the ferocity of an ardent gardener annihilating plant-eating pests. The café owner stood with her hands on her hips, her expression that of a mum dealing with a belligerent toddler.

'Oh, you're back.' The boss lady switched on a fake smile, as well she might; he'd hardly presented the nice version of himself on his previous visit. Not that Harvey knew if the nice version existed any more — or if it ever had. Perhaps Lindsey was the only one who'd chipped away enough gruffness to uncover something worth pursuing.

'Yes. Hello. Need some coffee.' Good God in Govan (a favourite expression of his long-deceased Glaswegian grandfather), why had his manners completely deserted him? 'Please,' he added, a little too late.

The younger woman finished her vicious assault on the tables and swooped into the back room, oblivious to Harvey's presence.

'Black, no sugar?' The owner had a good memory, though it probably wasn't hard to recall the order of someone as miserable as him. Dark, and bitter. She amped up the smile, and Harvey's frozen heart cracked a fraction. Her smile reminded him of Lindsey, but no one could ever replace her. No one would touch him with a ten-foot barge pole, to be honest. And that was fine. He'd tasted love in its purest form. Anything else would be a feeble substitute—

'Are you up for introductions? I'm Jo.' She stuck out her right hand.

Harvey hesitated. When had he last made physical contact with anyone? It had probably been a nervous pat on the back from his agent when Harvey announced his 'sabbatical' from the acting world. 'Probably for the best,' Arthur Petch had said, his rheumy eyes looking everywhere but at Harvey's face. 'Give it time, son. I'll, erm, let you know if anything decent comes up, but in the meantime…'

Needless to say, Harvey had heard diddly squat from his agent of over twenty-five years. Arthur wouldn't want his reputation further tarnished by association with—

Jo withdrew her hand. 'Fine. I'm not contagious, you know.'

Harvey kicked himself for yet more rudeness, even though it had been unintentional. 'I'm Harvey. Harvey Quinn. And yes, black, no sugar. Please.' He attempted a smile by way of an apology, but his facial muscles were sorely out of smiling practice.

'Anything to eat? Not chocolate, mind, but I do have a very nice Bakewell tart, or a cheese and onion bake if you fancy something savoury.'

Jo set about fixing his coffee and Harvey tried to recall when he'd last eaten. Last night: a round of toast with the mould trimmed off, smeared with the remnants of a jar of meat paste.

'A cheese and onion bake, please.'

Jo nodded, removing one from the heated display and popping it on to a plate. 'Take a seat and I'll bring these over.'

Harvey sat down at the table he'd occupied before. The only other customers were an elderly couple sharing a pot of tea and scones with jam and cream. They glanced over, raising their teacups in a welcoming gesture.

'Here you go.' Jo placed his food and drink in front of him, frowning at a dusting of sugar her assistant had failed to wipe away. 'Let me fetch a cloth.'

'It's fine.' Harvey swiped the offending granules into a paper napkin and handed it over.

'So, at the risk of sounding nosy, what brings you to Cranley?' Jo's tone was light, her hazel eyes curious, but not in a probing, spill-the-beans way.

'I needed a change of scenery,' replied Harvey. He broke off a corner of the pastry and popped it into his mouth. It was a big step up from mouldy bread and meat paste that resembled bathroom grouting.

'OK. Well, we're a friendly bunch, so just shout if you need anything.' Jo returned to the counter, leaving Harvey to sip his coffee and contemplate his lack of friends. He doubted anyone here would welcome him with open arms if they knew the truth. Or at least, the version that clung to him like a shroud…

CHAPTER 7

THREE WISHES. JO LAY BACK IN THE BATH, THE SCENT OF LIME and coconut permeating the air. Aaliyah was downstairs playing Candy Crush on Jo's phone, and a half hour's soak in the tub was a much-needed escape from her badgering.

'I've been here, like, two weeks and you haven't come up with a single wish!' Aaliyah's squawk was accompanied by a look of disbelief. *Squawk is about right*, thought Jo. Aaliyah reminded her of an exotic bird, released from its cage and determined to make its presence felt.

How do you decide what to wish for? Jo envied people who reeled off lists as readily as Jo rolled out puff pastry. Top ten movies? Top ten books? Jo's mind drew a blank every time. She loved movies, books and TV shows, but coming up with more than one or two favourites was beyond her.

Adjusting the inflatable pillow under her neck, Jo wondered how Jinnie had chosen her wishes. Had they randomly popped into her head, or been steered by her genie, Dhassim? Aaliyah didn't appear inclined to make any suggestions, though. She simply huffed and twiddled with her WIFI, when she wasn't raiding Jo's dressing table or bath-room cabinet.

Closing her eyes, and applying a masque that promised to soothe, lift and smooth out wrinkles, Jo crinkled her brow. That would do little to aid the anti-wrinkle treatment, but hey, she'd earned every single one. Badges of honour. Lines of duty. Wait, that was the name of a favourite TV show, wasn't it?

'Jo! Jo!' Aaliyah's strident tone pierced Jo's ears, making her wish (*here we go again*) that she'd inserted earplugs as well as the bath plug.

Jo squealed as the door opened and Aaliyah marched in. 'Haven't you heard of knocking?' She wrapped her arms around her upper half, grateful for the bubbles affording her a semblance of decency. 'You can't just barge in!'

'Calm your jets, pet. You've got all the same bits as me, just bigger.'

Feeling her breasts, a generous 38D, through the soapy water, Jo agreed that she was more generously endowed in that respect. However, she suspected her genie sidekick meant other parts of her anatomy. She'd be lucky to squeeze one leg into the skin tight jeans Aaliyah had picked out from Alison Gale's boutique.

Aaliyah had first appeared sporting a sequinned crop top and turquoise harem pants which screamed 'genie', but didn't exactly lend themselves to the sleepy streets of Cranley. Admittedly, some young women dressed in scanty outfits regardless of the temperature. Jo had seen them in The Jekyll and Hyde pub, with more flesh on display than a butcher's window. Luckily, Aaliyah fitted into some of Jo's more youthful tops, and Jo had ordered her a bunch of cheap undies and other bits from H&M.

'What do you want?' Jo frowned at the intruder, her feelings of zen-like calm evaporating as quickly as the bubbles. She grabbed the loofah and positioned it across her chest.

'I'm bored.' Aaliyah's expression reminded Jo of a toddler in need of a nap, and she prayed she wouldn't be subjected to a full-blown tantrum. 'There's nowt to do here, and you're no fun. All you do is work in a boring café and take stupid baths, and watch boring programmes about stupid cakes.'

Jo flinched. Yes, she loved the show *All Rise,* and had often dreamt of taking part. She'd applied during every year of its five-year run, but been rejected over and over again. Was she really so boring, or simply not camera-friendly? But most of the contestants were just ordinary folk united by a passion for baking. Last year's winner had been a seventeen-year-old boy from Dorset, who'd reduced the nation to tears with his story of being bullied. Baking amazing cakes meant nothing when your peers judged you by your prowess on the football pitch or your ability to chat up girls.

'I'm sorry I'm so boring, Aaliyah, but there's plenty to do around here. As you're a non-paying house guest, you could do some cleaning or tackle the ironing pile.'

Aaliyah raised a groomed eyebrow. 'I said I was bored, which means I want to do something interesting. That doesn't include scraping muck off your manky windows or using that horrible steamy thing to flatten clothes. It's bad enough that I have to work in the café and get all that yucky dough under me fingernails.'

Shooing Aaliyah out of the bathroom, Jo wrapped herself in a fluffy towel from the heated rail and perched on the edge of the bath. The water gurgled down the plughole, echoing Jo's sense of despondency.

She massaged the remnants of the masque into her skin, using a damp flannel to remove the residue. She peered in the mirror — her eyesight seemed to deteriorate daily, which at least meant lines were less visible — and added a song to her list of favourites. 'Blurred Lines' always got her bopping around the kitchen, even if the video made her cringe. Actually, the lyrics made her cringe, but she loved the tune. Did you have to analyse everything to the nth degree these days? Many songs from the past wouldn't stand up to present-day political correctness, but that didn't make them less enjoyable.

How can I stop Aaliyah's incessant moaning? Probably the only way was to come up with the first wish. Jo gazed at her feet, mottled pink and in need of a pedicure. Lots of bits of her could do with some TLC, but who cared? Certainly not her loyal customers, whose main concern was the lightness of her pastry or the gooeyness of her cakes. Jo's beauty routine consisted of a scrub with a flannel, a dab of tinted moisturiser and a quick lick of mascara. Unlike Aaliyah, who layered on make-up with expert ease, all of it purloined from Jo's meagre collection.

Jo grabbed a tube of body lotion and massaged some into her neglected tootsies. She'd never had a professional massage or any kind of beauty treatment in her life. Should she wish for an escape to some exotic location where she could be plucked, waxed, buffed and polished, all against a backdrop of shimmering sand and glittering ocean, with delicious cocktails and hot servers on tap?

Jo sighed, pulled on her bathrobe and went into the bedroom. There was no sign of Aaliyah, thankfully. No doubt she was holed up in her bedroom — Jo's spare room, which had previously doubled up as an office — listening to music on the ancient iPod Jo had unearthed from a drawer. She dismissed the idea of wishing for a decadent holiday. She had no desire to venture further than her native Scotland, and anyway, she had enough money to pay her own way if she changed her mind.

Heading downstairs for a cuppa, Jo's thoughts drifted

back to *All Rise*. She imagined herself in the distinctive chequered apron, wiping away tears of joy as she lifted the coveted trophy above her head. Admittedly, the trophy, which resembled a hand whisk, wouldn't win any prizes for aesthetics. Still, as the kettle boiled, Jo fantasised about her fifteen minutes of fame.

CHAPTER 8

JINNIE AND SAM HAD GOT BACK FROM THEIR HOLIDAY THE previous day. Out for a stroll, Jo had dodged out of sight when she spotted them unloading the car. They looked tanned and very much in love, Jinnie cheekily patting Sam's bottom as he bent over to wrestle a suitcase from the depths of the boot. Her heartstrings twanged with sadness at the look of adoration that passed between them. When had a man ever looked at her like that? Well, there had been one. Sadly, he wasn't the one who got away, but the one who could never be. Graham, her ex-fiancé of many years ago, had reserved such looks for a full Scottish breakfast or a Rangers win at the football.

Back at the café, Jo nodded at Aaliyah, who was serving a harassed young mum trying to placate a screaming toddler. To Jo's surprise, her normally haughty assistant got down to the child's level and pulled a series of ridiculous faces worthy of a world gurning champion. The little boy, scarlet-faced and snotty, eyed her with bewilderment.

Jo held her breath. Would the wee lad be traumatised for life? No: he chuckled in that delicious, infectious way only small children can, and the mum handed over a generous tip for the green tea, diluted juice and shortbread she'd ordered.

'Nice work,' said Jo, hanging up her jacket. 'I think you've found a new vocation as a children's entertainer.' Aaliyah harrumphed and stomped off to the back room.

Jo would have followed, but new arrivals meant that she needed to hold the fort. As she poured, sliced and chatted, she pondered how to approach Jinnie, and when. Good manners probably meant leaving it a day or two, but Jo's patience with the whole genie/wish situation was wearing thinner than filo pastry. She needed to find out what had transpired between Jinnie and Aaliyah's one-time beau, and she needed some guidance: a handbook would be nice. But that could wait until she'd given Jinnie a gentle bollocking for keeping shtum about the lamps' occupants.

Alison Gale entered the café, dressed to the nines as always. Alison had been widowed in her early sixties, and her local boutique, Gale Force, had certainly blown away the cobwebs of its tatty predecessor — so much so that customers travelled from Edinburgh to snap up her reasonably priced, effortlessly classy wares.

'Hiya, Alison,' said Jo. 'How's business? Did the move go OK?' Having lived in the tiny flat above the boutique for several months, Alison had recently purchased a three-bedroom property on the same street as Brae Cottage, Jinnie's former home before she moved in with Sam.

'All good, Jo,' replied Alison, unwinding a stunning scarlet scarf shot with gold from her elegant neck. 'I've sold three divine jackets, and one woman snapped up every cashmere-blend cardigan I had in stock. As for the move... Stressful, but I don't need to rush. The hardest part is going through Drew's stuff and deciding what to keep and what to throw away. I feel guilty binning anything, as if I'm erasing him from my life and putting memories in black bags. It's not easy.'

Jo nodded sympathetically. Not that she'd been widowed, but she remembered the gut punch of emptying her parents' house after they had died just six weeks apart. She'd sobbed over so many things: the fitted grey wool coat her mother wore on high days and holidays, her father's collection of vinyl records going back decades, and the boxes of Jo's childhood toys and clothes, down to her first pair of patent leather shoes. Stupidly, she'd kept them, tucked away in her wardrobe next to an embroidered bag containing some of her mum's make-up and toiletries. From time to time, Jo would take it out and inhale the fading scent of face powder and perfume, her sadness tinged with fond recollections of happier times.

'If you need a hand…' Jo smiled as she reached for Alison's favourite lemon verbena tea.

Alison shook her head, her auburn curls bouncing on the shoulders of her autumnal-hued coat. 'That's very kind, Jo, but I can manage. Ruairi, my eldest, is taking time off work to come and sift through his dad's bits, including the files crammed with ancient receipts and bank statements. Honestly, who needs to keep a record of a toaster and kettle bought in the early '80s?'

Alison took her tea and a buttered scone to a quiet corner — not that the wee fella was creating a scene any more. Taking advantage of the peace, Jo sought out Aaliyah. Instead of prepping sandwiches and paninis for the lunchtime crowd, she was curled up like a cat next to the industrial-size oven, positively purring, eyelids fluttering, oblivious to the hardness of the floor.

Jo stood over Aaliyah, her foot itching to give her a prod. Instead, she banged two pot lids together.

Aaliyah leapt to her feet, hissing like a tabby with its tail on fire. 'What's your problem? Can a girl not have a wee nap, seein' as you treat me like a slave?'

Jo let out a derisory snort. 'You have free accommodation, all meals included, and your toughest task is shelling hard-boiled eggs. Slave is a bit of an exaggeration, don't you think?'

'Whatever.' Aaliyah curled her lip and began slicing bread with unnecessary force. 'Was that the boutique lady I heard coming in? Has she got new stuff for me to check out?'

How Aaliyah knew who'd come in, considering her state of slumber, was anyone's guess. 'Yes, it was, and no, she hasn't. Alison's got a lot on her mind. She's clearing out her late husband's stuff.'

'Crikey, that's a bit brutal,' said Aaliyah, slathering butter on the bread. 'If the poor geezer's lost track of time, surely junking his possessions is a bit OTT?'

Not for the first time, Jo wondered how Aaliyah could be so streetwise and modern in some ways, yet fail to understand a simple expression. 'I didn't mean that kind of late,' she explained. 'He died, so she needs to sort out his things. You know, clothes and papers and … things.' Jo's eyes welled up, her thoughts back in her family home.

'Aww, pet, did you ken him well?' Aaliyah put down the knife and patted Jo's shoulder hesitantly, as if Jo might crumble at her touch.

'I didn't know him at all. It just reminded me of losing my parents — not in a "they've gone missing" kind of way, in case you were wondering…' Jo took a steadying breath.

Aaliyah's hand kneaded Jo's shoulder as if it was a stubborn lump of dough. 'I ken what that means,' huffed Aaliyah. 'Mind you, I never had parents, so nowt to grieve over. Although I did have a hamster once— Well, my master did. Loved that wee guy pedalling like fury on his wheel. I cried buckets when he climbed into the tumble dryer one

day and ended up dead. Very fluffy, like, but definitely
dead.'

Thanking Aaliyah for her concern, Jo nipped to the loo to
splash water on her face. A quick scan of the café revealed no
new customers: Alison was still sipping her tea and the mum
and toddler were engrossed in a picture book. Staring at the
mirror, she saw her parents' genes in her reflection: her dad's
cheekbones and chin dimple, her mum's hair colour (until
her mum turned grey and refused to dye it). She recalled the
photo albums crammed with pictures of her growing up:
with bucket and spade, on family holidays to the seaside;
blowing out the candles on her birthday cake; shy infant with
oversized blazer; sulky teenager with self-pierced ears and
lashings of lip gloss.

Jo had never considered how genies came to be. Did they
just manifest from thin air and take up residence in a
random lamp? The thought added another layer of sadness
to Jo's melancholy mood. She'd been so loved: the only child
of older parents who'd dedicated their lives to her happiness.
Not rich in the material sense, but abundant in wisdom and
generosity, they had instilled Jo with a true sense of self-
worth. What she'd give for one more day with them, to thank
them and say all the things you never do until it's too late.

CHAPTER 9

'AALIYAH?'

It was Sunday morning, and Jo had just surfaced after an unexpected but much-needed lie-in. For several years she'd opened six days a week (closed Mondays), rising at the crack of dawn to deal with deliveries and prepare food for the day ahead. What was the old saying again? *Early to bed, early to rise, makes a man healthy, wealthy and wise*. Jo had no health worries, but she certainly wasn't rich, and seriously doubted that anyone would seek her out for her wisdom.

'Aaliyah!' Jo raised her voice as she walked barefoot down the hallway. Her snap decision last night to open at midday today had gained her several hours of extra sleep, although waking from her deep slumber had taken some time. Thoughts of her mum and dad had swirled around her head, both their voices as clear as if they were in the room with her. Like any dream, though, the details faded quickly. All that remained was a familiar feeling of comfort mixed with loss, the two emotions jostling for supremacy in Jo's muddled mind.

Downstairs, the radio blared. Aaliyah normally slept like

a log. Jo yearned for the good old days when she could conk out for twelve hours straight, but like her ability to eat loads without gaining a pound, that talent had vanished over the years.

'Morning.' Jo's greeting went unheard, as Aaliyah was up, singing along to something upbeat and annoying. Jo liked to start her days with either total silence or classical music at low volume. So many adjustments had been needed since Aaliyah had gatecrashed her life, but at least Jo could adjust the volume control.

'Ee, that's one of my favourites!' Aaliyah grumbled, tossing her swishy ponytail around like a horse flicking away a cloud of flies.

Not for the first time, Jo marvelled at Aaliyah's luxuriant mane, the ponytail extending as far as her perfectly pert bottom. 'Do you have a hairpiece?' she asked. She had never been able to grow her hair past the top of her shoulders.

'Eww, that's like, totally gross and a bit personal.' Aaliyah shuddered before taking a bite of toast slathered in butter and Marmite. Jo wouldn't normally give house room to the vile concoction, but...

'Sorry, I just wondered—'

'No, I do *not* have herpes. Not the ones on the face, and certainly not the ones down under.' Aaliyah gestured to her crotch, her face contorted in horror. 'I knew someone once who had these horrible thingies all over their lips, like something out of The Plague. Revolting.'

Jo didn't know whether to laugh or cry. 'No, I meant a *hair* piece.' She enunciated the words carefully, pointing at her head then at Aaliyah's. 'It's a fake piece — well, sometimes it's made of real hair — that you attach for extra length or volume. I've never tried one myself, but they're pretty popular.'

'Not with me, sweetie. I am one hundred per cent au

naturel.' Aaliyah chomped through her toast, pushing the crusts to one side.

Jo poured herself cereal and a mug of coffee. 'We need to leave at 11.30 to open up,' she said. Aaliyah nodded, then turned the radio back up.

'Listen, I've been thinking.' Jo sliced a banana on top of her granola. 'About my parents, and about things to wish for. I wondered if—'

'You want new ones? I'm not sure my WIFI can conjure up replacement mums and dads. I did try to resurrect Horatio the hamster, bless him, but something went wrong and he wasn't the same.' Aaliyah shivered.

'What do you mean?' Jo's appetite shrivelled up at the thought of a dead rodent showing up. Not that she was a fan of live ones, either. Her only family pet had been a supercilious cat called Candy, who had walked into her parents' kitchen one day and never left.

'It was like something from a Stephen King movie. What's the one? Ah, yes, *Pet Sematary*. It fair gave me the heebie jeebies, Jo. All blood-red eyes and pointy teeth, snapping and snarling like a bad 'un.'

'What did you do?' Jo chased away both her vision of a demonic hamster and her surprise at Aaliyah's knowledge of the works of Stephen King. By now, nothing ought to surprise her about genies.

Aaliyah's expression was distinctly sheepish. 'Well, I couldn't let my master see it like that. Or his daughter, bless her. Cute little thing, but scared of her own shadow. So I disposed of it humanely, like. A quick whack with a shovel, buried it in the herb garden, and that was me done with raising the dead. So if you're asking—'

Jo shook her head so hard that her brain rattled. 'No, absolutely not. That's not what I meant. I'd just like the chance to spend one more day with them. Go back in time, I guess. Tell them how much I loved them. How much I *love* them. We rarely said it, I don't know why. We just weren't a family who said stuff out loud.' Jo closed her eyes, forcing back the tears. 'Stupid, isn't it. So many words spill out of our mouths every day, but the ones that really matter get stuck or swallowed because actions speak louder, as the saying goes.'

'No idea what you're on about,' said Aaliyah. 'Me and Dhassim were all about the action, if you catch my drift.' She winked, and Jo pushed away her untouched cereal. 'He liked to gush on a bit, mind you, did Dhassim. Dribble, dribble, waffle, waffle. Hard work, I tell ya!'

Jo didn't want to hear about Aaliyah's sex life, and especially not the dribbling bit. Her own remained a distant, rather dull memory. 'If I could have just a day, even a few hours, with Mum and Dad, it would give me closure. God, I hate that word, but I don't know how else to put it.'

Aaliyah yawned and whipped out her WIFI. *What did I expect?* thought Jo. An outpouring of empathy from a woman who'd bludgeoned a mutant hamster to death with a garden tool?

'Looks like it might be your lucky day, Jo.' Aaliyah pushed buttons in a shotgun fashion, the device tinkling and beeping as she jabbed away. How she managed to hit the right ones with such long nails remained a mystery. 'Reet, you have to say your wish out loud, like. Ready, steady, go!'

Jo closed her eyes and swallowed. 'I wish to spend one more day with my parents. As they were before, not after they died, obviously.' She garbled the last bit, thoughts of shuffling zombie-like creatures making her stomach churn.

There was silence, then... 'Your wish is granted.'

Jo's ears hissed and popped, her stomach lurched, then everything went dark.

CHAPTER 10

THE WARMTH OF THE DUVET ENVELOPED JO, HER HEAD cocooned by the fluffy pillow. The rhythmic glug of the radiator and the faint traffic noise barely registered as she stretched her legs and wiggled her toes. Ooh, still some residual heat in the fleece-covered hot-water bottle. Jo snared the bottle with her feet, brought it further up the bed, and—

Wait a minute. Jo's radiator didn't glug, hardly any cars passed her house, and she hadn't used a hot-water bottle in years.

She sat up so quickly that her vision blurred. Blinking furiously, she took in her surroundings bit by bit. The garish green and blue wallpaper. The white wooden dressing table with trifold mirrors. The wonky wardrobe, one door always slightly ajar.

She was home.

As if on cue, an achingly familiar voice came from below. 'Are you awake, love? Just popping some bangers under the grill, or Lorne sausage if you'd rather.'

Jo pulled the duvet up to her chin. She remembered shopping with her mum for the chambray cover. Its daisy design clashed with the walls, but that didn't matter. The combination of pretty flowers and paisley-patterned paper might have induced a headache in some people, but Jo had adored her bedroom and all its quirky charms.

Her gaze alighted on the pale-blue towelling dressing gown hanging on the back of the door. *Wait a minute.* That had been a gift from her mum when she finished school, purchased from an upmarket boutique in Glasgow. It even bore her name, hand-stitched in gold thread.

Throwing herself out of bed, Jo lurched towards the dressing table. She gasped in disbelief. Her reflection was that of a girl in her late teens, before almost three decades of life and its ups and downs had etched themselves on her face.

Touching her cheek, Jo grinned at the mop of badly bleached hair: a DIY job done on a whim when her parents were out at the local pub with friends. Her mum hadn't been best pleased at the state of the bathroom and the ruined towel, streaked with white patches—

'Are you decent?' Her mum at the bedroom door, never one to barge in uninvited.

'Two secs,' Jo replied, grabbing the robe from its hook and shrugging it on over her pyjamas. She tied the belt firmly around her waist — jeez, she'd been skinny back then — and opened the door.

There she stood: her gorgeous, caring, generous mum. She'd be around the same age now as Jo, in her mid to late forties. Beautiful, even without a scrap of make-up, and sporting her checked robe and ancient slippers.

'Did you sleep well, love?' Her mum smiled and Jo drank in her glowing good health, a stark contrast with her last days, when she'd faded to a shadow of her former self.

'I did, thanks.' Jo had no idea if she had or not. One minute she'd made her wish, the next she was in her childhood bed. Aaliyah's wish-granting gizmo had chosen to send her back in time, to her teenage years.

'I thought you might be hungry, so I've cooked both and some bacon. Dad's just popped out for fresh rolls. Fancy an egg?'

Jo's mouth watered at the thought of a good old Scottish fry-up. Nowadays she avoided such fat-laden delights, but at eighteen she'd had no need to count calories. 'That'd be great, Mum. A fried one, sunny side up.'

Leaving Jo to get dressed, her mum padded downstairs, humming. Jo closed the door and looked around for the clothes she'd been wearing when she made her wish. Slim black jeans, a grey cashmere jumper and suede ankle boots. There was no sign of them. She opened the wardrobe, grinning at the sight of the early nineties attire on display. Garish printed leggings that made her eyes water, with an array of flannel shirts and halter-neck tops in bright hues. Pastel pedal pushers, and corsets for nights out with the girls.

Jo slid some hangers to the side and wistfully stroked the faux-silk baby-pink slip dress and the black crushed velvet number she'd coveted for weeks, eventually saving up enough money from her Saturday job to buy both. She remembered going on a date with a lad to see *Jurassic Park*, followed by a meal at the local carvery. Looking back, the slinky pink number had been a tad over the top, but Jo had felt like a princess even in her denim jacket. Gavin Collins, that was him. A nice enough lad, a couple of years older, with slicked-back hair and a Volkswagen Beetle. Jo had grabbed his hand several times during the scary bits of the film, and he'd kissed her after driving her home. Conscious of the amount of garlic that had been in her chicken curry, Jo had responded nervously. She needn't have worried, though; Gavin's kissing technique had reminded her of a plunger unblocking a toilet. She hadn't gone out with him again.

Choosing a pair of high-waisted jeans and a long-sleeved cotton top, Jo dressed and headed downstairs. Delicious aromas emanated from the kitchen, and the radio was playing one of her favourite songs of the year, 'Dreams' by Gabrielle.

'Hi, Dad.' Her father sat at the table, the newspaper spread out in front of him. He was wearing his weekend uniform of polo shirt and chinos, his hair still damp from the shower. Like her mum, he radiated good health, the heart that would eventually fail him currently pumping blood round his body with military precision.

'Hi, love. Be an angel and butter those rolls, would you? My stomach thinks my throat's been cut. What's a man got to do to get fed around here, eh, Helen?' He winked at her mum, who whacked him with a tea towel.

'Less of your cheek, Neil! If it were down to you, we'd dine on fish and chips and jam butties day in, day out.'

'Guilty as charged.' Jo's dad was a highly respected plumber, with a roster of clients dependent on his expertise and his willingness to offer discounts to those in need. His culinary skills, however, were a source of constant amusement.

They tucked into their plates of food. Neil slathered his with brown sauce, Helen kept the mugs topped up with tea, and Jo tried not to gawp at them both. She pierced her egg, the yolk pooling around the crispy bacon rashers. She took a bite, her throat tensing as the food slipped downwards.

'All right, Jo?' Her dad looked at her quizzically.

She nodded, forcing the food down with a swig of builder's brew. *How long do I have?* The kitchen clock showed

10 am. A few hours, a day, or longer? She wanted to freeze time, postpone the inevitable, but something told her that time wasn't on her side.

'I'm fine, Dad.'

Tick, tock, went the clock.

CHAPTER 11

'IF I COULD TURN BACK TIME' BY CHER WARBLED IN THE background as Harvey sorted his pathetic selection of socks into pairs. Why was there always an odd one? Did its partner slink off into sock solitude, relieved to break free? A *conscious uncoupling:* that phrase coined by Gwyneth Paltrow and Chris Martin when they went their separate ways. That stuck in Harvey's throat and gave him the 'dry boak': the urge to vomit without actually doing the deed.

Tossing the lone sock to one side, Harvey folded a couple of shirts in the manner instilled in him by Lindsey. Straighten up the back, line up the sleeves and smooth everything down with careful precision. Collar neatly buttoned, all ready to put on a shelf. He had two shelves for shirts and T-shirts, a drawer for underwear, and a half-width wardrobe for hanging his two good suits, a handful of casual trousers and Lindsey's wedding dress.

It swung on its hanger, the sweetheart neckline and chiffon bodice so achingly pretty. The full-length embroidered skirt with swirls of mother-of-pearl and appliquéd flowers — Lindsey's favourite apple blossom — as fresh and vibrant as the day she'd stood next to him and said, 'I do'. He'd been the proudest, happiest, most sickeningly loved-up person that day. When Harvey had said 'I do', he'd wanted to repeat it over and over in case anyone didn't get the message. But Lindsey had. She'd taken his hands in hers, steadied him with a squeeze that spoke a thousand words, and sealed the deal with a kiss that had the tiny congregation whooping and cheering. The minister hadn't been best pleased, but who cared? It had been their day. The joining of two people who'd found each other, for better or worse, and everyone else could form an orderly line behind them on the road to contentment.

'Lindsey.' Harvey brushed away a tear. So many tears... He wondered when — if — they ever stopped. 'Girl, you make my heart break every single day. There are days when I think I can't go on. Without you, there's no point. I'm a husk, I'm broken, and no one can ever put me together again.' He paused. 'Is it time?'

Unbidden, the dress swayed a little, as if a gentle breeze had shifted the fabric. Yet the window remained closed, and nothing else stirred. Nothing apart from Harvey's heart, which pumped harder. He touched the dress, then brought his fingers to his nose. The faintest hint of Lindsey's signature perfume lingered — or was that his deluded imagination?

Don't even think about leaving this world yet.

Those words were in her voice. The voice he carried with him like a precious gift, as if everything she'd said over the course of their relationship had been stored inside. Every thought shared, every opinion expressed, all tucked away for posterity.

'I won't.' Harvey closed the wardrobe. He eyed the bed, its bottom sheet crinkled and the duvet piled in a heap. When had he last changed the covers? Two, three weeks ago?

A wave of exhaustion hit him and he slumped on the bed, pulling the duvet over his weary limbs. He had nowhere to go, no one to see, nothing that prevented him from seeking solace under a crumpled, stale quilt.

Closing his eyes, Harvey drifted off on a wave of bad smells and worse memories. How could a man have it all — the perfect wife, the perfect life, the perfect career — only for it all to collapse like a badly played game of Jenga?

Lindsey's illness had come first. A cough that persisted, stubborn against the various potions dispensed at the chemist. She'd insisted she was fine. Why wouldn't she be? The woman pounded out miles on the treadmill, made smoothies every morning, and had never smoked in her life. She was a poster girl for the fifty-somethings who stuck two fingers up at articles stating what women of 'a certain age' should wear, or how they ought to behave. A rebel with a clear cause: live life to its fullest, and bugger the naysayers.

Harvey flipped over, trying to turn away from the images of Lindsey's rapid decline and the diagnosis that had stunned them both. The unfairness of it all: his beautiful wife destined to wither away, despite all the drugs, treatments and technology available in the twenty-first century. She fought and she fought, but in the end, the slayer couldn't conquer the dragon.

What had come next? Harvey tried to sort the pieces in his mind. The months of grieving, of waking up and hoping it had been a bad dream. The support of colleagues, being on location filming and escaping himself for a little while. Inhabiting another skin, and shedding the one that kept you flailing around in misery. It had worked for a while to dull the pain.

Snatching the fresher pillow from the opposite side of the bed, Harvey craved a glass of something strong, but hadn't the energy to go downstairs. He'd kept a bottle of whisky by the bed for a while, but he knew that was a road best not travelled.

Funny how life dumps on you from on high, then comes back to dump some more. Harvey could never have anticipated the next cruel twist, and he'd been too numb with grief to see the signs.

A fellow actor went out of her way to cheer him up with small acts of kindness. Things like fetching him his favourite takeaway coffee, often with a sticky bun or a chocolate bar. He'd never admitted to disliking chocolate. He was too polite to say, and in hindsight, he'd been flattered by the attention. And where was the harm in going for the odd drink together once they'd finished a gruelling day of filming? If other people raised eyebrows, Harvey didn't care. It was when she started turning up on his doorstep, claiming she was 'just passing', that the alarm bells rang — but not loudly enough. By the time he realised what she was doing, things were already out of control.

Sod it! Harvey levered himself upright and groaned as his right knee refused to cooperate with the left. Hobbling, he cursed under his breath. He'd let everything slide since losing Lindsey, his job and his self-esteem. At least his friend Johnnie Walker didn't judge or pass comment. They'd sit together for a while, until the edges blurred and the world seemed a little more bearable.

CHAPTER 12

'ANY PLANS FOR THE DAY?' JO'S MUM ASKED AS SHE CLEARED away the breakfast bits. When Jo had been in her teens, her mum had worked part-time in the local library. A total bookworm, she usually had several on the go: everything from romantic novels and gritty thrillers to cookery books and biographies. Jo had inherited her love of baking from her mum, with Fridays after school set aside for a full-on cake-making session. Unsurprisingly, Jo's friends loved to drop by on a Friday evening to sample the goodies.

'Erm, not really.' Jo grabbed a tea towel and started on the drying up. 'What day is it?'

Her dad laughed, a sound she'd never imagined hearing again. 'You're a bit young to be forgetting things, love!' he said. 'Unlike me and your mum. Lucky I've got my trusty work diary to keep me on my toes, and your mum's always scribbling wee notes to herself.'

'It's Saturday,' said Helen, squirting the greasy frying pan with washing-up liquid. 'Are you not heading into town? I'd come with you, but there's a mountain of ironing to do and your dad's promised to fix the dripping tap in the cloakroom.

Married to a plumber, and I still have to join the queue to get a wee job done.'

'Could we do something together? The three of us, I mean.'

Both her parents stared at her. God, had she been such an awful daughter that the suggestion of spending Saturday with them stunned them into silence?

'Are you sure, love? Maybe you're coming down with something,' said her mum, reaching out to touch Jo's forehead. 'Barbara at the library had a shocking tummy bug last week. I swear she got through a month's supply of toilet roll, and you know how stingy the council is with basic supplies. And the gurgling noises when she—'

'Too much information,' chided her dad. 'If our girl wants to spend time with us wrinklies, that's what we should do.'

'But what about the tap? And the ironing?' Her mum's brow creased, reflecting her anxiety about the ironing.

'Mum, these things don't matter. Who cares if a tap drips for one more day, or Dad wears crumpled boxer shorts? Dad doesn't need razor-sharp folds in his underwear. Do you, Dad?'

Neil had the good grace to look embarrassed. For years, Jo had tried to persuade her mum that she spent too much time dealing with petty details instead of *living*. Her mum argued that attending to little things gave her pleasure: a sense of order in a world dominated by chaos, inequality and injustice. Helen Milligan couldn't change the world, but she'd tried to maintain her own quiet corner with dignity, fabric conditioner and slices of roly-poly pudding.

'Well, you're not at the supermarket today, so I guess we could go somewhere. Where do you fancy, love?'

Jo rifled through her brain, trying to think of a place. A happy place, that would give her new memories to cherish. Somewhere, when this wish ended, that she could revisit to hold on to the happiness and let it wash away the grief she'd carried for so long.

It came to her in seconds. 'Let's go to Largs. We can eat fish and chips and mushy peas and walk along the promenade. And then we can have ice cream — Italian ice cream, gelato — and hope the bloody seagulls don't swoop down and snatch the cones.'

Jo had always loved Largs. Under an hour's drive away on the Firth of Forth, it boasted stunning beaches, an elegant Victorian promenade, and possibly the best ice cream anywhere in Scotland. Not to mention Hasties department store, where you could buy anything from a kilt to tinned smoked mussels. A veritable Aladdin's cave, which brought Aaliyah to mind, it had closed down in 2015 or thereabouts. But this was 1993, and it would still be there in all its eclectic glory.

'I can drive if you like.' Jo's parents owned an ancient Ford Fiesta nicknamed Betty, as well as her dad's functional white van with *Milligan's Plumbing Services (No Job Too Big Or Small)* emblazoned on the side.

'You haven't passed your test yet, love.' Jo's mum gave her a puzzled look and felt her forehead again. 'She's a wee bit hot, Neil. Why don't you fetch the thermometer from the first-aid kit?'

The heat emanating from Jo owed more to embarrassment at her gaffe than any tummy bug. She'd gained her driving licence days before her nineteenth birthday, after more lessons than she cared to remember.

'Just joking, Mum! Dad, there's no need to check my temperature, honestly. I'm fine. Absolutely fine.'

'It's not exactly seaside weather,' said her mum, peering out of the window. 'Wouldn't you rather stay cosy indoors? We could watch something together, or play cards. We've plenty of cake, and I can rustle up something with leftovers.'

Jo stood next to her mum at the window. Sure enough, a smattering of rain streaked its surface, and the sky suggested a heavier downpour on the horizon. But Scotland prided itself on chucking more than one season in per day — and the Scots prided themselves on getting on with it, regardless of Mother Nature.

'Aw, come on, Mum. If the worst comes to the worst, we can eat our fish and chips in the car with the windscreen wipers going full pelt. Just like the old days.' *Swoosh, swoosh,* they'd gone, hypnotic in their rhythm, as a young Jo chewed a malt vinegar-soaked chip and listened to her parents' good-natured bickering about why they'd ended up dining in their car on a rain-lashed summer's day.

'If that's what you want to do, that's what we'll do.' Her dad nodded at her mum, who nodded back. Two peas in a pod; occasionally rubbing each other up the wrong way, but united in the things that mattered. *Mushy peas.* Jo giggled at the double meaning.

'Right, waterproof jackets needed, then. Neil, go and turn Betty's engine over; she's been playing up, and the last thing we need is for her to conk out en route. Jo, your hair could do with a brush, love. I'll just pop some lipstick on, and your dad could probably do with a shave.'

Neil rubbed his stubbly chin and got to his feet. 'Right, I'll crank up Betty and run my razor over this handsome face.'

Ten minutes later, they were on their way. Snuggled up in the back with a tartan throw over her legs, as Betty's heating was unpredictable, Jo savoured the moment. Her mum switched on the radio and the raspy voice of Rod Stewart singing 'Have I Told You Lately' filled the car. Jo hummed along, happiness filling her from head to toe.

CHAPTER 13

Jo and her parents strode along the Victorian promenade, buffeted by the wind, yet exhilarated by the bracing sea air. The weather had cleared, a watery sun peeking out from behind the clouds.

'Shall we skim stones?' said her dad, with all the enthusiasm of a young boy released from the stuffy confines of a classroom.

'You're a bit long in the tooth for that nonsense, Neil,' her mum said, good-naturedly.

'What do you mean?' her husband retorted. 'I'm barely a day over fifty, and all my teeth are my own.'

Jo linked arms with them both. Her dad's was solid and muscular, her mum's slender and surprisingly warm through her quilted jacket. She knew her dad was nearer sixty than fifty, but he was still as fit as a fiddle. At least, he was back then.

'Let's eat first; I'm absolutely starving,' said her mum. 'Besides, Jo and I will trounce you at stone-skimming.'

They stopped for a moment to look at the shingly beach. A few hardy souls were perched on plaid blankets. Armed with Thermos flasks and shielded by wind-breakers, they nibbled on home-made sandwiches and chatted.

'After all that breakfast you scoffed? Jo, I swear your mum's got a second stomach. Mind you, I'm peckish. There's something about the air here that stirs the appetite.'

Jo squeezed her dad's arm in agreement. Largs might not be big-city glamorous, but it wore a cloak of charm scented with salt, vinegar, and other smells that tickled the tastebuds. She hadn't been in years, too afraid to revisit the past. But now the past was the present: one special day to treasure for as long as she inhabited this earth. A gift that few received, unless they had a genie rattling round their home.

'Nardini's?' her dad asked, and raised an eyebrow.

'Nardini's,' they replied in unison. 'Where else?'

* * *

'THIS IS THE LIFE.' Jo's dad stretched out his long legs, nearly tripping a young waitress scuttling past with a laden tray. 'Sorry, love,' he said, drawing his legs back under the table.

'What are we all having?' Jo put down the menu. She'd decided on her choice before they'd set foot in the place: battered haddock, chips, mushy peas, and lashings of tartare sauce.

Another waitress appeared, notepad and pen at the ready. Are you ready to order?' she asked. 'We have scampi on the menu today, and our desserts include tiramisu and Black Forest gateau.'

Jo smiled inwardly. Such things were the epitome of sophistication back in the nineties, or possibly even earlier. Funny how the culinary world had evolved, with exotic ingredients now commonplace. Artichokes, avocados, quinoa and hummus, which Jo vaguely remembered her mum bringing home one day. Such excitement — although neither she nor Dad had been smitten by the taste.

'Haddock for me.' Jo reeled off her side-order requirements. Her mum opted for the same, while her dad dithered for a few seconds before settling on scampi. Drinks-wise, they each chose a shandy, then settled back in their chairs, eagerly anticipating the feast to come.

'This is nice,' declared her mum, scanning the Art Deco-style room. Babies squirmed in highchairs, their mothers spooning in indeterminate mush and attempting to shovel in their own cooling food between reluctant mouthfuls. Couples shared bowls of multi-hued ice cream, the intimacy of spoons being passed to and fro a painful reminder of Jo's single status. Not her current single status, of course. At eighteen, she'd never given a thought to being married or in a steady relationship. Boys had come and gone while Jo focused on her studies at Lanarkshire Catering School. Relatively new, it had given Jo the qualification she needed to pursue her passion for food, and eventually, run her own business.

'Aye, it is nice,' said her dad, taking a swig of his shandy. 'You can't beat a day by the seaside with two of the most gorgeous women on the planet.'

'You silver-tongued rascal,' chided her mum. 'Don't think I didn't spot you eyeing up that glamorous blonde in the corner when we came in.'

'What blonde?' replied her dad, sipping his shandy with casual indifference. 'Surely you don't mean that buxom creature over there?' He nodded towards a heavily made-up woman of around sixty, sharing a table with a younger man: perhaps her son or toy boy. No, definitely the latter, as she squeezed his knee in a most unmaternal manner. He gazed adoringly at her — or rather, her tanned, impressive cleavage.

'If he falls in there, he'll need a ladder to get out!' joked her dad, earning a dig in the ribs from Jo's mum.

The food arrived, piping hot and smelling divine. Jo's parents got stuck in, and she dunked a chip in the tartare sauce. It burned her tongue, and she took a cooling sip of shandy. Then something struck her like a punch to the stomach: her parents had less than twelve years to live. They'd both passed away shortly before her thirtieth birthday. They'd never met her fiancé, Graham — not that Jo imagined he or his control-freak mother would have met with their approval — or witnessed Jo's rise through the ranks of the catering industry. So many things had been missed, so much left unsaid. If only she'd known... But in her teens, she'd believed her parents would be around for much longer.

'You OK, Jo?' Helen put down her fork and dabbed at her mouth with a paper napkin. 'You're not eating much.'

Jo's throat tightened and she blinked away tears. 'The chips are hot; they're making my eyes water.'

Half an hour later they were on the beach, each with an ice cream cone, licking furiously to catch the drips.

'Right, stone-skimming time!' Her dad crunched the last of his cone and bent to locate a suitable pebble. Jo and her mum followed suit, taking turns to flick their stones across the water. Her dad's bounced a pathetic three times, her mum's a marginally more impressive five. Jo whooped with delight as she counted one, two, three, four, five, six, seven, eight, nine...

Before she got to ten, the stone sank. Her legs wobbled, and she grabbed her dad's arm as her vision blurred and the sounds of excited children and dogs faded away. *No, not now!*

'Jo, what's the matter?' Her dad wrapped his arm around her and she buried her face in his chest. *Please, Aaliyah, just a few more minutes.*

Buffeted by a sudden gust of wind, Jo disentangled herself

and stood swaying between her parents, their concerned faces swimming in and out of view. 'Mum, Dad, I love you so much. I wish I'd said it more often. You're the best parents anyone could ever have, and I will miss you every single day for the rest of my life.'

'Jo, I think you need a wee sit down and a cup of tea.' Her mum's words brought a weak smile to Jo's face, even as the beach shifted unnervingly beneath her. A cup of tea: the answer to all life's problems.

'Jo, you know we love you too. Maybe we don't say it enough, but—' Her dad's voice was distant and echoey.

'Of course we do! Neil, should we call for help?' Her mum, pragmatic as always, but rapidly disappearing.

'I love you!' Jo screamed at the sky. Then it swooped down and everything went black.

CHAPTER 14

'Could I have a little word with you, Jinnie?' Jo eyed her friend, whose arm was entwined with Sam's. 'In private.'

'I've stuff to do back at the shop, so I'll leave you two to it.' Sam winked at Jinnie, who blew him a kiss in return. They'd arrived at A Bit of Crumpet moments before, ordering slabs of tarte flambée, a recent addition to Jo's repertoire. Aaliyah was out back, purportedly making black-bean brownies. There was no sound of the food mixer, though, and Jo thought it extremely unlikely that she was mixing it by hand,.

Sam left the café, pausing to blow a kiss back at Jinnie, who play-caught it in her hand. Every fibre of her body screamed, 'Look at me, I'm a smitten kitten!' Jo resisted the urge to snarl like a grouchy dog — or bitch. Just because Jinnie had found her happy-ever-after didn't mean Jo should lift her leg and pee on her happiness. What she did want to do, however, was get to the bottom of the whole lamp/genie/wishes conundrum.

'What's up, Jo?' Jinnie perched on a stool, winding a strand of hair around her finger. 'You look a bit out of sorts.

Is everything OK?' Her voice sounded normal, but the hair-twisting suggested a certain twitchiness.

'How was your holiday?' asked Jo nonchalantly. 'Lucky you, being able to escape Cranley for a month.'

Jinnie shrugged, although her nervous smile lifted a notch. 'It was incredible, Jo. I always thought cruises were for older people — I mean, much older people — but I couldn't have been more wrong. We made loads of new friends and saw some amazing places. Oh, and the food! I ate more in a month than I usually eat in three.' She patted her slightly rounded stomach and giggled. 'That's a food baby, by the way, not a real one.'

The sound of the food mixer firing into action coincided with the arrival of a customer. Cursing under her breath, Jo told Jinnie to sit in the furthest corner of the café, then dealt with the order. She made them a pot of tea to share, and prayed for no further interruptions.

'Jo, I get the feeling you're mad at me. Can you tell me what's bugging you, please?'

Without a word, Jo pointed at the high shelf housing the two lamps. 'I bought them from Sam,' she said. 'But you know that already. And I guess you also knew these were no ordinary lamps, but you didn't tell me.'

Jinnie blushed and attempted to pour the tea, and hot liquid pooled in the saucers. Jo mopped up the spillage with a napkin and took over.

'I'm so sorry, Jo.' Jinnie's blush deepened. 'I was so shocked when Sam told me you'd bought the lamps that I didn't know what to do for the best.'

'So you did nothing?' Jo stirred her tea clockwise, then anti-clockwise. 'A wee warning would have been nice.'

'What would I have said? Oh, by the way, those lamps contain genies, so go easy on the cleaning. Either you wouldn't have believed me, or you'd have thought me madder than a box of frogs. Trust me, Jo, it took me a while to accept the insanity of it all.'

Jo reached out and squeezed Jinnie's trembling hand. 'Sweetheart, I understand. Well, kind of. But by the time I met my new *friend*, you'd sailed off into the sunset with Sam. I suppose you weren't to know I'd get polishing so quickly.'

'Jo, it comes as no surprise that you'd get busy cleaning them up. Not that they were in bad shape, really. Which one did you…?' Jinnie eyed the shelf again. 'I know they're similar, but I'll never forget Sam giving me the first one. That one.' She pointed at the lamp on the right. 'Which means…'

'I got the female version. She's currently working as my assistant, God help me. Apparently your genie's sulking. Not that I want both of them shacked up with me; a ménage à trois is definitely not on my wish list.'

They paused as several expletives emanated from the kitchen. A customer tutted and headed for the door.

'I didn't really know Aaliyah,' Jinnie continued. 'She only appeared right at the end, when Dhassim was getting ready to move on.' Jinnie wiped away a tear with the soggy, tea-soaked napkin. 'He drove me nuts, but his heart was in the right place.'

'Well, Aaliyah is a piece of work,' huffed Jo. 'She has no respect for privacy or property, and she looks down her nose at any task she feels is beneath her. And she has a Geordie accent, although that's veering towards Scottish now.'

Jinnie nodded. 'When we met, I figured she'd be a tricky one. Not that Dhassim was easy, but we muddled along.'

'Sounds like you got the better deal,' said Jo. 'So, how did the three wishes thing go?'

Jinnie gave a derisive snort. 'Three wishes my arse! Dhassim said that was so passé. He was adamant that things had changed — evolved, I think he said. He even insisted that the term genie was outdated. He preferred *personal wish-fulfilment assistant*, would you believe.'

A familiar figure appeared at the front window. Harvey, if Jo wasn't mistaken. He lingered for a second, then disappeared. Ah well, it wasn't like they were besties. And she had more to worry about than a gruff stranger with an attitude problem.

'Jo, are you listening?' Jinnie tapped a teaspoon on her cup. 'I got more than three wishes, and some of them were completely random. I can list them for you, if you like—'

Aaliyah swooped into the café, eyes glittering with annoyance. 'That black-bean mix looks like something you'd fertilise roses with. Not that I'm a gardening expert, mind...' She halted, taking in the sight of Jo and Jinnie huddled over their cooling cups of tea. 'Wait a minute. Don't I know you from somewhere?' Aaliyah stared at Jinnie, who stared back. Who would crack first? They reminded Jo of a couple of cowboys: guns at the ready, but neither quite prepared to take the first shot.

'Bingo!' Aaliyah punched the air in jubilation. 'You were Dhassim's mistress, right? Well, not in the sexual sense.' She grinned. 'As if he'd have the hots for you when he had little old me to play with. Who wants a burger when you can have a steak, if you catch my drift.' Leaving Jinnie gaping like a landed fish — and Jo gobsmacked by her cheek — Aaliyah turned and stomped off.

'Wow, you've really got your work cut out with that one.' Jinnie's face said it all. Two lamps meant a fifty-fifty chance of getting it right. Or almost right.

'I know.' Jo sighed. 'If she was made of chocolate, she'd eat herself.'

CHAPTER 15

THE TRAIN TO EDINBURGH RATTLED ALONG AS HARVEY STARED at a crossword puzzle on his phone. He tutted at a seven-letter clue: *Not solid or liquid*. Nothing came to mind, except that his diet recently had been more liquid than solid.

Already jaded with the scant charms of Cranley, he'd figured a trip to Auld Reekie might inject some much-needed excitement into his life. The capital's nickname, a throwback to its days of smoke pollution and sewage smells, brought to mind Harvey's need for new bedlinen. Not to mention a supply of decent coffee, a selection of ready meals and perhaps a couple of shirts. His pathetic wardrobe could do with something new, not that he was out to impress anyone. Lindsey would turn in her grave if she saw his day-to-day attire. Less shabby chic, more two steps away from vagrant.

As the train pulled into the station, Harvey switched off his phone and tucked it into his pocket. An elegant woman who looked vaguely familiar sidled past him, a fleecy-coated dog trotting at her heels. The unmistakable sound of a fart emanated from either the woman or her pet. Harvey coughed, his money on the pooch.

The woman smiled apologetically and hurried to the door. Harvey's nostrils twitched at the lingering odour, and the crossword answer came to him in a flash. *Gaseous.*

Born and bred on the West coast, Harvey's heart belonged to Glasgow, but he grudgingly admitted that Edinburgh's architecture and history were impressive. Its smoky, gothic buildings grafted on to the shoulder of an extinct volcano. Its castle looming large, the Edinburgh Tattoo centrepiece to the annual festival with all its glorious military pageantry. Harvey had only been once, many years ago. The heavens had opened, and umbrellas were not allowed.

Edinburgh was famous for many things, including its weather, but not for the right reasons. He recalled a dour taxi driver who had picked him up after a Fringe production, where he'd played Macbeth in a modernised version of the Shakespeare play. Set in a council estate, the three witches had been a trio of home-brewing harpies, and Banquo a ghostly drug dealer with a penchant for profanity. 'Another typical Edinburgh night,' the taxi driver had moaned, the windscreen wipers thrashing back and forth. 'Wet, windy and grey, and this is supposed to be summer.'

Today, the skies were gentler. Harvey strode along Princes Street, dodging the tourists high on tartan overkill and all things Scottish, and the locals seeking out lunches to go or a quiet pint in one of the hundreds of pubs that populated the city. Tempted though he was, Harvey kept going, smiling at a lone piper entertaining a crowd.

His first port of call was the iconic department store, Jenners. Nestled on a street corner, its rooftop boasted a collection of caryatids — sculpted female figures — acting as pillars. Holding things up, as women so often did. Lindsey had loved Jenners, though they'd only visited it a handful of times during their relationship.

Stepping through the doors, Harvey wished with all his heart that Lindsey was by his side. But she was, of course, and always would be. Death might have parted them, but she'd still give him a flea in the ear if he chose an unflattering shirt or failed to acknowledge a helpful shop assistant's attempts to steer him in the right direction.

The menswear department boasted an array of designer clothing, as well as more budget-friendly items. Since the acting roles had dried up, Harvey relied on his savings and the money from Lindsey's life-insurance policy. He located a rail of reasonably priced cotton shirts and grabbed three. He'd never been a fan of upmarket labels emblazoned with logos: they should pay *him* for advertising.

The next stop was a boutique coffee shop, where Harvey picked up enough quality java to keep him going for a couple of months. The cheerful owner persuaded him to try a new blend, enthusiastically proclaiming it a 'rich and nutty combination of beans from Colombia, Costa Rica, Brazil and Ethiopia.' As Harvey doubted he'd visit any of those countries, he added a bag to his collection.

Torn between Primark and Marks and Spencer for new bedding, he opted for the latter. Heading for the homeware section, he checked the scrap of paper in his pocket for the dimensions. Double, he reckoned, although he'd measured the mattress just in case. Ten minutes later, he had selected a cream fitted sheet and a geometric-patterned duvet cover with matching pillowcases.

Right, time to hit the food hall. Descending into the basement, Harvey drooled at the thought of a meal deal for a tenner. A main, side dish and dessert, requiring minimum effort, and a huge step up from his recent culinary attempts.

Awkwardly wrestling a basket from the pile, his shopping

bags now cutting into his arm, Harvey located the meal-deal section. What to choose? Perhaps roast duck à l'orange, or prawn and chargrilled chicken paella. Mind you, the steak and ale pie sounded tempting, with a side of truffled cauliflower cheese.

As he eyed the selection, he felt a tap on his shoulder. Turning, he came face to face with Jo from the café, her basket piled high with all manner of M&S goodies. 'I thought it was you!' she said. 'Now I'm busted, buying pre-cooked meals when I should be chained to the stove making everything from scratch.'

'No reason why you should,' replied Harvey. 'It's good to have a break when you spend most of your time baking stuff. Not that I mean you don't do other things; I just don't know what they are. And why would I? After all, your business is your own.'

Harvey wished he could pull a cork out of one of the wine bottles and ram it into his garrulous gob. He didn't mean to be rude to this woman every time they met, but somehow she brought out the worst in him.

'OK.' Jo stretched out the word, her expression neutral. And yet something, amusement or perhaps irritation, flashed in her eyes. Again, she reminded him of Lindsey. Not just the physical resemblance, but her spirit. In another life, Jo might have been the kind of woman he'd be attracted to. But stuck in this one, with all his baggage, that was a no-go area.

'I'll, um, leave you to it. Have a good day.' Jo lobbed a pack of triple-cooked chips into her basket and turned away.

Harvey stood for a moment, teetering on the brink. Lindsey's voice was in his head. *Stop being a complete eejit, H. You like her, and God help her, maybe she likes you too.*

Did she? He didn't even like himself, which made it hard to believe that anyone else would spare him a nanosecond of their time. He looked at his basket: the contents screamed

'Lonely guy about to eat on his own again.' Wouldn't it be nice to sit down with someone and just chat? A meal deal, with plenty to share. Nothing ventured, nothing gained...

'Jo, hang on a minute.' Harvey caught up with her at the till queue. 'I wondered if maybe ... if you didn't have other plans ... we could eat together? Tonight? At my place. Unless the thought of slumming it at Brae Cottage fills you with horror.'

Jo placed the last items on the belt. The sticky toffee pudding and profiterole stack glided by and she pulled a 'what's a girl to do?' face. 'That sounds good. I'll bring dessert and you can fill me in on the life of Harvey, the enigmatic stranger to Cranley and all its dubious charms.'

'Seven o'clock?' Harvey stammered, doubt trickling through his veins. This was insanity. This was a *date*.

No, this was not a date. This was a chance to prove that Harvey Quinn had a decent bone or two in his body. Not that many people believed that these days.

Jo swiped her credit card and packed away the purchases. 'So, see you at seven?'

Harvey nodded. 'Just one thing. Can you bring the triple-cooked chips?'

CHAPTER 16

Jo's trip to Edinburgh had been a spur-of-the-moment decision. She'd needed to get away, following the all-too-brief time with her parents. Such a bittersweet second chance; she wished it could have been much longer.

Jo had woken up dazed in her Cranley home, convinced it had been a dream. But it had been real. She'd found a scrunched-up Nardini's napkin in the pocket of her high-waisted jeans, folded neatly at the end of the bed alongside her teenage blouse and grown-up clothes. She had no memory of travelling back — or rather, forwards — in time, but she'd treasure every precious extra moment she'd had with the two people she loved most in the world.

Leaving Aaliyah in charge of A Bit of Crumpet had been a last-minute call that had filled Jo with terror. What if Aaliyah insulted someone, or served a gluten-laden cookie to someone with coeliac disease? Jo knew her regulars, and paid attention to dietary requests from the odd passing customer. Luckily, all seemed to have gone well.

Now, though, things were less smooth. 'You're not going

on a date looking like *that?*' Aaliyah looked Jo up and down with a lip so curled it made Elvis look like a novice.

Jo shrugged. She was wearing a simple linen top and comfortable jeans, unlike the high-waisted horrors she'd never fit into again unless she opted for gastric-band surgery. Her hair was in a loose topknot, her make-up not so much subtle as barely there. What was wrong with that? 'It's not a date. He's just a lonely guy with an attitude problem.' *Like someone else I know.*

'Whatever. I'm telling you, hun, if you're looking for some action, that outfit and face paint isn't going to deliver. Take it from an expert.'

'We're eating together, not indulging in rampant sex. And even if I was interested in him in that way — which I'm *not* — he'll have to take me as he finds me. Aaliyah, I appreciate your comments, but this is how I'm going out.'

Her genie sidekick shook her head, ponytail swinging. 'Not happening, girlfriend. What kind of Wish Fulfilment Assistant would I be if I didn't grant a few wee favours?' She opened Jo's wardrobe with a flourish and pushed the contents around, muttering under her breath.

'Aaliyah, I'm not getting changed, and that's that. Get your mitts off my clothes and get out of my—'

Jo gasped as Aaliyah gave a triumphant whoop and held up a stunning wraparound dress in dusky blue, embossed with tiny pink swallows. She'd never seen it before. Nor had she ever seen the cute navy suede ankle boots with heels just low enough to walk in.

Jo took the dress and boots, gazing at them. The silence was broken only by the unmistakable buzz and beep of Aaliyah's WIFI gizmo. 'This isn't a wish, is it? Because I'm pretty sure I didn't wish for a new outfit.' Jo couldn't deny how much she liked the ensemble, though. Without trying it on, she knew it would flatter her curves and give her a boost in the height department.

'Nah. I did an update on my WIFI last night and it's decided to go a bit mental, like. You've totally got two proper wishes left. Call this a bonus, but your coupon still needs some work.'

Coupon? Despite her Scottish heritage, it took Jo a few seconds to understand. As she'd said to Jinnie, the Geordie lass was segueing into a Scotswoman day by day. 'My face needs work?'

'All you need is a decent covering of foundation, a bit of eyebrow shaping, and some eyeliner and mascara. Oh, and a pop of colour to emphasise those cheekbones. Those need all the help they can get.'

Reluctantly accepting that Aaliyah was to tact what pollen was to hay-fever sufferers, Jo sat down and let Aaliyah get to work. Fifteen minutes later, Aaliyah stepped back with a satisfied sigh and passed Jo her hand mirror.

Jo blinked in amazement. She might not look ten years younger, but Aaliyah had worked miracles. Her skin looked dewy and fresh, her eyebrows no longer resembled a pair of disgruntled caterpillars, and she'd been spot on with the cheekbone comment. Amazingly, Aaliyah had opted for subtlety, with just a hint of liner and enough mascara to achieve an eye-popping but not overdone effect. 'Crikey, I'm stunned. I look like myself, but a shiny, improved version. What can I say but thank you!'

Aaliyah gave a swooping bow. 'You're very welcome. I did my best to fill in the cracks but I'm a genie, not a plasterer.' Before Jo could howl in protest, Aaliyah winked and cracked a genuine, from-the-heart grin. 'I'll step out while you get dressed. I suggest you accessorise with silver jewellery and let your hair down.'

Literally or figuratively? Jo pondered, as she stripped to her undies and slipped on the dress. It fitted perfectly, as did the ankle boots, once she'd located an unopened pair of tights. She had no intention of letting her hair down in Harvey's presence, though. A simple meal, a bit of harmless chat, then home for a camomile tea and deep slumber.

Unclipping her hair, Jo raked through it with her fingers. Remarkably, it fell into place. Had Aaliyah arranged that, too? Probably not, though her erstwhile partner in beautification still mystified her. *Of course she does. She's a genie, and you don't come across one of those very often. Maybe I should embrace the madness and just accept it.*

Jo checked her watch. Just time to pop to the loo, say her goodbyes and head to Harvey's. Oops, mustn't forget her contribution to the meal. She headed to the kitchen, where she found Aaliyah stir-frying noodles and swigging a beer. 'Lookin' mighty fine, boss,' she said, lacing her noodles with a glug of soy sauce and a sprinkling of chilli flakes. 'Have fun, and don't do anything I wouldn't do.'

Jo dropped the triple-cooked chips and sticky toffee pudding into a plastic carrier bag. 'I've never quite got that expression, but I'll be on my best behaviour. And I'm sure Harvey will be too.'

'Whatever. Just enjoy it, Jo, and don't worry about me. I'll dive into the delights of Netflix and perhaps partake of those profiteroles for dessert.'

Striding along the street towards Brae Cottage, Jo wondered what the evening held in store. If Harvey proved as dour as ever, though, she'd leave him to it. Life, as she well knew, was too short to waste on misery.

CHAPTER 17

HARVEY CHECKED THE OVEN. THE STEAK PIE WAS BROWNING nicely and the truffled cauliflower cheese bubbled away. All that remained was to pop in the triple-cooked chips, and Bob's your uncle. Whoever bloody Bob was.

The minuscule table and two folding chairs didn't exactly scream fine dining. Harvey had attempted to pimp them up with an old tablecloth he'd found in a cupboard and a pair of cushions, to lessen the hardness of the chairs. A bottle of white wine was in the fridge and an opened red breathed on the kitchen worktop. Stupidly, he hadn't asked what Jo preferred. Perhaps she didn't drink. He had sparkling water and some cans of Irn Bru, described as Scotland's other national drink apart from whisky. And he had plenty of that, too.

He inspected himself in the mirror. He was freshly shaven, wearing one of the new shirts and a decent pair of chinos. He fingered the scar on his cheek, as familiar now as an old friend — or a sworn enemy.

Not for the first time, Harvey marvelled that no one in

Cranley had recognised him. Admittedly, he hadn't been the star of *Chasing Shadows*, but over its four-year run it had brought in audiences of several million. In between series, he'd acted in a few low-key stage productions. He preferred live theatre to TV roles, but he couldn't deny that the show had paid very well.

He glanced at the mantelpiece, Lindsey's photo conspicuous by its absence. Taking it down felt like a betrayal, but Harvey didn't want to field questions about his wife. He didn't plan on revealing much about himself, but he wanted to know more about Jo. Hardly fair, but that was how he wanted it to be. How it *needed* to be.

A knock on the door signalled Jo's arrival. Harvey hurried to answer it, not that reaching any point in Brae Cottage required more than a few steps.

'Hi. Hope I'm not too early.' Jo swung a plastic bag from her left hand, her right held out expectantly.

For a mad moment, Harvey imagined grabbing it and twirling her around as he used to twirl Lindsey on the dance floor. He blinked away the memory and shook Jo's hand. At least that was an improvement on the last time she'd tried to instigate a handshake. 'Not at all. Perfectly punctual, as one should be.' Jeez, every time he spoke in this woman's company it came out wrong.

Stop being a pompous prick and act normal! Lindsey again. Except that Harvey had forgotten how to act, normally or otherwise.

'Erm, can I come in?' Jo hopped from one foot to the other. Harvey noted her cute boots: exactly the kind of footwear Lindsey went crazy for.

'Sorry. Please, come in.' He stood back, allowing Jo to enter. She dropped the bag and removed her coat, hanging it on one of the pegs in the hallway. Harvey admired her dress and the way her hair sat on her shoulders. Not over the top, but natural and very attractive.

'Here's the chips and pudding,' said Jo, proffering the bag. 'Something smells delicious, by the way. Can I do anything to help?'

Harvey took the bag and shook his head. 'All under control. I'll just get the chips underway while you make yourself at home. Not that it's much of a home, but…'

Jo touched his arm, and Harvey's resolution to treat the evening as a casual get-together took a battering. That touch ignited feelings he'd put on ice for a long time. 'It looks lovely to me. Home is where the heart is, right? That's what my parents used to say.' Her eyes misted over and Harvey sensed a deep sorrow behind her smile.

'It's a nice expression, but I'm not sure where my heart lies these days,' he replied, bitterness souring his words. 'Let's concentrate on our stomachs instead.'

Jo followed him into the kitchen and removed the packaging from the chips. Harvey wrangled them into the tiny oven alongside the other dishes. He offered Jo a drink, and she opted for a glass of red.

'Here you go.' Harvey poured two glasses, steered Jo into the lounge, and gestured for her to sit down in one of the sagging armchairs.

She raised her glass in a toast. 'What should we drink to?'

Harvey shrugged, still pondering why this woman's presence unnerved him so. It wasn't just her physical resemblance to Lindsey; her mannerisms and her obvious warmth threatened to chip away the stone wall around his heart. 'To friendships,' he replied. 'Rarer than hens' teeth, in my opinion.'

They clinked glasses, sipping quietly and contemplating the next conversational gambit.

Jo made the first move. 'I have a feeling that talking about yourself isn't something you're comfortable with, Harvey.'

Nail firmly hit on the head. Harvey nodded, taking another, more generous, swig of wine.

'That's fine by me. Some people spill their entire life stories in the time it takes to open a packet of biscuits. I'm always happy to listen, but if someone doesn't want to talk, that's their choice.'

An awkward silence descended for ten minutes, until Jo sniffed the air. 'I think something's burning.'

Bollocks! Harvey sprinted into the kitchen, grabbed the oven gloves and opened the oven. The pastry was a little dark and the cauliflower cheese a tad charred around the edges, but the chips were golden and crispy. 'Let's eat,' he said, scooping food on to his two least offensive plates. 'You bring through the bottle, I'll get these on the table.'

To her credit, Jo didn't attempt to squeeze information out of Harvey as if he were a tube of toothpaste. They chatted about inconsequential things like the weather, the Scottish parliament and First Minister Nicola Sturgeon: 'a right wee nippy sweetie' in Jo's opinion. She spoke briefly of her parents' passing, Harvey admitting that his own parents were still alive but had little contact with him.

'I always envied people with close bonds to their folks,' he said, loading his fork with pie filling and cauliflower cheese. 'They're in their mid-eighties now, but fit as the proverbial fiddle. They're living it up in a retirement village on the outskirts of Glasgow: all CCTV cameras, shuttle buses and on-site medical care. They never really wanted a child, to be honest. They'd have been better off with a dog: more obedient and less demanding. Still, that's the way the cookie crumbles.'

'Speaking of sweet things, shall I warm up the pudding?

It'll take about twenty minutes and I brought some cream to go with.'

Harvey gave a thumbs up and added more pie and chips to their plates as Jo went to deal with dessert. Swirling the remains of the red around his glass, he felt something he hadn't felt for a long time. Dabbing at his lips, he realised what it was. Contentment.

CHAPTER 18

DESPITE HER MISGIVINGS, JO HAD TO ADMIT THE EVENING WAS going well. They'd devoured the sticky toffee pudding and opened a second bottle of red. Not normally a big drinker, she welcomed a top-up. It helped take the edge off any lingering anxiety about dining with a man she barely knew and hadn't particularly warmed to in the beginning.

The alcohol seemed to have a similar effect on Harvey, whose relaxed and attentive manner was in sharp contrast to the gruff, antisocial creature she'd first encountered. 'It must be challenging, running a business single-handed,' he said, refreshing his own glass. 'But you have an assistant, right?'

Jo nodded, and dabbed at a dribble of wine on the table-cloth. Her thoughts of Aaliyah and genie madness had faded as the evening progressed. For an insane moment, she contemplated taking to Harvey about it, then dismissed the idea immediately. Being carted away by men in white coats would not be ideal end to the evening. 'Yes, the daughter of a good friend. She's just helping out temporarily.' *Until she grants me two more wishes and buggers off back where she came from.* 'The lovely Angela worked with me for a while, but now she's running The Jekyll and Hyde with her partner, Ed.'

'I've never set foot in the place,' said Harvey. 'Not really one for crowds, to be honest. This is nicer. I've always preferred one-on-one chats, like I used to have—'

His mouth clamped shut faster than a freshly tapped mussel. Jo didn't press him further. The fleeting look of sorrow on his face had told her all she needed to know. 'It's a lovely pub,' she said, 'but hordes of beer-swilling locals with loose tongues and long noses might not be your thing.' She winked at Harvey, who gave a wry smile.

'You're not wrong there,' he said. 'I've already encountered Janette in the corner shop on a few occasions. I suspect she likes to keep tabs on what folks are up to round here.'

'She's a good soul,' replied Jo. 'Salt of the earth, as they say. Every small village has its eccentrics, and Janette definitely fits the bill.'

'Indeed she does,' said Harvey. 'Last time I was in looking for a few bits, she told me off for floating around like a fart in a spacesuit!'

Jo spluttered on a mouthful of wine, and Harvey hurriedly refilled her tumbler of water. Her equilibrium restored, she regaled Harvey with colourful tales of life in Cranley. They laughed together, two people enjoying each other's company with no pressure or expectations.

Feeling it was his turn, Harvey divulged a little about his pre-Cranley life. 'I dabbled in this and that,' he said. 'I studied philosophy at university, but soon realised the job opportunities were limited unless I became a lecturer.'

'Or sat around with your chin on your hand, looking deeply pensive,' teased Jo. 'Like the Rodin statue.'

'Very droll.' Harvey adopted a Rodinesque pose. Then his elbow slipped off the table and he came perilously close to nose-diving into his empty pudding plate. 'That's enough vino collapso for me!'

'So, what did you end up doing?' Harvey's features tightened a fraction and Jo hoped she hadn't overstepped the mark. Perhaps he'd got into financial trouble or gone off the rails somehow. Drinking, maybe, or something worse…

'I, erm, I took a short course in film and TV production and picked up a few gigs over the years. Behind the camera, mainly low-budget, but I enjoyed it. Nothing you'd have heard of,' he added, a slight flush warming his cheeks.

'I could always Google you,' retorted Jo. Not that she planned to. The energy now radiating from Harvey was less cosy, more 'barricades up, approach at your own risk'.

Perhaps sensing Jo's discomfort, Harvey disappeared to the loo. She fidgeted in her chair. Would now be a good time to yawn excessively, make her excuses and leave? As if on cue, she yawned — an absolute gaping belter.

Harvey reappeared and looked at her with a mixture of comprehension and sadness. 'Sorry if I've rambled on,' he said. 'You look like you need your bed, Jo.'

She did. For a fleeting second, Jo imagined Harvey's lips pressed against hers, and her destination his bed, not hers. But like her never-could-be relationship with Ken, such thoughts needed bottling up. Genies might emerge from lamps, but Jo had no intention of letting her libido loose. Certainly not with a man she barely knew, who played his cards very close to his chest.

'I am pretty tired,' she said. 'I've an early start at the café, and a ton of prep to do for a kid's birthday party I'm catering for. I'll be drowning in coloured sprinkles and butter icing!'

'Won't your friend's daughter give you a hand?' asked Harvey. 'That's a lot to deal with on your own.'

Jo harrumphed, easing herself to her feet. 'Sure, but

Aaliyah's idea of hard graft is a bit different to other folks'. She needs a lie-down after beating egg whites.'

Harvey barked out a laugh. Jo definitely liked the sound of his laugh. She liked a lot of things about him. But as with Ken, she couldn't allow herself to blunder down a dangerous road.

'I could help,' Harvey blurted out, looking as surprised as Jo felt. 'I've done a bit of baking in my time. Nothing fancy, mind you, but I can follow a recipe and I promise I won't collapse in a heap after a bit of mixing. Lindsey always said—'

Again, the shutters came down. Harvey began stacking plates and Jo went to retrieve her coat from the hallway. She'd decline his offer politely, and muddle through as she always did.

'Jo, I'd like to help.' Harvey took her coat from its peg and held it as she wriggled it on. 'There are things I can't talk about. Not because I don't trust you: it's just too painful. But I can lend a hand, if you'll let me. What do you say?'

Jo belted her coat, shouldered her handbag and stared Harvey straight in the face. She saw a maelstrom of emotions, but the overriding one was desperation for her to say yes. Every fibre of her being screamed *no* — what if Aaliyah let something slip about her true identity? — but Jo's heart kicked her head into touch. 'OK. Thank you. See you at seven?'

Back home, with Aaliyah already asleep and unlikely to have set her alarm, Jo made a calming herbal tea and curled up on the sofa. *What have I done?* Sipping her drink, she flicked on the TV, then turned it off again. Tomorrow she, Aaliyah and Harvey would don aprons, measure out ingredients and work together in perfect harmony. What could possibly go wrong?

CHAPTER 19

'AALIYAH, YOU HAVE PRECISELY TWO MINUTES TO HAUL YOUR bony arse out of bed before I drag you out myself.'

Jo stood on the landing, her temper reaching boiling point. After last night at Harvey's, she'd questioned the wisdom of the three of them working together at A Bit of Crumpet. She'd even considered giving Aaliyah the day off, before discovering that Aaliyah had eaten the entire profiterole stack, used the last of Jo's wax hair-removing strips, and signed up to an online dating site with Jo's credit card.

'Stop being such a drama llama,' Aaliyah had huffed, massaging Jo's favourite oil into her hair-free legs while clicking through potential suitors on Jo's laptop. 'Did you have fun with Harley?'

'His name is Harvey, and yes I did. You do realise you can't possibly date in the real world? How are you going to introduce yourself? I'm Aaliyah, normally a lamp-dweller, of indeterminate age and origin, with the ability to grant wishes. Fancy a kebab?'

Now, with less than half an hour until Harvey showed up at the café, Jo chose not to question why she'd put on make-

up and given her hair more than a perfunctory brush.
Nothing to do with trying to impress Harvey. No sirree. The
fact that she normally pulled an early shift bare-faced and
tousle-headed meant nothing. Not a thing.

Aaliyah slunk out of the bedroom, looking as if she'd
spent several hours in a beauty parlour. Damn the young,
and their ability to stay fresh-faced and uncreased after a
night's sleep. Although Jo had no clue how old Aaliyah was,
or if magic came into to play somehow.

'Calm your jets, Jo. Once you've made me a cuppa and
some toast, I'll be ready to rumble. Oh, and I'll need a few
minutes to check if any lush lads have viewed my dating
profile.'

For the sake of peace, Jo made Aaliyah a sugar-laden
coffee and slammed two slices of wholemeal bread in the
toaster. She had no appetite herself, which she put down to
the mountains of sickly sweet delights they'd shortly be
preparing.

'Eww, as if I'd be interested in someone like that!' Aaliyah
swivelled Jo's laptop around and pointed disdainfully. 'I've
seen better-looking camels. And this one isn't much of an
improvement. Face like a well-slapped arse.'

Granted, neither young man had posted the most flat-
tering profile pictures. There *was* something vaguely camel-
like about the first one, with his protruding bottom lip and
goofy stare. As for the other...

'There's no need to be so mean, Aaliyah,' retorted Jo, gathering up her bag and keys. 'I'm sure they're perfectly nice
boys — men — and it's not like you'll be dating them anyway.
Surely it's against genie law or something to fraternise with
humans in that way?'

Aaliyah guzzled the toast, gulped down the coffee and
tapped her nose. 'That's for me to know and you to find out.
Don't worry, pet, this is a thirty-day free trial and I won't

have you wasting your money on a gallery of gawky no-marks. Maybe there's someone in Cranley who fits the bill...'

Shuddering at the thought, Jo led the way to A Bit of Crumpet.

* * *

AT SEVEN O'CLOCK on the dot Harvey entered the café, looking very dapper in a smart shirt, faded blue jeans, and brogues so shiny Jo suspected he'd given them a military-style buff and polish. 'Morning, Harvey.'

'Morning, Jo, and ... sorry, brain like a sieve. Nice to properly meet you, erm...' Harvey extended a hand to Aaliyah, who eyed it like a venomous snake, then shook it limply.

'Aaliyah,' she replied, emphasising every syllable. 'Ooh, hang on a sec. Let me get some scissors.'

Jo and Harvey regarded each other with alarm. What on earth did she need scissors for?

The answer came a moment later when Aaliyah reached around Harvey's back, performed a surgical snip and produced a price tag. 'Thirty quid for that? You were robbed, mate.'

Getting off to a good start, thought Jo. Perhaps she should remove all sharp objects, lest a bloodbath ensued. But they needed knives to chop and slice, and skewers to stab cakes and ensure they were cooked all the way through.

'Right. I have a list.' Jo waved a piece of paper in front of them. 'The brief is: butterfly cakes with silver and pink sprinkles, chocolate chip traybake, polenta pizza bites and sticky hoisin sausages. I've already baked two sponges to fashion into a dinosaur birthday cake, God help me. The mum assures me she's stocked up on fruit and healthy snacks, which I have no doubt will remain untouched.'

Jo unfolded a printed-out recipe with a picture of a garish green dinosaur, smothered in Smarties and baring white icing teeth. Aaliyah grabbed it excitedly. 'Ooh, can I make this? Better than the boring stuff you usually have me do. Hmm, it reminds me a bit of you-know-who. All prickly, and green with envy. Prat.' Aaliyah shot a glance at the lamp on the shelf.

'Aaliyah, it's not easy. I don't want little Tommy sobbing his eyes out because his dinosaur cake looks like an R-rated swamp monster.'

Harvey coughed discreetly and pulled Jo aside. 'Look, Jo, why not let her have a go? You can supervise while we get on with the rest of the menu. It'll be fine. Pass me an apron and let's get cracking.'

Two and a half companionable hours later, the job was done, all bar Aaliyah putting the finishing touches to Dhassim (as she insisted on calling him): spiky red spines along his back and enormous googly eyes. She stood back and admired her handiwork, gaining a high-five from Harvey.

'Nice job,' he said, wrapping the dish of sausages in tinfoil. 'Aren't you meant to be open for business now, Jo?'

'Eek!' Jo dashed to the door, flipped the sign over, and mumbled an apology to the lone customer shuffling outside. Leaving Aaliyah to take their order, she went through to the back with Harvey and they stacked the party food into crates.

'Thanks so much,' Jo said, carefully manoeuvring the birthday cake on to a sturdy board which she covered with a plastic dome. 'All done and dusted in record time. Your help made a big difference.'

Harvey gave Jo a hand to load her van while Aaliyah, supposedly, washed up the party food debris. 'Would you like me to come with you?' he asked. 'I've no big plans for the day, so if you'd like a bit of company…'

Jo's first thought was to say no. She appreciated Harvey's help, but she could manage the delivery on her own. Before she could reply, though, he opened the driver's door and gave Jo a beseeching smile. Something inside Jo gave a dangerous wobble. She opened her mouth to turn down the offer, but instead, the words 'That would be lovely' slipped from her lips and Harvey climbed into the passenger seat. As she pulled away from the kerb, Jo glimpsed Aaliyah at the café door, fluttering her fingers, with a smug look on her face.

CHAPTER 20

'Oh, wow! That's amazing, Jo! It makes all my wishes seem a bit pathetic. I guess you're a deeper person than I am.'

Jo and Jinnie were at The Jekyll and Hyde pub for a lunchtime catch-up. Jo had filled Jinnie in on her successful first wish: to spend more time with her parents.

'I still have to pinch myself to believe it happened, but I have souvenirs to remind me.' Jo welled up and Jinnie swiftly produced a pack of tissues.

'All right, ladies?' Ed McCroarty approached their table with two plates of sesame-seared salmon and stir-fried veg.

'All fine,' said Jo. 'Just something in my eye.' She pulled out her compact mirror and made a show of dabbing away the imaginary object.

'When are your folks back?' asked Jinnie. 'They've been away for ages.'

Ed put down the plates and straightened up the condiment rack. 'Tomorrow, I think. I'm losing track of the days, trying to keep this place running and working on my business at the same time.'

'I'd be happy to do a few shifts again if you need me,' said

Jinnie. 'I miss pouring pints and having in-depth discussions about life and the universe with Jamie.'

'Sure you do,' replied Ed. 'We both know that getting more than a grunt out of the boy is like squeezing juice out of a rock-hard lemon. Still, he's come round to his mum and I being together. Well, he doesn't mutter "twat" under his breath quite so often.' Ed wandered back to the bar where Angela and part-timer Rose held the fort.

'I seriously cannot believe I fancied Ed at one point.' Jinnie cut into her salmon, groaning with delight at its flaky tenderness.

'Why ever not? He's a good-looking guy and obviously very fond of you. In a purely platonic way now, of course.'

'Agreed, but I was so muddled in my head when I first moved here. I was licking my wounds after being dumped by my fiancé, not expecting to find myself torn between two men.'

Jo had no desire to be torn between any men. She contemplated mentioning her meal with Harvey, but decided against it. Better to operate on a 'need to know' basis, and Jinnie didn't need to know a thing about Jo's private life. Apart from her visit to her childhood home, obviously, and the fact that she had a temperamental genie invading her personal space.

'You're in love, Jinnie, and that's a wonderful thing,' she said. 'Every time I see you with Sam you're lit up like a Christmas tree. He's one of the good ones. Any plans for a wedding?'

Jinnie giggled, and fiddled with the simple ring adorning her finger. 'Not yet. We're still getting to know one another; there's no rush. Heck, who says we even *have* to get married? Except my gran will kill me if I don't march down the aisle in a frou-frou dress one day, escorted by my dad and praying Archie doesn't belch during the marriage vows.'

Jo knew a little about Jinnie's family. Her doting parents, Rob and Kath, her wildcard gran Wilma, who preferred to age disgracefully, and her brother Archie, making megabucks in the music industry but still an uncouth, socially inept teenager at heart. 'Does Sam… Have you ever told him about the lamps?'

Jinnie shook her head so vigorously that one of her dangly earrings plopped into her Diet Coke. 'Whoops!' She fished it out with a spoon and put it back in. 'No, absolutely not. He has his suspicions about them, but I can't tell him. He'd think I was away with the fairies. That's not exactly grounds for a stable relationship, is it? Although…'

'Although what?' Jo ate a mouthful of fish and waited.

'Well, just after Dhassim and Aaliyah shimmied back into their lamps, I had a lightbulb moment. About Sam, I mean. I always wondered why they'd ended up with him when they could have gone anywhere. That's when I clocked his name, and it all made sense. OK, none of it makes sense really, and I could be putting two and two together and making five, but…'

Jo regarded her younger companion with amusement. 'What possible link could Sam have with Dhassim and Aaliyah? OK, he picked up the lamps somewhere and gave you one, but what does that prove? And what's his name got to do with it?'

Jinnie scrabbled in her bag, produced her purse, and rummaged through plastic cards and crumpled bits of paper. With an exasperated sigh, she fanned them out on the table until she found what she was looking for. 'Look!' Jinnie thrust a card under Jo's nose.

Jo wrangled her glasses from her head and read: *Samuel A. Addin, Out of the Attic Antiques.*

'Still not getting it, sweetie. Hang on, I need to eat more

fish before it gets cold.' Jo took a bite, then squinted at the card again.

Jinnie looked on the verge of exploding with frustration. 'His middle name is Alistair. But you probably knew that already, seeing as his alter ego is Alistair Scott, author of bestselling gritty crime thrillers.' Two dots of pink flared in Jinnie's cheeks and she took a hasty gulp of water. 'Erm, you did know that, right?'

Jo knew Sam preferred to keep his writing stuff close to his chest. She also knew it was one of the worst-kept secrets in Cranley. Unless you counted the unconfirmed rumour that Janette had once worked as a nightclub hostess in London, stuffing tips down her bra and hanging out with gangland bosses. From big-city glamour to franking Jiffy bags and flogging out-of-date baked beans at a discount. Who knew?

'OK, give me a moment. Alistair Addin. Is that supposed to mean something? Am I being thick, because I don't get it.'

'If you shorten his first name, then say the whole thing together...' prompted Jinnie.

At last the penny dropped. As did Jo's fork, which bounced on the table and clattered to the floor.

'Bingo! Al Addin. Say it quickly. It must mean something!' Jinnie's eyes glittered.

Jo retrieved the fork and gave it a wipe. 'Jinnie, Aladdin is a fictional character from a book hundreds of years old, if my memory doesn't fail me. Sam is a flesh-and-bone, down-to-earth human. I think you're getting carried away, which isn't surprising, considering how—'

The doors of The Jekyll and Hyde burst open and two familiar figures were greeted with whoops and cheers by both staff and customers.

'They're early!' Ed, who'd swooped by on a mission to gather up empties, gave a lopsided grin.

'Hey, son.' Ken McCroarty slapped Ed heartily on the back. 'Did you miss us?'

Winking at Jo and Jinnie, Ed pulled a 'you must be joking' face. 'Like the proverbial hole in the head. That's you, not Mum, of course.'

Ed's mum Mags hovered nervously behind her husband, her tanned features creased with confusion. 'You didn't pay for the taxi, Ken. Where are we, and why are these people making so much noise? Can you please ask them to stop?'

Ed gathered his mum into a comforting embrace. She resisted for a moment, then succumbed as Ken gestured to everyone to get back to their business. 'It's OK, Mum. You're home.' Ed spoke quietly, but Jo heard the slight wobble in his voice.

Her eyes met Mags's as she peered around Ed's broad shoulder. A flicker of recognition passed across Mags's face, and Jo smiled. Whatever life had to throw at her, she prayed dementia wouldn't be on the list.

CHAPTER 21

'ONE WISH DOWN, TWO TO GO.' AALIYAH TWIRLED STRANDS OF spaghetti round her fork and devoured them with a noisy slurp.

Jo had never been able to cope with spaghetti, resorting to chopping it into bite-sized pieces. She scooped some up with a slice of garlic bread and shrugged. 'I don't know what to wish for, Aaliyah. You picked a no-hoper, I'm afraid.'

'*You* picked *me*, remember? Honestly, you humans don't know a good thing when it bites you on the bum. Ooh, I have three wishes and I don't know what to do with them. Ooh, I'll pretend I don't like Harley when I've clearly got the hots for him.'

'I do not have the hots for him! And his name — as you know — is Harvey. He's a man, not a bloody motorbike.' Jo bit into the garlic bread and cursed as a dollop of bolognaise sauce slithered down her front.

'Wind your neck in, Jo, I'm just having a laugh. Pop that off before the stain sets and I'll give it a soak.'

If Aaliyah had announced that she'd ditched make-up and intended to spend the rest of her life in trackie bottoms, Jo could not have been more surprised. Aaliyah didn't do laundry. Aaliyah didn't clean toilets. Aaliyah regarded domestic chores as things someone else did — that someone being Jo. Now she was making an impatient 'get it off' gesture, her hands flapping up and down. Jo didn't know what else to do but wrestle the blouse over her head and pass it over.

'Blimey, I hope Harley — sorry, Harvey — never cops a look at that monstrosity. Less Wonderbra, more Blunderbra. Jeez, they're like two bald guys fighting for headroom in a hammock!'

Jo looked down at her bra. Pinky and Perky, as her long-gone fiancé had once dubbed them, nestled uncomfortably in the cheap nylon fabric, seemingly plotting their escape in opposite directions. 'Fine. My underwear is a disaster. My love life is a disaster. I have a genie who reckons I'm as much use as a chocolate fireguard and I dribble pasta sauce like a toddler. Anything else you want to throw into the mix?' Jo grabbed the oven gloves and covered up her upper half.

Aaliyah scrunched up the blouse, stomped into the utility room and made a performance of running the taps and presumably adding a liberal dose of stain-removing product. Jo scampered upstairs, located a clean T-shirt and tugged it over her head. When would the madness stop?

The answer came with lightning speed. *When you wish for two more things. Then she'll disappear, and life will be...*

Life will be what? Jo had no idea. Probably the same old, same old: running the café, catering the occasional party and spending evenings flicking through Netflix. She needed a holiday, an escape from the humdrum, but there was a snowball's chance in hell of her leaving Aaliyah to run the ship for a week. She might suddenly have developed a passion for stain removal, but Jo didn't fancy the chances of A Bit of Crumpet staying afloat with Aaliyah at the helm. Maybe Harvey could take charge? As quickly as the notion entered

her head, Jo shook it loose. Neither Aaliyah nor Harvey, she
suspected, had professional catering qualifications. Yep, slob-
bing on a beach while the authorities ticked off a list of
misdemeanours and shut her business down didn't exactly
give her all the happy feels.

A fleeting image of herself and Harvey by a sparkling
pool, sipping cocktails and basking in the sun, nudged its
way into Jo's capricious brain. She shut that one down too
and returned to the kitchen.

'All done? Or do you want to dribble more sauce down
your front?' Aaliyah stretched like a cat, her plate well and
truly licked clean. Jo shook her head and tipped the remains
of her meal into the bin.

'Pet, you mentioned a TV show you liked. The cake one,
right? Although why someone who spends their life baking
would want to do it on live television in front of millions of
people is beyond me. It's like taking bloody coals to Newcastle, if you catch my drift.'

*Because just once, I'd like a wee taste of being in the spotlight.
Not just Cranley Jo, purveyor of pasties and scones, sad singleton
without the snarky wit of Janette, the fabulous wardrobe of Alison
Gale or the youthful exuberance of Jinnie, Ed and co. Someone that
people cheered on and applauded as she proudly accepted the
winner's trophy.*

Jo didn't say any of that, though. She ignored Aaliyah's
questioning look and went into the lounge. Locating the TV
remote under a pile of glossy magazines, she flicked through
the saved programmes until she found the last series of *All
Rise*. Jo scrolled through to the final, and the moment a
disbelieving teenage victor sobbed all over the three judges
as well as presenter Kelvin Brady, who made a show of
mopping his shoulder with a tea towel.

'His winning cake was incredible,' Jo murmured. The
camera panned in on a fairy-tale castle complete with intri-

cate turrets, tiny detailed flags and a shimmering moat of blue fondant icing. He'd dedicated it to his wee sister, born with a rare degenerative illness, whose biggest dream was to meet a princess at Disneyland Paris. A short video clip showed the girl, all golden ringlets and hesitant smile, waving at her brother. Their parents were in the background, about to explode with pride.

'Not bad,' conceded Aaliyah. 'I stayed in something like that, once upon a time.'

Really? Jo looked at Aaliyah, unsure whether she understood anything about actual fairy tales. But her expression remained neutral, verging on bored, as usual.

'Yeah. Got me a wish-granting gig for a prince who was so up his own back passage he could probably have counted his internal organs. Shame the one between his ears didn't function too well. As for the one between his legs…' Aaliyah guffawed, holding her thumb and second finger close together.

'I'm not sure I want to hear any more,' said Jo, flicking the TV off. 'Right, I've some admin to deal with, so if you'll excuse me—'

Aaliyah blocked Jo's escape, arms folded and biceps bulging alarmingly. 'Not so fast, pet. Is this thing on your wish list, or not? Time's a-ticking.' She whipped out her WIFI and it gave a despondent beep.

'I don't know!' Jo squared up to Aaliyah, in no doubt of who'd win if they embarked on an arm-wrestling contest. 'It seems a bit … fatuous, I suppose. I should just apply again and hope I get picked before I collect my pension.'

'Nah. I know you're knocking on a bit, but why wait another five years when yours truly can have you icing your way to national glory in a jiffy?'

Five years? Jo gritted her teeth so hard that she feared they'd snap. Did Aaliyah really think Jo was a stone's throw from her sixties? 'As I said, I have paperwork to sort and I'm feeling a bit...' Jo massaged her temples, a headache tip-tapping its way into her skull. 'It can wait another day, can't it?'

Unprompted, Aaliyah rummaged in a drawer, pulled out a pack of paracetamol, and handed Jo two with a glass of water. Her behaviour confused Jo: one minute the prickly, self-opinionated, self-absorbed woman she'd become accustomed to, the next a mixture of domestic goddess and Florence Nightingale. Would the real Aaliyah please step forward?

'Sleep on it, Jo. Me WIFI can wait. Just not sure if our true master can, though. Buggered if I know who that is, mind.'

Jo took the stairs slowly, waiting for the painkillers to work their magic. *Their true master.* She assumed Aaliyah meant the boss of both her and Dhassim... A thought flitted through her clouded mind. Something Jinnie had said; something that made no sense. Something to do with Sam...

CHAPTER 22

'GRAN, MEET JO,' SAID JINNIE. 'JO, THIS IS MY INFAMOUS GRAN, Wilma.'

Jo extended a hand to the older lady, who grasped it firmly, flipped it over and peered at Jo's palm. 'Good strong life line there,' she declared. 'Hmm, the heart line starts in the middle; that means you fall in love easily.'

'Gran, give Jo her hand back and stop with the palm-reading nonsense.'

'Ye of little faith, Jinnie. You weren't such a doubting Thomas when I predicted how you'd meet yer man. Hit the nail on the head then, didn't I?' Wilma gave a jubilant grin before heading to a free table, wheeling her tartan shopping trolley behind her.

'Give me strength,' muttered Jinnie, as Jo filled a teapot and slid two pieces of millionaire's shortbread on to plates. 'It was bad enough when she insisted on reading tea leaves, whether you wanted it or not. Now she's obsessed with palm readings, accosting total strangers in the supermarket and asking if they'd like to know their future. As if random lines mean anything.'

Jo dragged her thoughts back from Wilma's assertion that she fell in love easily. Total twaddle, of course. Looking back, she'd never been head over heels for her former fiancé, Graham, and as for Ken … better not to go there.

'So what did Wilma see in the leaves for you, Jinnie? A hunky antique-shop owner with a nice bum? Oops, sorry about that!'

Jinnie pulled a faux frown, then giggled. 'Nah, you're fine, Jo. Sam does have a very nice bum, not that other people should be noticing. And the shapes in the tea leaves are never that precise. Gran just saw a horse's head and said it signified love.'

Leaving Jo to ponder that correlation, Jinnie took the tray of tea and cake to her gran's table. Jo dealt with another customer, relieved that she'd given Aaliyah the morning off. Her genie pal had appeared for breakfast looking pale and complaining of exhaustion; perhaps her brief burst of domesticity the night before had sapped her energy. Jo had sent her back to bed with a bowl of muesli and a glass of orange juice.

'Gran! You can't do that it in here.' Jo glanced up to see Wilma blowing out a plume of smoke. The couple on the next table tutted loudly and glared at Jo. Jinnie shrugged helplessly and fanned the air with a rolled-up newspaper.

'Wilma, I'm really sorry, but you can't smoke in here.' Jo smiled apologetically, although the indoor smoking ban had been in effect for almost fifteen years. However, when she caught sight of the wording on Wilma's shopping trolley — *You're a long time deid!* — Jo decided Wilma had little truck with petty rules and regulations.

'It's disgusting,' said one half of the couple, a man in his mid to late-forties, his lips puckered in distaste. 'Do you realise the harm caused by passive smoking?'

Wilma swung around, eyes sparkling with mischief. 'Aye,

son, I do, which is why I've switched to this shite. What you see here' — she expelled another cloudy puff — 'is vaping. Stinky steam, but no' the kind that clings to your clothes or makes twats like you hyperventilate. My father and his father and probably all the fathers down my dubious family tree smoked, but I'm trying to break the habit 'cos it costs a wee fortune and will probably kill me. Then again, something has to. Two things in life you cannae dodge: death and taxes.'

Wilma took a last, triumphant suck and tucked her vaping device away. Jinnie, meanwhile, put her face in her hands, not quite hiding the flush of colour in her cheeks.

'Well, OK. That's good. We're all good here now.' Mr Angry made a hasty exit with his partner as Wilma rubbed her nose and gave his back the middle finger.

'Gran! Can you please behave yourself for once?' Jinnie poured their tea, giving Jo a watery smile.

'No harm done,' said Jo. 'I've a couple of tables outside if you want to carry on vaping, Wilma.'

They turned towards the window and watched a passer-by struggle to keep their umbrella from turning inside out. In the past few minutes the rain had set in, and it was blowing a hoolie.

'Nah, you're all right.' Wilma took a bite of her cake, nodding approval at Jo. 'Lovely. Now, are you up for a wee tea-leaf reading, Jo? Fetch another cup, and—'

'Much as I'd love to, I need to get back behind the counter,' Jo said hurriedly. 'Enjoy your tea, ladies.'

Watching Jinnie and Wilma chatter away, Jo's mood took a downward turn. She had no grandparents, no parents, no children, no partner. Just a madcap genie haranguing her about wishes. How had it come to this?

Slipping out back to fetch more milk and a new batch of cheese scones, Jo's thoughts drifted to Harvey. How did he fill his days? He'd mentioned writing in the passing, but apart from that and the mysterious Lindsey, she knew nothing about him. Why had he ended up in Cranley, of all places? He was an enigma wrapped up in a puzzle, with an impenetrable outer layer. *Do I really want to get involved with someone like that?*

'Jo! Come and have a gander at this.' Wilma flapped her hand impatiently, Jinnie staring at the ceiling as if waiting for an escape ladder to appear.

'Erm, what am I supposed to be looking at?' Jo wiped her glasses on her apron and squinted at the teacup. It was empty, apart from a smattering of leaves that could be anything from a small colony of squashed ants to one of those weird ink-blot tests.

Wilma harrumphed as Jinnie dabbed at biscuit crumbs with a dampened finger. 'It's a ring! Honestly, I despair sometimes. Here's me in my eighties, and you two youngsters cannae see what's in front of your noses.'

'Gran, it looks nothing like a ring. At best it could be a mangled doughnut, but even that's a stretch.' Jinnie gave Jo a helpless look. 'And I know exactly what your game is, so wipe that butter-wouldn't-melt smile off your face.'

'Ach, it's clear as a bell. It's a ring, which means you and Sam are going to tie the knot and your poor old gran might see you wed before she shuffles off her mortal coil.' Wilma sat back, gave a hearty cough, and grinned.

'Gran, Sam and I are perfectly happy as we are. I know you've been bookmarking fascinators — I've seen your saved stuff on the computer — but it's not happening. Absolutely not.' Jinnie sighed. 'You don't need to put a ring on it these days, anyway. Something like sixty per cent of marriages end in divorce. I don't want to be another statistic, not when things are fine as they are.'

Hmm, thought Jo. *Methinks the lass protests too much.* Still, it was none of her business. What *was* her business was the café, and the pressing need to get a certain genie off her back.

CHAPTER 23

'FEELING BETTER?' JO LOOKED UP FROM HER PHONE AS A bleary-eyed Aaliyah shuffled into the kitchen. She'd been sound asleep when Jo got back from the café two hours ago, her faint snores emanating from the bedroom.

'A bit,' Aaliyah replied. 'I just need some decent scran and a shower. Mind if I hop in the shower first, pet? Before you use up all the hot water, like.'

That would be a first, thought Jo. Aaliyah inevitably used up virtually all the hot water, leaving Jo to cower under a tepid stream with shampoo stinging her eyes. How anyone could take so long washing their bits defied belief. Did she soap each toe individually? Use a loofah to forensically scrub every inch of her gleaming skin?

'Be my guest.' Jo saw a WhatsApp notification and opened the message. *Harvey.* Her heart did a little skippety-hop as she read it:

Loved helping out for the party, Jo. Just wondered if you'd like to meet up again soon. Maybe bite the bullet and try the local pub? Whatever works for you. No pressure. Harvey

There was no kiss or smiley emoji, and an underlying

sense of things being slightly off. Insecurity? Demons? And yet...

Jo realised that Aaliyah had headed to the bathroom, the rumble of the boiler signalling the probability that Jo would have a mere dribble of water left to perform her ablutions. She loved that word, even if Aaliyah did put the 'blue' into it.

Her fingers hovered over the phone. Her options were simple: a reply in the affirmative or a gentle let down. *Thanks, but no thanks. See you around.* She imagined Harvey's face if she went for the latter. She just couldn't do it. Jo told herself her motives were purely altruistic, one human being kind to another. Her inner voice — her mum's voice — screamed 'You like him, so stop analysing and get on with it!'

Jo typed: *Sounds good. How about Saturday at The Jekyll and Hyde? Say 7, and the first drink's on me...* She hit *send*, and sat back.

Music blared from upstairs, and Jo contemplated what to eat. A seedling of an idea sprouted in her brain. She didn't want to cook, Aaliyah needed feeding, and the pub did a more than decent selection of grub.

An hour later, Jo and Aaliyah were seated at a quiet table. It was Thursday evening and only a handful of punters lined the bar. A crowd of giggling women in their twenties occupied a large table piled high with platters of chicken wings, cheese-smothered nachos and an eye-popping collection of empty and half-empty wine bottles.

'Someone's birthday?' Jo asked when Ed arrived with their drinks: a glass of Pinot Grigio for her and a Porn Star Martini for Aaliyah.

'Nah, I think Kylie got a promotion. To what, I haven't a clue, but they're making serious inroads into the rosé.'

Aaliyah toasted Jo with her drink and gave Ed the benefit of her bewitching smile. He grinned back before asking if they'd made their food choices.

'What do you fancy, Aaliyah?' asked Jo. 'I can recommend the Thai green curry, and the fish and chips is pretty spectacular too.'

'Ray and Liz have whipped up an incredible rabbit stew laced with cider and cream as today's special,' added Ed.

'Eww! There is no way I'm eating a fluffy bunny,' protested Aaliyah. 'That is gross.'

So says the hamster killer, mused Jo. And Aaliyah hadn't recoiled in horror when she'd served up lamb chops the other day.

Placing their order — two Thai green curries — they sat back and surveyed the scene. Out of the corner of her eye, Jo spotted an inebriated Kylie tottering towards them. Her gait reminded Jo of a long-ago rough ferry crossing with passengers swaying from side to side as they attempted to stay upright.

'Just wanted to say that I love your dress,' Kylie slurred at Aaliyah. Jo had tried to dissuade Aaliyah from wearing the skintight body-con number with cut-out panels at the waist, arguing that they were going to the local pub, not a nightclub.

'Thank you.' Aaliyah regarded the young woman haughtily. 'I like yours too. Didn't it come in a bigger size?'

Jo gasped as Kylie crinkled up her nose, her booze-addled brain struggling to process the comment. Just as realisation dawned, one of her equally sozzled cronies hollered across the room. 'Kylie, get your arse over here. We're out of pink and Ed says the prosecco's not chilled. We'll have to chuck ice in it.'

Steadying herself on the back of Aaliyah's chair, Kylie leaned forward, her too-tight dress straining at the bust. 'I think you just said something very rude to me. I'm out celebrating with my mates, though, so I'll let it slide. This time. But don't think I didn't see you giving Ed the once-over. He's taken, you know.' She straightened up, a side seam splitting as she did so. Clutching the fabric, she muttered 'bitch' under her breath and stomped off.

'Aaliyah, that was totally uncalled for,' Jo admonished. 'Women need to support one another, not make derogatory remarks. You should go over and apologise.'

'Not happening.' Aaliyah gave a faux yawn and stood up, smoothing the sides of her dress. Her move was timed to perfection, as Ed arrived at the table with two plates of curry and sides of steaming jasmine rice. 'That looks so amazingly edible,' purred Aaliyah. Whether she meant the food or Ed remained to be seen. *She knows Ed and Angela are a couple*, thought Jo, *so what's her game?*

'Bon appétit.' Ed set the plates down, made sure they had everything they needed, and skirted past Kylie's table.

'Have you got tattoos on your bum too, handsome?' One of Kylie's friends, all hair extensions and trout pout, sniggered and pointed at Ed's tattooed forearms.

Ed paused, made as if to pull his trousers down, then shimmied back to the bar.

'He's cute.' Aaliyah drained her cocktail. 'But those inkings are not to my taste. When skin is perfect, why spoil it?'

Jo had often wondered that, too. But some people just seemed to suit tattoos, as if they'd been waiting for a way to express themselves. Their body art said things they couldn't. Angela had got one, and it spoke volumes about her transformation from a lonely alcoholic and single parent to an independent woman with courage in spades.

'Speaking of cute.' Aaliyah pointed her fork at the bar. 'Who is that vision of hotness?'

Jo looked up. Currently at the bar were a couple of red-faced regulars well into their seventies. Not one of them, then. Behind the bar, Angela's son measured out shots of whisky.

'You don't mean the barman? Jamie?' Jo had never in a million years thought of Jamie as cute. Then again, he was barely out of his teens, and his normal countenance bordered on the downright dour.

'He's well fit,' replied Aaliyah. 'Look at them biceps straining through his T-shirt. And I bet he's got a six-pack too. Dhassim tried for one, bless him, but his abs were less than fab.'

Before Jo could reply, Aaliyah picked up her empty glass. 'I'll just get a refill, pet. You all right?'

Jo nodded mutely and watched as Aaliyah homed in on Jamie like a scantily clad heat-seeking missile. Smiling coquettishly at the two older gentlemen, she leaned over the bar, gestured to Jamie and whispered something in his ear. Whatever she said, it transformed Jamie's sullen features like sunshine breaking through clouds. Yes, he was a good-looking lad, but... Jo necked the rest of her wine. The last thing she needed was a budding romance between those two. It could only end in disaster.

CHAPTER 24

'IF YOU NEED HELP FINDING ANYTHING, JUST GIE ME A SHOUT.'

Harvey put down the pack of hot cross buns — hadn't Easter been months ago? — and gave Janette a stiff smile. He'd only popped in for eggs, milk and bacon, and now he was browsing through the 'bargain' bin with its plethora of dodgy delights. Meanwhile, Janette followed him around under the pretence of dusting. More like ensuring he didn't stuff an out-of-date sausage roll up his jumper. Good lord, did he look like a shoplifter?

'You know, you remind me of someone.' Janette flapped her pale-blue feathery thing in Harvey's general direction. He sneezed, apologised and carried on rummaging. Battered tins, Mr Kipling cakes, Yorkshire pudding mix and crumpets with a suspiciously green tinge all nestled on a pile of tatty magazines several months old, if not older.

'And who would that be? Mel Gibson? Michael Douglas? That old codger off *Eastenders?*' Harvey kept his tone light, but his insides contracted and he tugged his scarf further up his face. Why had he named bloody actors? If this nosy old biddy recognised him, he might as well pack up and leave.

Game over: time to start afresh somewhere else. Except that he didn't want to leave. Not now he had a possible reason to stay...

'Aye, you're a big hit for yourself, laddie. I can't quite put my finger on it, but it'll come to me: I never forget a face. But don't even mention yourself in the same breath as Michael Douglas. He's Hollywood royalty, with a chin chiselled tae perfection. Now, I'll have to leave you to it.' She shouted a welcome to a young mum clutching a baby to her bosom. 'Grab a basket and I'll sort you out in a minute.'

Harvey did as he was told, wrenching a basket from the stack by the door. He added the items he'd come in for, as well as a bottle of HP Sauce and a tub of spreadable butter. He fancied a bacon buttie when he got home, and no buttie was complete without a dollop of the brown stuff.

Returning to the bargain bin, Harvey rifled through the magazines. All trashy tabloid-style fodder, featuring vacuous celebs waxing lyrical about their oh-so-perfect lives. He'd turned down several requests for interviews in the past; he had no desire to have a camera crew poking around his house and some journalist prying into his business. Of course, he'd had no control over the stuff written after Lindsey died, or the scandal involving—

Harvey paused, an icy shard of horror prickling his spine. Staring up at him was a photo of Abby Kinsella, the architect of his downfall. He'd played his part, of course, but only as a bereaved innocent taken in by her cunning ways. Ridiculous, considering that he was a man in his fifties, but stupidity didn't come with an expiry date, unlike the hot cross buns.

'You all right there?' Janette sidled up, casually adjusting an errant bra strap. 'I've a two-for-one offer on baked beans, if you're interested. They'd go down a treat with the bacon. What's that you're looking at?'

Harvey quickly shoved the magazine beneath the others.

The article pre-dated his fall from grace, but he didn't want Janette to see it and put two and two together. Or rather, put *them* together, and draw the distasteful conclusion that so many people before her had. 'Nothing. Nothing at all. Can I just pay for these and … a bottle of whisky, please?'

Janette's cabinet of booze stayed under lock and key behind the counter. She gave a disapproving sniff and opened the cabinet. 'Are ye after the cheap stuff or a decent 12-year-old? This one's not bad, although I only drink the stuff when I've got a cold. It's no' good to drink alone, you know.'

Harvey bit his tongue, and pointed at the 12-year-old whisky. Now the old bat was giving him a lecture about solitary drinking!

Back at the cottage, he unpacked his supplies and popped a few rashers of bacon under the grill, then stowed the whisky away and made himself a coffee. As the bacon sizzled and popped, he opened his laptop and clicked on the screenplay-in-progress. Not that he'd *made* much progress in recent days. His head was too full of other things, not least Jo and their approaching date. Was it a date? If two people agreed to meet in a pub, did that constitute a progression in a relationship?

Harvey had only dated two other women before he'd met Lindsey. Shy in his late teens and early twenties, he got tongue-tied around the opposite sex. Ironic that he'd fallen into acting, but he preferred pretending to be someone else. His fragile confidence grew when he stepped into the shoes of a fictional character. Drama school had been the making of him.

Did you line the grill tray with tinfoil? It'll be a bugger to clean otherwise.

Harvey laughed. He hadn't, of course. Lindsey always had the answers, no matter how complicated the questions were.

She'd approached him after a performance of a play based loosely on the life of Scottish poet Robert Burns. Three years out of drama school and still fumbling his way around, he'd played the role of the bard to an average of twenty people a night. No one usually hung around at the end, so he was surprised to see a petite brunette hovering in the foyer of the tiny theatre.

'Erm, can I help you?' Harvey approached her, raising his voice over the vacuum cleaner being wielded by a sour-faced man. The other three cast members had legged it the minute the curtain came down.

'Nice wig,' said the woman, who looked around the same age as him. 'Or is it all your own?'

Harvey fingered one of the poorly glued-on sideburns and laughed. 'I'm actually as bald as a coot, but thanks for the compliment. Are you waiting for a taxi?'

The woman, eyes dancing with mischief, shook her head. 'I was waiting for you, actually. I'm a sucker for a poet, even a dead one. Fancy going for a drink?'

And that was how it had started. One drink led to two, then a dodgy curry down a side alley. They shared stale poppadoms and watery chicken vindaloo and tried to outdo one another with literary quotes. Lindsey trounced him every time, her knowledge far superior to Harvey's. 'I have what you might call a memory for the useless,' she'd said. 'Song lyrics and famous film lines all lodge themselves in my brain. Ask me to remember what I had for breakfast, though, and I'm a no-hoper.'

'Well, I hope you don't forget about me.' Harvey half-sang the sentence, in homage to the band Simple Minds, and immediately wished he could stuff the remainder of the poppadoms in his mouth.

But Lindsey reached over, touched his hand and sent shivers through his body. 'Not bloody likely. In the words of

George Sand, "Don't walk in front of me, I may not follow. Don't walk behind me, I may not lead. There is only one happiness in life, to love and be loved." That's my philosophy, Harvey: I believe things happen for a reason. I was given a ticket for your show and I had no intention of coming. But I did, and I'm glad I did.'

Harvey rubbed at the remaining glue on his cheek, unable to believe that someone so beautiful, so eloquent, saw something in him. Or did she just have a fetish for Rabbie Burns lookalikes?'I'm glad you did, too.' He'd never believed in love at first sight, but now the evidence suggested it existed, even in grotty venues and grottier restaurants. 'That's a beautiful quote. George Sand isn't a name I recognise, but he's clearly a very talented man.'

'*He* was a she,' said Lindsey.

'Oh,' said Harvey.

CHAPTER 25

'So, you've got a date with lover boy on Saturday?' Aaliyah perched on the edge of the sofa, an old towel at her feet and a foot file in her hand. Jo watched as shards of dead skin floated down like snowflakes. They weren't particularly attractive snowflakes. In fact, they reminded Jo of Parmesan shavings, which meant pasta was off tonight's menu.

'As I keep telling you, Harvey is just a friend. And I wish you'd do that in the bathroom or your bedroom.'

Aaliyah grunted and grabbed a pot of Jo's hand cream. 'It's more comfy here, pet. If you like, I'll give your tootsies a once-over too. Haven't seen hooves like that since me and Dhassim once hung out with a couple of old donkeys. It's a bit of a long story, but that's the last time I ever kip in a barn. Bloody straw everywhere, and who knew that donkeys made so much noise when they—'

'Too much information,' said Jo. 'And my feet aren't *that* bad.' She glanced down at the aforementioned feet, currently clad in her favourite Birkenstock sandals. OK, she wouldn't be signed up as a foot model any time soon, but head-to-toe maintenance wasn't high on Jo's agenda. Keep it simple, don't

frighten the horses (or donkeys), and focus on more important stuff. Like the upcoming date — that absolutely wasn't a
date — and... Maybe a wee pedicure wouldn't do any harm.

Minutes later, Jo had her feet in a basin of warm, soapy
water. Aaliyah laid out an array of implements with the zeal
of a surgeon about to carve into a sedated patient. Clippers:
check. Scissors: check. Nail file: check. Some random instrument of torture Jo had never seen before: check. Jo hoped
she'd still have some skin and nails left when Aaliyah had
finished.

'Jeez, your big toenails are as tough as rhino hide,'
whinged Aaliyah, attacking them with distaste.

Jo flinched as the clippers nicked a piece of flesh. 'Ouch!
Go easy, Aaliyah. And, by the way, while my nails might be as
tough as a rhino, my feelings are a little more delicate. You
can be very cruel, you know. Maybe try to be a little more ...
thoughtful ... when you open your mouth.'

'Moi? I am the epitome of thoughtful. Well, Dhassim
sometimes told me off for being too direct, but what does he
know about anything? I say it as it is, right? The thing is, Jo...'
Aaliyah resumed her clipping, pausing now and again to
spritz Jo's feet with a cooling spray. Or a can of WD40,
perhaps.

'What's the thing?' Jo winced as another slice of skin fell
victim to Aaliyah's trimming.

'You're spending your life sitting on the fence. I think
that's the right expression. And when you sit on the fence, all
you get are dents in your buttocks. Not cellulite: you've
already got that. Oops, I've offended you again. Sorry.'

Aaliyah didn't look remotely sorry. She carried on with
the job in hand, thankfully moving on to massaging and
filing. 'You have a second wish you're too scared to ask for,
and a man you want to get to know better, but you're
pretending you don't. I'm a genie, pet, but I don't just grant

wishes. I can sense things, and I sense you're holding back. Give me something to work with, and we can move forward.'

Jo closed her eyes and leant back on the sofa. She let Aaliyah's firm but soothing caress wash over her, and tried to focus on what she wanted. What she *really, really* wanted. Seeing her parents again had been so special, but now she needed something lighter. Something fluffier, that would give her ego a much-needed boost. Yes, she did want to get to know Harvey better, but that man couldn't be described as 'fluffy'. He was pricklier than a hedgehog, with the occasional flash of marshmallow. Damn it! All she could think of now was cake. Light, fluffy cake, baked to perfection and drawing gasps of admiration from an appreciative audience of sugar-lovers. A place on *All Rise,* where Jo could demonstrate her skills in front of devoted viewers up and down the country.

'You're thinking about that show again,' said Aaliyah, tutting as Jo wriggled free of her grasp.

'Sorry. I've got cramp in my leg.' Jo hopped up and down until the pain eased. 'Yes, I am, but it's a totally daft wish. You pretty much said so yourself. And how would it work, anyway? Wouldn't people I know see me on screen and wonder what the heck is going on?'

Aaliyah gathered up the towel and its unpleasant contents. 'There are ways to make things happen in an alternate world. I can grant the wish, but only you would know it is happening. It will be real in *your* eyes, and those of the people around you at the time, but only you will retain the memory.'

Jo's mind boggled at Aaliyah's words. *All Rise* returned to TV very soon. She had the date noted on her calendar: how sad was that? But if she wished to be on it now, what did that mean? Would she be an early participant? One of the first twelve, sweating into their cake mix and praying to the gods of baking to make it to the next stage. Or one of the three finalists, all bonhomie and backslapping, when everyone knew they'd flail their opponents with a sharpened spatula if it meant victory?

'Jo, my patience is wearing thin. Do you want to be on the show or not?' Aaliyah stomped into the kitchen, the sound of the pedal bin signalling the disposal of the dead skin collection.

Do I? Jo sat down and attempted to gather her muddled thoughts. If only she knew it had happened, did that make it less worthwhile? *If a tree falls in a forest and no one is around to hear it, does it make a sound?* Stuff like that made Jo's brain hurt. Thinking about Harvey made her brain hurt. Having a genie lodger with an attitude problem definitely caused cerebral pain. But ... it was only a wish. An inconsequential droplet in an ocean of much bigger things. What did she have to lose? Apart from the coveted *All Rise* trophy, of course.

'Aaliyah. I'm done with procrastinating. Let's get this show on the road.'

Aaliyah reappeared, stuffing a chocolate digestive in her mouth. 'Reet, pet. I believe syrup of figs get things moving. Do you need a minute?'

Yet again, Jo wondered how Aaliyah was so savvy with words sometimes, then came unstuck. 'My bowel movements are fine, thank you. I meant that I'm ready to make the wish. To appear on *All Rise*. Wait...' As Aaliyah scrabbled in her crop top for her WIFI, Jo made a time-out sign with her hands.

'What are you doing? Is that some silly dance move like those guys I saw on the telly?' Aaliyah performed a speedy rendition of 'Y.M.C.A.' her pigtail bouncing as she flexed and stretched.

'No. I just need to understand how this works. I can't miss work at the café and I've got a date ... a get-together ... a rendezvous with Harvey coming up.' Jo's cheeks flamed.

She'd slipped up and mentioned a date and now Aaliyah would—

'It will be fine.' Aaliyah crouched in front of Jo, her eyes filled with concern. 'I know I'm a gobby mare, but I promise this will be a blast. And you won't miss a thing in the real world. Like I said, it's in a parallel universe, where time has no meaning. Just enjoy it. Do you trust me?'

Jo swallowed. *Do I?* Her first wish had helped heal her aching heart. Perhaps her second could inject some much-needed excitement into her life. What did she have to lose?

'OK. Go for it.'

CHAPTER 26

'Ladies and gentlemen, let's be upstanding for the terrific trio ready to bake up a storm tonight. We've got eggs, we've got flour, we've got ingredients I've never even heard of, but most importantly, we have you! So make some noise and *all rise* for our fabulous finalists.'

Thunderous applause rang in Jo's ears. The heat and glare of the studio lights assaulted her senses, as did the familiar surroundings. Familiar in the sense of seeing them on TV, but definitely unfamiliar in every other way.

She fingered the iconic apron, trying to ignore the beads of sweat gathering on her brow and in her armpits. Her fellow contestants looked more relaxed. One, a woman she reckoned to be in her early twenties, beamed at the audience. Easy to beam when you had youth on your side and a sheen of sweat made you glow, rather than look like you'd been dipped in a vat of oil. The other, a man possibly in his late fifties, seemed a little more nervous. His smile was pasted on, and he exuded a twitchiness that suggested either fear of being on camera or a desperate urge to pee.

The host of *All Rise*, Kelvin Brady, signalled for quiet. The audience obeyed, resuming their seats, and a hush fell over the studio.

'And now, without further ado, please welcome the three people whose job it is to sort the wheat from the chaff. Or rather, the baking flops from the magnificent masterpieces. Give it up for … the judges!'

The trio of judges descended the sparkly staircase and the applause started again. Unchanged since *All Rise* began, they comprised comedian Lee Russell, author and broadcaster Katie Nkosi, and cookery writer and owner of the highly successful Sweet Nothings chain of cake shops, Lily Mancini.

'Looking gorgeous as always!' cooed the host, oozing his trademark charm with a side order of smarm. 'That's Katie and Lily, of course. Lee, did the cat have his work cut out today?'

The audience roared with laughter. It took Jo a few seconds to make the 'look what the cat dragged in' connection.

'Better than looking like an oven-ready turkey,' retorted Lee, nodding at Kelvin's shiny silver suit.

'Ooh, the cat's got claws! Just kidding, my darling. Boho chic is just another way of saying vampish vagrant, right?'

The banter over for now, Kelvin moved on to introducing the contestants. 'Our finalists are raring to get mixing and fixing. Only three rounds stand between them and victory. There's everything to play for. So, before battle commences, let's meet the team chasing the dream!'

Kelvin urged them forward, one by one. First, he thrust his microphone under the nose of the younger woman. 'Becky, tell us a little about yourself, just as a reminder to those with the memory of a goldfish.'

Becky giggled and blushed. 'OK, I'm Becky from Beaconsfield, I'm twenty-four and I work as a midwife. I've loved baking since I was little, and winning *All Rise* would mean the absolute world to me. I'm engaged to the wonderful Dean and I can't wait till we get married. And of course, I will be making our wedding cake!'

Kelvin faux-wiped a tear from his eye and Jo fought back a wave of nausea. What on earth was she going to say when put in the spotlight? *I'm Jo Milligan from Cranley near Edinburgh. I'm only here because a genie granted a wish, and even if I win, it won't be for real. None of this is real, but I want it so badly.*

Luckily, Kelvin turned his attention to the fifty-something man, still fidgeting and tugging at his trousers. His face was redder than a ripe tomato and he looked on the verge of galloping off the set. 'Let's hear from our second finalist, folks. Marvin, tell us a little about yourself.'

Kelvin waited as Marvin composed himself. Jo's heart went out to him, though she wondered why he'd chosen to be on a live television show. Or had he? How did this work, if Jo's participation was all down to Aaliyah's mystical powers?

'Erm ... my name's Marvin. I live in Manchester with my partner, Giovanni, and we have a poodle called Noodle.'

Kelvin swivelled round to face the audience, a few titters audible from the back. 'Well, thank goodness you didn't get a duck,' he deadpanned, prompting a fresh wave of hysterical laughter.

Poor Marvin looked bewildered. Jo got the joke a little quicker this time and prayed she wouldn't be at the mercy of Kelvin's cutting comments.

'And when did you start baking, Marvin? Didn't you tell us that your beloved gran introduced you to all things moist and spongy at an early age?' Kelvin winked, Marvin squirmed, and Jo fought the urge to take the host's microphone and perform a rudimentary endoscopy.

'Yes, she did. My gran brought me up when my mum died, and she taught me everything I know. How to cook, do the laundry, grow vegetables, and most of all, how to be kind.' Marvin flashed a look at Kelvin, his nerves replaced with a steeliness surely instilled by his beloved gran.

'And being kind is what it's all about, folks! That, and getting your mitts on the glittering prize this evening. Which brings me to our final contestant. Last but definitely not least, we have … we have … just a moment.'

In all her years watching *All Rise*, Jo had never witnessed its host lost for words. Kelvin fiddled with his earpiece, a rictus grin plastered across his face. 'Sorry about that, folks. Let's welcome the lovely Jo, all the way from bonnie Scotland!'

Jo straightened her shoulders and smiled as broadly as her tense facial muscles would allow. Her fellow contestants clapped along with the audience and she allowed herself to relax a fraction.

'Apart from being a wee Scotch lass, what else can you tell us about yourself?' Kelvin smoothed down an imaginary crease in his suit jacket and pretended to do a Highland jig.

Give me strength! Jo adored her native country, but loathed the twee tartan-and-trews image it conjured up for others. And as for 'Scotch'…

'Well, Kelvin, I'd just like to point out that Scotch is a drink and a person is described as a Scot. I'm proud to be the latter, although not fond of the former. I run my own café just outside Edinburgh and I'm single and very happy with my life.'

Kelvin pursed his lips, glancing at the judges now seated to his right. Lee rocked in his chair with undisguised mirth, while Katie and Lily maintained an air of cool detachment. 'Well, that's me told! Here's hoping you'll not be hurling a haggis or tossing a caber in my direction by the end of the show.'

Jo felt like hurling, but in the vomiting sense. Watching

Kelvin on screen was one thing; being on the receiving end of his toe-curling quips made her skin crawl.

Introductions over, the three finalists took their places at their baking stations. This round of the final called on them to create a character cake based on a prompt contained in a golden envelope.

'From the moment you open the envelope, you have ninety minutes to prepare your masterpiece. Everything you need is in front of you — except the magic that only *you* can provide.'

A hush fell over the audience as Becky, Marvin and Jo picked up their sealed envelopes. Lee, Katie and Lily moved forward to line up with Kelvin and the famous countdown clock appeared behind them.

'Get ready to open your envelopes!' The clock ticked loudly, the audience and celebrities counting down in unison. 'Ten, nine, eight, seven, six…'

Jo ripped open the flap and gasped. *This just might be a piece of cake after all…*

CHAPTER 27

JO SCOOPED THE CAKE BATTER INTO THE MOULD, SMOOTHING it off with a spatula. She popped it into the pre-heated oven while she set about prepping the icing and the other bits and pieces that would bring her creation to life.

'How are we all doing, my lovelies?' Kelvin strutted around the previously immaculate stations, now smeared with flour, marzipan trimmings and droplets of food colouring that resembled a gruesome crime scene — if blood came in crimson, lurid green and dayglo orange.

'It's fine. I'm fine. Totally fine.' Becky's perky persona had dissipated rapidly, her reply laced with a side of tartness. The state-of-the-art Kitchen Aid mixer lay abandoned, the creamy mix dribbling forlornly on to the worktop.

'Hmm, sounds like Becky needs a boost. What do you think, All Risers?'

On cue, the audience stamped and whooped, the judges acting as cheerleaders. Flashing a quick smile at the nearest camera, Jo focused on the task in hand. Four separate bowls of icing, each needing careful colouring to adorn the finished product.

'Looking good, Becks,' cooed Kelvin. 'Maybe better in the oven than out, eh?'

'It's *Becky*,' she hissed, upending the bowl of mixture into two rectangular trays. With an almighty clatter she shoved the trays into the oven and slammed it shut.

'Moving swiftly on,' chirped Kelvin, gliding over to Marvin. He'd clearly regained his equilibrium and seemed at ease twisting strands of liquorice into an intricate design. 'Any guesses from the audience as to what divine concoction marvellous Marvin is making?' Kelvin cupped a hand around his right ear as various suggestions were shouted out.

'A caterpillar?'

'It's a horse's tail!'

'Princess Leia's hair!'

'Kelvin's toupée!'

Kelvin swept a hand through his lustrous locks, giving them a tug for good measure. 'How very dare you! I'll have you know that every inch of me is real, unlike others I could mention. Hmm, Katie?'

The three judges were circling the workstations like cake-loving piranhas, pausing to scribble notes. Katie stuck her tongue out at Kelvin, and made a show of thrusting her enviable bosom in the host's direction.

'And what have we here, bonnie lass?' Kelvin halted next to Jo, still stirring colouring into her various mixes.

Jo gritted her teeth and resisted the urge to flip a dollop of flesh-coloured icing at Kelvin's annoying face. 'That would be telling, wouldn't it?'

No one, apart from the behind-the-scenes crew, knew what the cards contained. Kelvin pretended to peer over Jo's shoulder and she did a passable impression of a pupil trying to hide their exam answers from a cheating classmate.

'Thirty-five minutes to go!' The booming voice of the show's narrator prompted an upsurge in activity. Becky whipped a bowl of something with lightning speed, her expression somewhere between beatific and deranged. Marvin had moved on to slicing and dicing, wielding the knife with all the fervour of a serial killer.

You can do this. Jo upended the mould, still hot from the oven, and gingerly eased the contents onto a rack to cool it as quickly as possible. The image of what she was about to create filled her mind, as did an all-too-familiar voice. *You're on to a winner, pet. Mind you don't balls up the finishing touches.*

As if, huffed Jo. She glanced at the audience, but it was so difficult to pick anyone out under the harsh glare of the studio lights. For a brief moment, she thought she saw the flick of an ebony ponytail and a flash of pearly teeth. But it wasn't Aaliyah, just a teenage girl wedged between an older couple.

'While our contestants add the wow factor, let's hear from our illustrious judges.' Kelvin made his way to the area dubbed 'Cosy Corner', where Lee, Katie and Lily huddled round a pot of tea and the selection of petit fours made in the opening round of the final. 'As these little darlings take a while to set, tradition dictates that our finalists make them earlier in the day,' explained Kelvin. Devoted fans of the show already knew that. Jo certainly did; she just couldn't remember anything about it. Somehow her wish had landed her right at the end of the show, meaning that she had no memory of the opening round.

'Let's have a quick recap of the scores as they currently stand.' A giant screen displayed photos of the three finalists. Becky oozed confidence, her cross-armed stance at odds with her current state of panic. Marvin gave a tight-lipped smile, hands jammed into the pockets of his apron. Jo, to her horror, resembled a rabbit caught in headlights. A jowly rabbit, with an inane smile that suggested village idiot rather than potential *All Rise* victor.

'With just the final round to go, Becky's in the lead with a score of seventeen, Marvin's in second place with fifteen, and Jo is trailing behind with a total of thirteen. Shame your dumplings didn't quite rise to the occasion, Jo.' Kelvin shot her a sideways glance, his look laced with a side order of sneer.

The screen changed to show the finalists holding their second-round efforts. Sure enough, Jo's platter was more trodden-on pancake than the fluffy mounds of point-scoring perfection presented by her rivals. What on earth had gone wrong? If she didn't up her game now, she had no chance of lifting the *All Rise* trophy.

'These are simply to die for,' simpered Katie, taking a mouse-sized nibble of Becky's mandarin-scented white chocolate and cranberry lollipops.

'Hmm, I found them a tad sickly, to be honest,' said Lily. 'I preferred Marvin's absinthe and peppermint truffles. Such an interesting merging of flavours: the ideal after-dinner treat.'

'A tough call,' added Lee. 'Personally, I felt Jo's goat's cheese and lemon ganache ticked all the boxes in terms of creativity and eatability, if that's even a word. Well, it is now!'

Goat's cheese and lemon? Where on earth had that combo come from? A faint snigger tickled Jo's ear and she suppressed one herself. There was no doubting who'd nudged Jo in that unexpected direction. Still, the unorthodox mix had given her an overall score of eight in the opening round. Shame about the five in the second round, though. Now she needed a real showstopper to seal the deal.

'Not long to go now,' announced Kelvin, making a show of checking his flashy watch. 'Contestants, it's time to pump up the jam, let loose with the juice and get those master-pieces in front of the nation!'

Jeez, the man talked absolute drivel. All pre-scripted, of

course. Jo had seen him interviewed once when the autocue had gone on the blink. He'd stumbled over his words, relying instead on simpering over his fellow guest, a well-known Shakespearean actor who'd quietened Kelvin with an imperious eyebrow.

Jo glanced at her rivals: busier than bees on amphetamines. She closed her eyes, conjuring up an image of how her cake would look. Unbidden, a picture of Harvey appeared, his features replacing the ones Jo needed to add, and fast.

'You've got this.' Jo said the words to herself, but pictured Harvey egging her on. Victory was within her grasp...

CHAPTER 28

'IT'S NOT EASY BEING A GENIE WHEN YOUR MASTER IS A meanie,' warbled Aaliyah, squirting vivid blue liquid into the toilet bowl. Proud of her impromptu lyrics, she snapped on a pair of rubber gloves and wrestled the toilet brush from its holder. 'I dream of being human, just an ordinary woman, but it's hard to decamp when your home is a lamp.'

OK, maybe the words needed some work, but at least it distracted Aaliyah from the task at hand — or rather, the long *list* of tasks at hand, provided by Jo before she did the magical skippety-hop to TV land.

As Aaliyah scrubbed the bowl, Jo's experience in front of the cameras played on a loop in her head. The silly bint thought she might lose! As if that would happen on Aaliyah's watch. Genies' wishes came with a cast-iron guarantee of success. Dhassim's didn't always hit the mark, mind, but his heart was in the right place even if his brain resided elsewhere.

Satisfied that the bloody loo gleamed, Aaliyah skipped downstairs and put the TV on. Fiddling with the remote and her WIFI, she brought up the episode of *All Rise* featuring Jo.

For her eyes only: an episode fulfilled in a dream land where anything was possible if you wished hard enough.

Aaliyah pressed *pause* and dashed to the kitchen for corn chips and salsa. Back in the lounge, she hit *play* and guffawed at the image of Jo hunkering by her workstation. Blobs of icing spattered her apron, and if she frowned any harder, the furrows on her forehead would resemble troughs.

Only minutes remained till the winner was announced. The other two contestants — a young woman and a sweaty old geezer — lined up with Jo. The show's host pranced around while the three judges gave the final-round creations a last taste.

'Get on with it!' screeched Aaliyah. 'I've got some serious flirting to do.' In Jo's absence, she had decided on a solo trip to The Jekyll and Hyde. Cleaning duties could wait; what she needed was a healthy dose of girl/boy banter. Attractive lads were in short supply in Cranley, and that Jamie wasn't too shabby a specimen.

Aaliyah punched the air as Jo finally accepted the winner's trophy. The losers clapped on either side of her, the man with the fervour of a seal on uppers. The woman, however, was sour-faced, and her hands barely made contact. Jo beamed at the camera and held the trophy aloft.

'Pretty impressive, Jo,' murmured Aaliyah as the camera panned in on the winning cake. 'Mind you, I think me boobs could have been bigger.'

Leaving Jo to bask in her glory, Aaliyah scooped up the remaining crumbs with a damp finger. A little primping was in order before she dazzled Jamie with her assets, physical or otherwise.

After checking that no rogue crumbs had nested in her cleavage, Aaliyah headed upstairs, and safe in the knowledge that Jo wouldn't be back for a while — she'd set the WIFI accordingly — snuck into Jo's room. Perched at the dressing table, she applied a lavish coating of mascara that claimed to be 'orgasmic'. Nope, not so much as a tingle. For good measure, she doused herself in Jo's favourite evening perfume — not that Jo went out much after dark. A bit pungent, but the bottle claimed aphrodisiac qualities. Poor Jamie didn't stand a chance.

Minutes later, Aaliyah strutted into the pub. She revelled in the head-turning response, even from those old enough to be … well, who knew? Birthdays didn't figure on a genie's calendar and if they did, she reckoned the fire brigade would need a lot of hoses to extinguish all the candles.

Aaliyah smirked as she clocked Jamie cleaning glasses behind the bar, but her smirk flagged a little when she saw who was sitting on a stool facing him, ample buttocks fighting for space. Bloody Kelly, or Kylie, or whatever her stupid name was. Still, Aaliyah didn't need magic powers to make sure *she* grabbed Jamie's attention. Skintight leggings and a slouchy off-the-shoulder top totally trumped the over-stuffed sausage-skin creation sported by her nemesis. Why did so many women dress so badly here? Not that the men did much better, Aaliyah thought, eyeing an unfortunate example with his trousers at half-mast and his belly straining against a stained T-shirt.

'Hey, nice to see you again.' Aaliyah started at the rich voice behind her. She turned, coming face to face with the very easy-on-the-eye Ed. 'No Jo today? I guess she's holding the fort at the café.'

Technically, Aaliyah should be there. She glanced at the large clock on the wall: just after midday. By her calculations, Jo would zap back from her *All Rise* triumph in around an hour, which was plenty of time for Aaliyah to wind Jamie round her little finger. Ha, as if she needed that long! And anyway, Jo's adventure had lasted a nanosecond in real time. No one would notice her blink-and-you'll-miss-it absence.

'Yeah, Jo's busy doing cakey things,' said Aaliyah, letting her top slide down another inch. Ed's expression remained unchanged. Jamie, however, ceased his glass buffing and caught Aaliyah's eye. She winked, and his pale cheeks flamed red. As did the tips of his ears, poking out under his mop of dark curls. *How adorable!*

Ed glanced at Jamie, who dropped his gaze as well as a pint glass. The resulting crash disturbed a slumbering mutt, who gave out a sharp yelp. Jamie's bar companion wriggled off her stool, her leopard-print number creeping up towards her waist.

'Be gentle with him,' murmured Ed, heading over to help clean up the breakage. 'He doesn't have a lot of experience with women.'

Aaliyah followed, pausing only to pat the pooch, still whimpering by its owner's feet. 'There, there. Calm your jets,' she cooed. The dog flipped onto its back and Aaliyah threw in a tummy rub for good measure.

'Any chance I could get one too?' The owner — a scrawny individual with a remarkable resemblance to his pet — leered over his whisky tumbler.

Aaliyah straightened up and blew him a kiss. 'Ah, that would be lovely, but my heart belongs to another.' *And I'd rather crawl over that broken glass than touch your icky body.*

Reaching the bar, she slid onto the stool vacated by Kylie/Kelly. Still warm from the heat of her generous buttocks, it brought Aaliyah face to face with Jamie.

As Ed vanished with a dustpan full of glass shards, Aaliyah pushed aside the drinks menu. 'I've got a right thirst on, so fix me a pint of your finest ale.' Remembering Jo's jibe about manners, Aaliyah added a purred 'please'.

Jamie nodded and began pouring, although a faint frown creased his youthful forehead. 'Erm, are you sure you wouldn't like a cocktail instead? Not that I'm saying girls shouldn't drink beer, but … well, Kylie and her mates always have cocktails.' Jamie blushed again, and the beer foam spilled over the top of the glass.

'Yeah, that's what *real* ladies drink round here.' The scrape of another stool being pulled up signalled the return of Kylie. 'Not that a rude cow like you could be described as a lady. And you're sitting in my chair.'

A flustered Jamie carried on pouring the pint, his eyes darting between Aaliyah and Kylie like a table-tennis spectator. Unfortunately for Kylie, though, there would only be one victor in this game.

'Really?' Aaliyah made a show of examining the back of her stool. 'I don't see a plaque with your name on it. And my choice of drink is exactly that: *my choice.* As is my choice in men.' She accepted the pint from Jamie's shaky hand and took a satisfying gulp. 'So why don't you tootle off back to your girlie pals and let me and this fine specimen get better acquainted. What do you think, Jamie?'

Before Jamie could speak, Kylie stabbed a French-manicured nail at Aaliyah. 'You've got a bloody nerve, swanning in here like the Queen of Sheba and thinking everyone's going to fall at your feet. Well, I've got news for you. We don't take kindly to up-their-arse newcomers and their fancy ways. Wise up, or you'll wish you'd never crossed me.'

Aaliyah wiped a smidgeon of froth from her upper lip. 'Thank you so much for the advice. Speaking of wishes, I happen to be something of an expert on those. And right now, I just wish you'd disappear.'

CHAPTER 29

'RIGHT. YOU ARE *NOT* GOING TO BEHAVE LIKE A CURMUDGEON with a rampant dose of indigestion.' Harvey paced the floor of his bedroom for the umpteenth time, annoyed that a jagged nail had snagged one of his best socks. Best, as in not having holes in the heels. He perched on the edge of the bed and surveyed the damage. Just a pulled thread: no need for a meltdown.

One of his mother's favourite expressions when he was young came to mind: *If the wind changes, your face'll stay like that!* He massaged his freshly shaven cheeks, hoping the motion would rearrange his features into something more attractive.

'Ah, you're not bad-looking when you smile. Shame your smiles are as frequent as Scotland winning at the footie these days.'

Harvey smiled and checked the time on the watch Lindsey had given him during their last Christmas together. A jokey one, featuring Mickey Mouse with his gloved hands pointing at the numbers. They'd both known it was her last. Curled up together watching *It's A Wonderful Life*, knowing they'd never pull a cracker together again — Lindsey always got the silly trinket and insisted on wearing the paper crown — or make a wish with the turkey wishbone. Harvey had won that time, securing the bigger end. He'd wished as hard as possible, Lindsey teasing him as he shushed her, wanting to believe that a stupid age-old tradition might halt the cancer's uncaring assault.

Wiping away a tear — they hovered, ever-present, sometimes marshalling themselves into platoons so that Harvey had to seek cover — he knew his grieving had to stop. No, not stop, but take a seat further back in the bus of life. He'd promised Lindsey that the show would go on, the irony of those words coming back to bite him when his career hit the skids. And by inviting Jo out tonight, he had the chance to move up a seat or two. As long as Jo didn't leg it from the pub after ten minutes, in which case he'd be slumped in the back row again with a bunch of rowdy schoolkids twanging chewing gum and laughing at fart jokes.

'You're babbling, man,' he muttered to himself. 'Get a grip and focus on having a nice time. Like bloody buses, they don't come along too often these days.'

The walk to The Jekyll and Hyde took no time at all, and a pleasantly balmy evening meant an outside table was an option. Would they eat together, or just have a drink or two? Harvey's stomach gave the growling equivalent of a thumbs up. His pathetic diet of toast and whisky needed to change. A lot needed to change for him to stand a chance of getting to know Jo better. And that was something he knew was important.

* * *

'OVER HERE!' Jo raised her voice over the hubbub of drinkers and diners making the most of the mini heatwave. Anything over seventeen degrees Celsius constituted a heatwave in

Scotland. Acres of white flesh were on show, eager to boast a tinge of sunburn or a decent tan, to show their Spanish time-share mates they didn't have the monopoly on mahogany.

As Harvey approached, Jo battened down a frisson of excitement. It was all a bit much, considering what had happened on *All Rise*. The trophy, stuffed in her handbag, made it real, even though it wasn't.

Her genie-inspired cake had sealed the deal, her rivals left with a unicorn and a mermaid. The judges were less than impressed when the unicorn's cream-filled horn ended up on the floor, and they pronounced the green-tinted flower petals of the mermaid's tail 'chewy and tasteless'. Using Aaliyah for inspiration, Jo had crafted a curvaceous butter-milk sponge base with a hint of cocoa to reflect her dusky skin tone. Black gel food colouring gave the hair the right look, and a gold-leaf bra top added just the right amount of glitz.

'Hi, Jo. You look, erm, lovely.' Harvey stuttered over the words, making Jo smile. Compliments didn't slip easily from his mouth. Not that she was any better at accepting them. She normally replied with, 'This old thing? Had it for donkeys' years,' or 'Have you been to Specsavers recently?' But she'd put on a new dress, taken longer with her make-up than usual, and knew that much of her sparkle owed itself to her unsharable win in front of the cameras.

'Thanks, Harvey. I took the liberty of ordering drinks. Well, a bottle of fizz. I wanted to celebrate.' *Oops*. What exactly was she celebrating? She could hardly 'fess up to her *All Rise* win, and celebrating being on a date smacked of desperation.

Harvey nodded, took the bottle of prosecco from the ice bucket, and filled two glasses. 'Celebrating isn't something that comes naturally to me, but whatever you want to toast, count me in.'

They chinked glasses, neither sure what to say. Jo fiddled with a cardboard coaster, and Harvey smoothed back a rebellious strand of hair. Out the corner of her eye, Jo spotted Jinnie and Sam sliding onto a bench, Angela and Ed joining them. She contemplated waving, but didn't want to intrude on their cosy foursome. Better to focus on the not-so-cosy twosome she was currently part of.

'Have you had a good day?' Jo longed to scream and shout about her unbelievable experience, wave the trophy around, and revel in gasps of admiration from The Jekyll and Hyde faithful. But only Aaliyah could share her joy, and she'd been conspicuous by her absence. She certainly wasn't at A Bit of Crumpet, as Jo had legged it there in a panic after her head-spinning return to reality. It was all closed up — and rightly so, at six pm.

'What's a good day?' Harvey folded a corner of his coaster. At this rate they'd be trying to out-origami one another. Who said romance was dead?

'One when something nice happens, I suppose, or when bad things don't. When you get out of bed and feel positive instead of wanting to kick your cat. Not that I have a cat or would injure a defenceless creature, just to be clear.'

Harvey took a contemplative sip of his fizz and gave Jo a wan smile. 'I never imagined for a moment that you would. Feel free to kick me instead. I came here with the intention of being Prince Charming and I've already ballsed it up, haven't I?'

'That depends.' Jo ditched her coaster in favour of the bar menu. 'Maybe if we stuff our faces with food then the awkward pauses won't matter so much. I can't stand people chatting with their mouths full. Are you hungry?'

Right on cue, Harvey's stomach gave a snarl worthy of a *Jurassic Park* dinosaur. Jo took in his embarrassed expression and her heart melted faster than dark chocolate in a bain marie.

'Hey, how are you?'

Jo jumped and turned round. The speaker was Jamie, his smile stretching from ear to ear. *Wait a minute.* Jamie's smiles were thin on the ground and he never asked how anyone was.

'Erm, we're fine. Just trying to decide what to eat. Harvey, what do you fancy?'

Before Harvey could utter a word, an all-too-familiar figure came into view. Planting a kiss on Jamie's cheek, Aaliyah regarded Jo with a look of triumph. 'Seems like we're both winners, eh, Jo? And I've already got exactly what I fancy!'

CHAPTER 30

'HADDOCK AND PRAWN PIE?' HARVEY TRIED TO CAPTURE JO'S attention, but her gaze was fixed on the retreating backs of her assistant and the young barman. Speaking of fish, her mouth was opening and closing in a passable imitation of a gulping goldfish. 'Or maybe the lamb dhansak? You can't go wrong with a good curry, in my humble opinion.' Still no response. Jo seemed transfixed by the loved-up duo, Aaliyah fondling the lad's bottom as they re-entered the pub.

One last try. 'OK, let's go for the goat's intestines with a side of sautéed eel and witchetty grubs.'

Finally! Jo's head whipped around, a look of horror on her face. 'Please tell me you made that one up,' she gasped, snatching the menu from Harvey. 'Thank goodness. I was worried for a moment that Ken had gone weird on the food front.'

'You don't look very happy about Aaliyah and that young man. Don't you approve of their relationship?' Harvey topped up their glasses.

'No, I don't. I mean ... Aaliyah's free to see whomever she

wants, but it's just not right. I can't explain: it's complicated. Anyway, I'm not here to discuss somebody else's love life.'

'Ah, that's a shame, because I was hoping to talk about mine.'

Where in the name of the wee man had that come from? Harvey absolutely did not want to discuss his love life. He didn't want to open his battered heart and spill out the whole sad tale of Lindsey and how his life had turned to dust. Maybe he should leave now, and let Jo find a decent man without enough baggage to give a Heathrow handler a hernia.

'I'm all ears.' Jo tucked her hair behind said ears and gave them an impressive waggle.

'Can you touch your nose with your tongue too?' asked Harvey, in an attempt to change the subject.

Jo stuck her tongue out — not too far — and crossed her eyes for good measure. 'Now you've seen my full repertoire of silliness, why don't you tell me about your wife? I get the feeling that talking might help, unless you'd rather I attempted a couple of backflips to lighten the mood. And as I'm distinctly rusty in the gymnastics department, that might not be wise.'

Harvey inhaled sharply. The wound he carried ached, and memories of his wife pierced his soul like hot needles. And yet something about Jo acted as a balm, tempering the pain and dulling its ferocity.

'Should we order some food first? Full confessions aren't good on an empty stomach.' Not that Harvey planned on sharing the whole sad tale of his screwed-up life.

Ten minutes later, with two plates of lamb curry steaming fragrantly in front of them, Jo took the lead. 'So, I know you were married, but I suspect she passed away and there's an ocean of grief inside you. She was your everything, Harvey, and it's been an almighty struggle to get back on your feet.'

A statement, not a question, which hit the nail firmly on the head. Harvey leant over the curry, hoping that the steam masked the dampness threatening to blur his vision. But something else threatened his equilibrium: the realisation that this woman — this attractive, kind-hearted woman — had the power to change his life. If he was brave enough to let her.

'Lindsey was my soulmate. A cliché, perhaps, but when I met her it was as if all the jumbled pieces of me fitted together. She loved the best parts, buffed up the worst ones, and every day spent with her felt like a gift. I still can't believe that she's gone. Although sometimes, I—'

'Talk to her?' Jo reached between the plates and took Harvey's hand. He wrapped his fingers around hers, marvelling at their delicacy in contrast to his meaty paws. 'I understand, Harvey. Even after many years, I still have conversations with my mum and dad. Not out loud, but inside my head. It brings me comfort to share things with them and imagine what they might say.'

'Do you think we both need professional help?' Harvey barked out a laugh, aware of the heat from Jo's hand warming his skin.

'No, but I think we need to be honest with each other if we're going anywhere with this.' She paused, an emotion Harvey couldn't read clouding her face. 'I don't believe in ghosts, but there are things in this world that can't be explained. Harvey, I like you. I really do. I believe you're a good person, even if you try to hide it.'

'I don't try to hide it,' said Harvey. 'My natural charm chooses to live behind a wall of self-indulgent misery.'

Jo took her hand away. It felt like winter's grasp pushing aside the residual heat of autumn. He fought the urge to seize it back again.

'We can talk *and* eat. Come on: you women are famed for

multi-tasking. Lindsey always juggled so many things and rarely dropped a ball. I, sadly, find it hard to match my socks. And don't get me started on passwords.'

Jo scooped up a helping of curry with a torn-up piece of naan bread and groaned as she ate. For the briefest of moments, Harvey imagined he'd caused the groan. He often made people groan, but not necessarily in a good way. 'This is delicious,' said Jo. 'Come on, eat up.'

Harvey joined Jo in demolishing the curry and chatting between mouthfuls.

'Have you ever considered bereavement counselling?' asked Jo. 'I know someone whose partner died and they found it really helpful to talk to someone neutral.'

Harvey shook his head. 'No disrespect to people who go in for that kind of thing, but the idea of lying on a couch and laying my soul bare to a total stranger fills me with horror. Thanks, but no thanks.'

Jo gave an exasperated sigh. 'I don't think that's how it works, Harvey. But different strokes for different folks, as they say.'

Harvey's thoughts again leapt to a place out of whack with the current situation: him and Jo snuggled up, his hand stroking the nape of her neck.

You naughty wee devil! Lindsey, scolding him with the teasing tone she'd always used when he did something wrong. But was this wrong? Was it time to dip a tentative toe in the dating pool and see what happened?

'You've got that faraway look in your eyes again,' said Jo. 'We don't have to talk about Lindsey, and I promise I won't try and psychoanalyse you. How about we just enjoy each other's company and the sunshine?'

Harvey nodded. 'Sounds good to me. Are you up for a dessert?'

Before Jo could answer, Aaliyah reappeared and plonked

herself on the bench next to Harvey. 'Budge up, there's a darling. Ooh, am I playing gooseberry?' She poked him in the ribs, her unfeasibly long nail making him wince.

'Aaliyah, don't you have better things to do? Like toy with that poor lad, although you know how I feel about that.'

Harvey watched the exchange with curiosity. Jo had said that Aaliyah was the daughter of a friend. Was she adopting the role of surrogate mother, and being over-protective of her young ward?

'Jamie's working, so I thought I'd hang with you guys for a bit. Did I hear mention of dessert?'

As Harvey accepted that two had now become three, a shriek behind them signalled the arrival of another.

'Jo! How lovely to see you! And your friend — Harvey, isn't it?'

Harvey shuffled further along the bench, quite sure he'd end up on the ground in a moment. *There were three in the bed, and the little one said, move over...*

'Hi, Jinnie, Sam. You've both met Harvey, I believe: he lives in Brae Cottage now. We're just—'

'You!' Aaliyah cried, a coiled snake ready to attack. 'It is *you*. The key to everything, the conduit to all that has happened. I feel it — I know it. I wish I understood it, but—'

Jo and Jinnie wore the same startled expression. Sam, however, looked as if he'd experienced his first alien encounter. Harvey wanted to run. To keep running, until he reached the humble shack he called home and make sense of it all.

'Shall we call it a night?' Jo slapped down some cash, hoisted her handbag over her shoulder, and manhandled Aaliyah off the bench.

'Jo, I need to pay my share.' His words fell on deaf ears. Everyone had left before he was off the starting blocks. Not quite the evening he'd envisaged...

CHAPTER 31

'WHAT WAS *THAT* ALL ABOUT?' JO FUMBLED WITH THE DOOR KEY as Aaliyah pulled out her compact mirror and checked her reflection.

'You mean me seeing Jamie, or that other man? Jinnie's squeeze, although what she's doing with *him* is anyone's guess.'

Jo opened the door and waited as Aaliyah huffed about a microscopic pimple on her nose. 'I meant Sam. He's a lovely man, and the perfect match for Jinnie.'

If Aaliyah rolled her eyes any harder, they'd come loose from their sockets and skitter across the hallway like marbles. 'He's not who you think he is,' she said darkly. 'Trust me, Jo, I got a right old case of the willies when he stood there like butter wouldn't melt. Pah! There's something rotten in the state of Cranley, and I'm not talking about Janette's out-of-date eggs.'

Leaving Aaliyah to hunt out some spot cream — 'better deal with this blighter before it goes for facial domination' — Jo collapsed on the sofa. Poor Harvey. It had been going well. OK, there had been the odd sticky moment, but he'd opened up about Lindsey, which was a good thing. And there'd been a couple of occasions when Jo had felt their friendship creep up a notch. When they'd held hands; when he'd looked at her and blushed as she gave a primal groan at the tastiness of the curry. Jo didn't need a degree in psychology or psychotherapy to know what was going through Harvey's mind. Men! Easy to read, most of the time — except when the shutters came down and the print size required a magnifying glass.

'Jo! I can't find me Clearasil anywhere. Can you pop to Janette's and get some?'

'No, I bloody can't.' *Two wishes down and one to go*. Then it would all be over, normality resumed, and village life restored to its previous soporific state. 'Dab some toothpaste or perfume on it. That'll stop it in its tracks.'

There was no reply from upstairs. Jo imagined Aaliyah smearing Colgate over her nose and finishing with a spritz of Jo's beloved Miss Dior. She pummelled a deflated cushion and kicked off her shoes as thoughts swamped her brain.

Who is Sam? The mild-mannered owner of Out of the Attic Antiques and a quietly successful author, but what else? Jo frowned as she tried to recall what Jinnie had said some time before. *Al Addin*. Sam's middle and last names blended together. She'd pooh-poohed it, of course. What possible connection could Sam have with two genies? Yes, the lamps had ended up with him, but only by coincidence. If Jo had had to bet on anyone in Cranley possessing mystical powers, she'd put her money on Janette. *She* knew things about people before they knew themselves.

Massaging her aching toes, Jo picked up the TV remote and flicked through the channels. A trailer came up for *All Rise*: the next season was starting soon. Kelvin's mahogany face filled the screen, his unfeasibly white teeth threatening snow blindness. 'Will our contestants make the audience swoon at their swirls, drool at their decorations and marvel at their marzipan manipulation? Or will their efforts be more flash in the pan than fantastico? Tune in next Saturday for the show that's got a nation lovin' their ovens!'

Jo switched off the TV. She'd won, but only in a land of make-believe. Then again, wasn't TV often a place where dreams or wishes came true? Was her success any less valid because no one knew about it?

Dragging herself into the kitchen for a much-needed cuppa, Jo halted at the ping of an incoming WhatsApp message. Her bag lay in the hallway, next to a stack of unopened post. Bills, of course, and a letter from Carole. Old-school, but Jo always enjoyed seeing the familiar pastel-pink envelope and her dear friend's scrawly handwriting.

Leaving the kettle to boil, she dithered between the phone message and the letter. One to read in a glance, the other to savour.

'Just heading out for a walk with Jamie.' Aaliyah peered over Jo's shoulder, reeking of Miss Dior with a hint of mint. 'He's finished work, so we thought we'd go hold hands and make plans.'

'Are you off your actual rocker?' Jo's blood pressure, usually well within safe limits, threatened to come to the boil in sync with the kettle. 'He's a human, and… Well, you're not. It's like pairing a piranha with a puppy.'

Aaliyah snorted. 'Are you saying I'm like some killer fish? That's rich, coming from the woman who's always telling me to be nice. Anyway, we're just having fun. That's *definitely* in short supply around here.' Aaliyah flounced out, slamming the door so hard that the windows rattled.

Jo took a calming camomile teabag from the caddy and dropped it into a mug. Waiting for it to infuse, she fetched her phone and opened the message.

Hi Jo. Sorry our evening came to an abrupt end. No idea what happened but I did enjoy our time together. Might not always have been obvious, but I did. If you fancy doing it again, just let me know. Maybe a wee trip to Edinburgh if you fancy. Less chance of interruption there! H x

Sealed with a kiss! Heavens, he'd be proposing next. Jo fanned herself with Carole's letter, which she decided to put aside until bedtime. For now, she'd sip her tea and muse on the evening's events. Could Sam really have a connection with the lamps? If so, why had Aaliyah reacted so negatively? Was he a malignant force, manipulating his genies for his own nefarious ends? And where had that word come from?

Jo sat in the dark for a while. It soothed her, the absence of light allowing her mind to still itself. On the surface, her life remained as steady — as dull — as ever. But the ripples below, the ones others couldn't see, threatened to surge up and drown her. A genie housemate playing silly beggars with an innocent young man. A fellow Cranley resident who might or might not be some kind of mythological master. The memories of being with her parents again, and of winning something she could never share but would always treasure. And then, the man who'd snipped off a little piece of her heart and carried it home.

Tossing the dregs of her tea into the sink, Jo clutched the letter to her chest and switched on the hallway light for Aaliyah. She would read Carole's wise and witty words later and try to tuck everything else away until the morning. Even a reply to Harvey. That could wait, too.

CHAPTER 32

THERE WAS STILL NO REPLY FROM JO. HARVEY HAD LOOKED AT his phone a dozen times between sending the message and getting up the next morning. He'd checked it was fully charged and put it next to the bed, where he'd spent a restless night. When he did drift off to sleep, weird dreams plagued him. Lindsey, dressed as a devil, prodding him with a pitch-fork and cackling maniacally. Jo, wearing only a skimpy apron, brandishing a whisk dripping in cake batter. And strangest of all, something about a lamp. Not an everyday table lamp, but the kind genies emerged from. In fact, a bit like the ones Jo had on display in the café.

'You're losing your marbles, mate,' he muttered under his breath. 'Either that, or someone laced that curry with magic mushrooms.'

Three stand-a-spoon-up-in-it coffees later, Harvey's brain cells gave up yawning and sprang to life. He fired up his computer and opened the neglected screenplay. More abandoned than neglected: an unloved, one-eared mutt looking for a good home.

Harvey scrolled to the last sentences he'd written. *And*

through the mist he trudged, his destination unknown. He travelled
without hope, a nomad by nature and a pessimist to his core. 'This
isn't a bloody screenplay, it's a piece of navel-gazing shite.' He
deleted the words, his finger crushing them with the key.

A wave of nausea hit him, a combination of said curry
and excess caffeine combining to attack his stomach lining.
He needed to eat.

He shuffled into the kitchen, trying to recall what awaited
him. Ah, yes. Pop Tarts: another gem from Janette's cornu-
copia of culinary delights. 'See, you just bung 'em in the
toaster and Bob's your uncle.' She'd insisted on selling him
two packs: strawberry and chocolate chip flavours.

Harvey waited as the latter cooked — if that was the
correct term — making little hissing noises. He downed a
glass of water and checked his phone again. Zilch.

The tarts duly popped, he returned to the lounge. Instead
of carrying on with the doomed screenplay, Harvey signed in
to his internet bank account. It made for equally unpleasant
reading. Far too many outgoings and very little coming in,
just some residual royalties from previous acting roles and a
couple of TV commercials he'd agreed to at the peak of his
fame. Nothing to be proud of, but they'd paid well. If it was
good enough for George Clooney...

Harvey bit into a Pop Tart, then spat the mouthful back
onto the plate. It tasted like hot, sickly sweet cardboard. He
tossed the whole lot in the bin and grabbed some digestive
biscuits instead.

Back at the computer, Harvey shut down the screenplay
and Googled 'new restaurants in Edinburgh.' He didn't know
the city's dining scene well, and wanted to find somewhere
to impress Jo. Mind you, he didn't know if she would eat out
with him again...

Scrolling through a list of possibilities, he paused. The
Crooked Cauldron had only been open three months, but

already had plenty of five-star ratings from happy customers. It was situated in the New Town, and the photos showed a semi-Gothic interior, with lots of black and red, offset by trendy Perspex chairs and slate-topped tables.

About to scan the menu, Harvey started when his phone signalled a new message. Reaching hurriedly across the table, he sent it skidding onto the floor. He retrieved it, cursing, and noted another set of cracks and scratches marring the screen.

Hi Harvey. Sorry for the delayed response — had an early night. Dinner out in Edinburgh would be lovely. When and where did you have in mind? Jo x

The corners of Harvey's mouth twitched upwards and the revolting aftertaste of the Pop Tart faded from memory as he clicked on The Crooked Cauldron's menu options.

Rum-cured salmon, passion fruit, lime & coriander dressed spring-onion salad, pickled coriander seeds.

Cider-braised lamb shoulder, courgetti & pickled apple salad, toasted pine nuts & tomato sauce.

Harvey paused. A bit too pretentious? How did you pickle coriander seeds, and what the heck was courgetti? Still, the rave reviews and reasonable prices swung it. He checked table availability before firing off a reply to Jo.

Does this Friday work? I was thinking of The Crooked Cauldron, a newish joint with rave reviews. It's a bit fancy-sounding, but check it out and let me know if it's a pickle too far :-) x

Now he was adding a smiley face! Appropriate, as Harvey's grin now stretched across his face. Bugger stupid screenplays and scratched phone screens, this rare foray into fun felt good. Better than good. It felt like stepping out of an icy downpour into a cosy pub with a roaring fire and a sea of friendly faces.

Harvey paced the room, anxious for Jo's response. He pictured her face, perhaps with a little frown making way for a full-blown grin to match his own. Or … she'd changed her mind. His mood flailed around for a foothold, then hit the floor. He opened his computer again and searched for some music. Radiohead?

You need to be uplifted, sweetheart, not mired in misery. Put on something romantic or positive. One of our songs. Just not the Bocelli one about saying goodbye.

Lindsey. Harvey wondered if he'd ever stop hearing her voice. If he'd ever want to stop hearing her voice. Or would a new voice eventually drown out his imagined conversations?

He decided on 'Reach' by S Club 7. Cheesier than a cheese factory, but they'd always loved it. They'd dance to it after a few drinks, Lindsey singing along and failing miserably to reach the high notes. Refreshingly upbeat, it reminded him of the times when he felt as if he'd grabbed the entire solar system in his fist. He kept the volume low, though, just enough to satisfy his need for nostalgia.

Bopping around, Harvey contemplated a wee dram to oil his dodgy dance moves. Just a snifter, nothing more. He shimmied into the kitchen, the air still heavy with the smell of toasted Pop Tarts. An upturned glass lay by the sink, the whisky bottle within easy reach. He poured a generous measure, its golden lushness luring him in, raised the glass, and—

'Harvey, are you there?'

Harvey froze. A voice at the front door. Muffled, but unmistakably Jo's. He shoved the glass in the fridge, beads of sweat peppering his brow. Why was she here? Had her phone conked out? Did she want to tell him face to face that they had nothing in common and only complete weirdos ate courgetti? He went to the door, his heart pounding.

'Hi!' Harvey didn't know what to do with his arms. He went for a casual propped-up position against the door frame, but it seemed unnatural. He crossed them instead, now guarding his territory.

'Hi.' Jo's stance mirrored his own. 'I hope you don't mind me dropping by unannounced, but I felt we had unfinished business.'

'We do?' Harvey loosened his arms a fraction.

Jo's arms dropped to her sides, her face telling a story Harvey didn't know how to read. 'We do. We... I don't quite know how to say this, but I need you to kiss me. Right now. Before we go out again. I really want to go out again, but I need to know if there's something there. Physically, I mean.'

As gobsmacked went, Harvey's gob felt well and truly smacked. Never in a million years — light years, even — could he have conjured up this scenario. A woman he liked — more than liked — turning up on his doorstep and asking to be kissed? And he'd been fretting about overly fussy ingredients?

'Erm, please come in.' Harvey stepped aside, allowing Jo to enter. The closing bars of the song played, about dreams coming true. Seconds later, he wrapped his arms around Jo and they kissed, and kissed, and kissed again...

CHAPTER 33

'Jo and Harvey sitting in a tree, K-I-S-S-I-N-G.' Aaliyah kept singing the annoying playground ditty, interspersing it with equally annoying squelchy kissing noises.

'Would you please give it a rest?' It was Monday morning at the café and Jo was ready to scream, or alternatively, shove Aaliyah into the industrial-sized mixer. Why, oh why had she confessed to kissing Harvey at all? Not that a confession had been needed, as Aaliyah had immediately clocked Jo's flushed cheeks and smudged lipstick.

For the past twenty-four hours she'd been teased relentlessly and bombarded with questions.

'Was he a good kisser?'

'Did you use tongues?'

'Did he have nice breath, or did it honk like a monkey's armpit?'

'Who went first? Ooh, you did, you saucy mare!'

Jo resorted to the playground response of sticking her fingers in her ears and chanting, 'I'm not listening!' With ten minutes until opening time, she needed to crack on — and Aaliyah needed to zip her gob and get on with her job.

'You know, for someone in their forties, you really need to give up your membership to Old Fartsville,' shouted Aaliyah. 'You kissed a guy, woo hoo! Honestly, Jo, sometimes you make nuns look flighty.'

Ouch. That stung. Jo knew she could be a bit set in her ways, but that didn't make her an old fart. Did it? And there had been nothing remotely nun-like about Saturday night's episode. One minute she'd been sitting at home, musing over the turn of events, then she'd grabbed her coat and marched to Harvey's cottage. OK, it was out of character, but she remembered wishing that they could have kissed—

Jo removed her fingers from her ears. 'Aaliyah, did you by any chance engineer the whole kiss thing?' Jo adopted a stern headmistress pose which probably reinforced the 'old fart' criticism.

'Moi?' Her face a picture of innocence, Aaliyah picked up a tray of freshly baked cinnamon buns and showily arranged them on the display shelf. 'You know how the wish thing goes. If you happened to wish for a snog, how would I know about it?'

Leaving Aaliyah to carry on setting things up, Jo flipped the café sign to 'open'. Did she believe her? Not that it mattered, unless… Would that count as her third wish? But surely that would mean the end of the road for her and Aaliyah?

Nope, Aaliyah showed no sign of vanishing into the ether. Jo eyed the his 'n' hers lamps and wondered how Dhassim was doing. He couldn't be having much fun stuck in there. Then again, Jo pitied the poor soul (or souls) who inherited them next.

'Hi, Jo.' Jinnie, wrapped up in a fluffy coat, hurried through the door. Yet again, the east-coast weather had flipped from moderately warm to freeze-your-bits-off overnight.

'Hi, Jinnie. No Sam?'

Jinnie's gaze skittered around the room, alighting on Aaliyah, and the cosy atmosphere in the café dropped as the two women squared up to each other.

In the red corner we have Aaliyah. Genie, monumental pain in the arse, prone to the odd moment of unexpected kindness.

And in the blue corner, we have Jinnie. Gorgeous, warm-hearted girl, engaged to Sam, with her own personal experience of lamp dwellers.

Lordy, she didn't need this right now. She'd received a lovely message from Harvey shortly after they'd locked lips. That was all they had done, although the heat level between them had reached thermometer-busting levels. His decision, or hers? Probably more evidence of Jo's 'get thee to a nunnery' status.

'Aaliyah, if you could grind some coffee for the machine, that would be lovely. Give me and Jinnie time for a quick natter.'

Aaliyah backed down and stomped off to find the coffee beans. Jinnie, meanwhile, slumped in a corner, unwinding a multi-coloured scarf from her neck.

'Are you all right? Is everything OK with Sam?' Jo pulled up a chair, regarding her younger friend with concern.

'Yes. No. Oh, I don't know.' Jinnie's bottom lip quivered and Jo's heart sank. Surely not trouble in paradise? Sidling closer lest Aaliyah's flappy ears tune in to the conversation, she urged Jinnie to continue.

'It's probably nothing, but Sam was really rattled by her reaction on Saturday night.' Jinnie put extra emphasis on 'her', twisting her scarf around her fingers into a noose. 'He's been acting strangely ever since, disappearing into his study for hours and barely eating.'

'He's probably working on his latest book,' said Jo. 'Don't

all writers get a bit hermit-like if they've got a deadline approaching?'

Jinnie shook her head. 'It's not that, Jo. I sneaked into the study when he went to bed last night and peeked at his search history. It's full of genie stuff and masters and mythological weirdness.'

'Maybe you should tell him about Dhassim. And the other one.' Jo nodded at the counter, where Aaliyah's bean-grinding meant little chance of her overhearing.

'I can't! Jo, he'd think I was a sandwich short of a picnic. He's always been suspicious about Dhassim, and never really bought the whole long-lost cousin thing. But I can't believe Sam has anything to do with them, aside from picking up the lamps from some old dear's house.'

Jo pondered the whole bizarre situation. A stray thought meandered through her brain, halted, and demanded to be heard. 'But when Dhassim met Sam he didn't react that way, did he?'

'No, but Dhassim wasn't exactly the brightest bulb on the Christmas tree. OK, he was a sweetheart, but Aaliyah's definitely got the edge in the brains department.'

Before Jo could continue her train of thought, Janette stomped into the café, a beanie hat pulled over her brow and a dog in tow. 'Sorry, Janette, no pets allowed.'

Janette tutted loudly, her canine companion letting out a supportive yelp. 'Och, he'll be no bother, Jo. Compared tae some of those wee ankle-biters that run around the place, he's a cherub.'

'I didn't know you had a dog,' said Jinnie, as Janette blithely ignored Jo and let the dog off the leash. He promptly charged at Jinnie and propelled himself into her lap. 'Oof! Thank goodness he's not a Great Dane, or I'd be flattened.' She stroked the dog's silky ears.

'He's a Cavalier King Charles Spaniel,' announced Janette, looking as proud and devoted as a mum showing off her newborn. 'And he's no mine. Alison from the boutique got him to keep her company after … you know. I'm just minding Hector for the day.'

'Still, he really shouldn't be in here,' reprimanded Jo. Her resolve crumbled as Hector began licking Jinnie's face, prompting a fit of giggles.

'I'll only be ten minutes, and I doubt health and safety are about to burst through the doors,' said Janette. 'A pot of tea and a slice of gingerbread, please. Oh, and a wee biscuit for Hector.'

Recognising defeat, Jo fetched Janette's order and a cup of turmeric and ginger tea for Jinnie. 'How does Alison manage normally?' she asked.

Janette broke off a piece of biscuit and fed it to a delighted Hector. 'Well, she's cut down to three days a week in the boutique for now and she's got a dog sitter. The wee lass is poorly with the flu, so I offered tae help.'

With half an eye on the doorway, just in case, Jo rejoined Jinnie. 'Where were we? Oh yes: Sam's worried about something and you're worried about Sam. I just don't see the name thing as anything but a daft coincidence. Maybe he's incorporating something about genies in his book.'

Jinnie raised a dubious eyebrow. 'He writes gritty thrillers, Jo. I doubt a genie's going to pop up in the middle of a gruesome crime scene.'

Finishing her tea, Jinnie paid for it, along with two cheese and onion pasties. 'Hopefully one of these will tempt Sam into eating,' she said. 'Sorry, Jo, I jabbered on so much about myself that I didn't even ask how you are. Is life treating you well?'

Popping the pasties into a bag, Jo recalled a line from one of Harvey's WhatsApp messages.

I feel like I've woken from a very long, very dreary sleep. Thank you. I don't normally welcome late-night visitors, but for you I'll always make an exception. H xx

Jo passed over the bag and smiled. 'Oh, yes. Very well indeed.'

CHAPTER 34

SMEAR TEST DAY. IT WAS CIRCLED IN RED ON JO'S CALENDAR, along with other dreaded appointments like the dental hygienist and the podiatrist. Having toenails thicker than rhino hide wasn't a source of pride. At least Aaliyah had proven handy in the foot-care department.

After a five-minute wait in the reception area, Jo got the nod to go through. 'Good morning, Jo. How are you today?'

Oh, you know, feeling like the electric chair might be a better proposition than the one I'm about to hop on to. 'I'm great, Dr Abbott. How are you? I hope the family are all well.'

Jo's doctor of many years pushed his smeared glasses up his nose, squinting at the file in front of him. He was a nice enough man, but with all the personality of a mouldy potato. Not that general practitioners needed the smarm and showmanship of *All Rise* host Kelvin, but a bit of cosy bedside manner wouldn't go amiss. The man was chillier than the horrible tool he used to scrape at her bits. Well, not scrape so much as excavate, with a revolting, sucky sensation...

'All fine, all fine. Now, just pop yourself behind the screen and remove the bottom half of your clothing. I'll be through in a moment.'

Jo did as instructed, wriggling out of her trousers and knickers. She contemplated keeping her socks on, since the room was freezing, but decided to go for the (almost) full monty. Not for the first time, she wondered why doctors performing smear tests insisted on privacy at this stage, when they were about to get up close and personal with her vagina.

'All ready? Excellent.' Dr Abbott appeared, wiping his manky glasses with a tissue. Jo spread her legs, the sense of dread accelerating along with her heartbeat. It only took a minute, it could save her life, people went through far worse things on a daily basis… She closed her eyes, conjuring up a happy place. Harvey. Cake. A relaxing massage with scented oil. Harvey administering said massage. More cake.

'That's nice and shiny.'

What? Jo squeezed her eyes more tightly shut. Had he just referred to her cervix as *shiny*?

'Did you polish it?'

Right, that's off the chart weird! The man needed reporting, or sectioning, or—

'It reminds me of my wife's.'

Jo gasped and opened her eyes. If she could, she'd scurry out the room right now and scream for security. But each leg was hoisted in the air and her knickers lay forlornly on the floor.

'Your ring.' Dr Abbott completed his examination. 'It reminds me of when I asked Esme to marry me. She said no at first, but I wore her down with my charm.'

Jo followed his gaze to her right hand and her mother's engagement ring, a single sapphire surrounded by tiny diamonds. She wore it only when she needed comfort. On days like this, when its presence anchored her to the past and made the tough more bearable. She'd dipped it in cleaning solution this morning, and buffed it with a toothbrush. 'Can I get down now?'

Dr Abbott signalled his assent. Jo grabbed her knickers, hopped around on one leg getting them on, and wondered where Dr Abbott's alleged charm had gone.

* * *

BACK HOME, Jo delighted in crossing out the appointment with a thick, black pen. She made herself a tuna and mayo sandwich and settled down to read Carole's letter that she'd been too tired to focus on before.

Hi Jo!

Greetings from sunny south Wales. Well, it's actually pouring right now, but I caught a glimpse of sun yesterday when I was out for a walk with my book club buddies. It lasted about ten minutes, but you know all about changeable weather in Cranley.

How are things? Hope the café's doing well and you're taking care of yourself. I really need to get my butt in gear and visit you. I'm such a timid traveller — I panic when I have to drive from Mumbles to Swansea!

The big news from me is that I'm getting married! I can't quite believe it myself after all these years of being a sad singleton. Not that I'm suggesting you're sad in any way. Honestly, I can put my foot in it without leaving the house.

Anyway, the lucky man's called Austin and we met two months ago at Verdi's. You know, the fabulous restaurant and ice-cream parlour on the seafront here. I'm sure I've babbled on about it before.

I know you're shaking your head right now and thinking: Carole's lost the plot, marrying someone she's known for a heart-beat. But trust me, when it's right, you know.

Austin grew up in Mumbles but moved away in his twenties.

He's divorced, no children, and moved back here six months ago. I bumped into him, quite literally, on the way to the ladies' loo and we got chatting. Next thing I know, we're tucking into salted caramel and shortbread sundaes and chatting like we'd known each other forever.

He popped the question two days ago and gave me the most gorgeous ring. I promise I'll take a photo and send it to you. You know how rubbish I am with mobiles and computers! I'm much happier with pen and paper, or a proper chat on my landline. Austin thinks it's sweet that I'm a throwback to the seventies, minus the flares!

The rest of the letter contained more gushing about the wonderful Austin, wedding plans, and Carole's new job as an assistant in an optician's. 'Must have picked up a pair of rose-tinted spectacles on your first day,' grumbled Jo, before rebuking herself for being so cynical. Carole was in love after her fair share of disastrous relationships. Who was Jo to rain on her misty-eyed parade?

Jo twiddled with her mum's engagement ring and snorted with laughter as she remembered the bizarre conversation with Dr Abbott. Hesitating for a moment, she slipped the ring off her right hand and put it on her wedding finger. She allowed herself a little daydream about someone getting down on one knee and asking her to marry them, then producing a velvet box and flipping it open to reveal a beautiful ring. Nothing too flashy: more class than crass.

'For goodness' sake, you'll be skipping down to Janette's next to buy bridal magazines!' Jo switched the ring back to her right hand. She'd been engaged once, and that hadn't ended well.

With Aaliyah holding the fort at A Bit of Crumpet, Jo didn't have any pressing tasks. She pondered what to do next. Obviously, visiting the corner shop and stocking up on bridal magazines was a no-no. Firstly, tripping down the aisle in a haze of matrimonial bliss just wasn't on the cards. Secondly, word would spread like wildfire and Jo would be the subject of knowing looks and not-so-subtle comments.

'Didn't know you were seeing someone. Anyone we know?'

'Ah, how lovely. So nice to see older people finding happiness.'

'Are you pregnant?'

Jo decided a soak in the bath and a few chapters of a book would help soothe both body and mind. It would keep her focussed, instead of allowing random, crazy notions to swamp her brain.

Jo settled in the tub, but found it impossible to read as her glasses kept steaming up. She slid down until the bubbles enveloped her entire body and concentrated on her breathing — in, out, in, out — until she felt relaxed. She closed her eyes and drifted into a state of semi-consciousness.

Jo, would you make me the happiest man in the world and be my wife?

She slipped under the bubbles and allowed herself to dream a little longer...

CHAPTER 35

'Wow!'

Jo's reaction delighted Harvey — assuming that 'wow' always meant a good thing. Could there be a negative version? No, she'd clapped her hands together in delight, her sparkling eyes scanning every nook and cranny of the restaurant.

'You like it?' Harvey had spent yet another restless night wondering if The Crooked Cauldron would pass muster. OK, that wasn't the *only* reason for his inability to sleep more than four hours at a stretch.

'It's like being on the set of a Halloween movie, or an adaptation of Macbeth,' said Jo. 'Except with a modern twist.'

'And minus the witches,' added Harvey, placing a hand in the small of Jo's back to steer her towards the beaming young woman waiting to seat them. 'Table for two, under the name of Dempster.' Harvey's breath snagged in his throat as he imagined the whole restaurant grinding to a halt, beady little stares piercing his flesh like red-hot needles. A slip of the tongue, but a dangerous one.

'I'm sorry, sir. I can't seem to find a reservation under that—'

'Quinn. The name's Harvey Quinn.' Jeez, now he sounded like a bargain-basement Bond. Very shaken and definitely stirred by the woman next to him, who — thank the lord of small mercies — had wandered out of earshot.

'Ah, yes.' The maitre d' drew a neat line through the booking and gestured to a fellow staff member. 'This is Alfonso, who will be looking after you tonight. Your first time with us, Mr Quinn?'

Harvey nodded as Alfonso, all chiselled jawline and impossibly tight shirt, clutched two menus to his honed chest and gestured towards a dark corner of the restaurant. Not that any areas of the place were brightly illuminated. Perhaps they provided miners' helmets to peruse the menus.

Jo reappeared. 'Sorry, I just needed to pop to the loo. I have a thing about toilets.' She thanked Alfonso who'd guided her to their table. He pulled out her chair and waited until she was seated. 'Not in a "that ballcock needs changing" way or "shouldn't the toilet roll go the other way round?" way.' Jo laughed and the sound calmed Harvey's rattled nerves.

'We're all allowed our quirks and foibles,' he said, pointing to a top-of-the-range Malbec on the wine list and requesting a jug of water. 'And don't those two words sound really strange when you say them out loud?'

Jo giggled. 'Yes, they do! Like an upmarket gentleman's outfitter, or something. Does sir need his crotch adjusting?'

'Perhaps sir needs to become better acquainted with his feet before he attempts to squeeze his girth into a fitted waistcoat,' added Harvey. He didn't know where this was going, but hearing Jo's laughter meant the world to him. Laughter had been absent from his life for so long, but now...

'We've gone off track. All your fault, you naughty man.' Jo

composed herself, dabbing at her cheeks with the linen napkin. 'I was about to tell you about my toilet fetish. No, I don't have a thing about loo brushes, so don't give me that look. I just like it when bars or restaurants get imaginative. Instead of ladies and gents, they come up with alternatives.'

'Like "For Those Who Stand" and "For Those Who Sit"?' said Harvey, as Alfonso painstakingly uncorked the wine bottle. 'Although you might need to be careful with pronouncing the latter.'

Jo looked puzzled for a second, then burst out laughing again. 'Exactly! I once saw a "Ladles and Jellyspoons" in a cute café on holiday, and my all-time favourite was "Sausage" and "Eggs", in a pretty upmarket restaurant down south.'

'Glad we're not having a full Scottish breakfast, then.' Harvey nodded to Alfonso, who poured a tasting measure. 'Would you like to sample the wine, Jo?'

Jo swirled the wine around and took a quick sniff, then plunged her nose deeper into the glass and inhaled again. *Impressive*, thought Harvey. Mind you, Lindsey called him a wine philistine, and maintained that he wouldn't recognise a rare vintage if it bit him on the arse. 'Lovely. Thank you.'

Alfonso filled their glasses, stepping discreetly away when Harvey asked for a few more minutes to choose their food. 'So, did the toilet signs here pass muster?' he asked.

Jo grinned. 'Not bad. Ghouls and Gals, which fits with the theme.'

'I take umbrage at being called a ghoul,' said Harvey, raising his glass to Jo. 'Mind you, you haven't seen me at 5 am after a rough night between the sheets.' *Oh, bugger and bollocks.* Why had he alluded to the bedroom?

Luckily, Jo didn't pick up on the comment, or chose to ignore it. She took a sip of wine and ran an elegant finger down the entrées section of the menu. 'We'd better get ordering before Alfonso thinks we're only here for the booze. What do you fancy, Harvey?'

Oh, what a leading question. Harvey could hardly say, 'You. I fancy you!', even though he did. Besides, the verb didn't do his feelings justice. Jo, whether she realised it or not, had pierced a hole in the armour he'd consciously donned after Lindsey's death. Like it or not, this woman had seriously got under his skin.

'What about sharing some nibbles first, then choosing mains?' Jo's face glowed in the flickering candlelight, her fitted top accentuating her shoulders and the tantalising hollow at the base of her neck. It had a name, but Harvey couldn't recall what it was. He just wanted to touch it, smell it, kiss it—

Harvey barely listened as Jo reeled off the order to Alfonso, who made all the right noises as he jotted it down. 'Good choice. Ah, you cannot go wrong with the pistachio and feta dip. And some artisan bread on the side? Of course.'

With a little nudging from Jo, Harvey had gone for Parmesan-stuffed chicken supreme as his main. She'd opted for the cider-braised lamb shoulder with all the trimmings. Quite honestly, though, Harvey could have chowed down on a doormat and not noticed. Being here, with Jo, felt so right. Scarily so, considering he'd doubted he would ever find real happiness again.

'Mmm, this is delicious. Have a taste.' Jo waggled a forkful of lamb at Harvey and he willingly accepted the juicy morsel. He nodded his agreement, all the time gazing at Jo. He no longer saw any similarity to Lindsey, at least not in the phys-ical sense. Jo was Jo, and his heart did a little tattoo of joy as she returned his gaze with undisguised longing. Or did she just want a bite of his chicken?

The rest of the meal passed in a companionable haze, with a side order of sexual tension. Harvey barely tasted the food, his mind galloping ahead to the end of the evening. Would they kiss again? He sincerely hoped so. Would they go any further this time? He'd be a total liar if he denied that it had crossed his mind. Not that Harvey wanted to jinx things between them. He'd be more than happy to share a kiss or two, or three. He wanted things to work out, not fall apart before they'd really got going.

After sharing an apricot drizzle cake and indulging in a digestif each, Jo and Harvey squabbled over the bill.

'I'm paying. End of. It was my idea to come here, so my credit card's going on the plate.'

'Let me pay half. Or at least cover the wine and grappa.'

Harvey swatted away Jo's fistful of cash. 'You can make me a coffee back at yours if you like. Unless you'd like to get to bed straight away.'

Remove foot from mouth and pray to be struck by a lightning bolt. Yet again, he'd mentioned the bedroom, and revealed himself to be a horny old sod with a one-track mind.

'I might do.' Jo slid into her coat, held by Alfonso. Harvey shrugged on his own, unsure which suggestion had received the tentative thumbs up.

Forty-five minutes and a breathless, kiss-filled train ride later, he had his answer.

CHAPTER 36

'Not such an old fart now.' Jo sighed and snuggled down under the duvet. If only Aaliyah could see her now… Well, maybe not in her current state of wanton nakedness. Jo had no doubt her make-up was smeared across the pillow-case (luckily dark blue), and she dreaded to picture her hair.

Next to her, Harvey stirred. He emitted a kitten-like snore and turned over, his right arm draped over Jo's middle. She wriggled closer, until their bodies were perfectly aligned. Ooh, lovely heat coming from his leg and torso! It certainly beat her childhood hot-water bottle with its fleecy tartan cover.

Tempted as she was to wake Harvey for a rematch, Jo let him sleep. The worry lines on his forehead had softened, as if someone had given them a once-over with a steam iron during the night. He looked like a man without a care in the world, not the grumpy old sod she'd first met. Jo touched his cheek, a fairy-breath caress, and glanced at the digital clock on the bedside table.

Shit, it was already eight o'clock! She needed to get up, get dressed and get home to repair her damaged face and hair. Stupidly, she hadn't primed Aaliyah to deal with the café opening. Heck, she hadn't known how the evening would pan out... Except she had. Deep down, she'd known they'd end up in bed together. The attraction between them was palpable, the kisses they'd shared last night and before deliciously tender and sweet.

Jo reluctantly slid out from under the duvet, taking care not to disturb Harvey. She tiptoed around the room, gathering up her clothes and underwear. She picked up Harvey's too, stifling a giggle at his Superman boxer shorts. She hadn't noticed them last night; they'd both been in such a hurry to undress. Jo folded his clothes and placed them on a wicker chair in the corner.

Once dressed, Jo snuck downstairs: she needed a strong cup of tea before making her way home. Popping the kettle on, she wandered into the lounge where Lindsey's photo, absent before, took pride of place on the mantelpiece.

'He loved you very much.' Jo looked at the woman who'd first captured Harvey's heart before being cruelly snatched from his life. 'I hope you're OK with us,' she said, tears filling her eyes at the sadness of Harvey's loss. 'I don't know where we're going or if it'll last, but I'll do my best to make him happy.'

Cup of tea in hand, Jo heard the unmistakable sound of post plopping through the letterbox. She hesitated, unsure whether or not to pick it up. It would be strange to just step over it on her way out, so...

The small pile comprised several flyers and one plain white envelope. Jo scooped them up and carried them into the kitchen. As she propped the pile against the toaster, the name on the envelope caught her eye: *Mr H Dempster*. Strange, unless he used that name professionally. She'd ask him, but she didn't want to appear nosy. Despite their wonderful night together, Jo feared that Harvey still teetered on a precipice of emotions. One false move, and their fledgling relationship might shatter.

Checking she'd got everything, Jo psyched herself up for a verbal assault from Aaliyah — assuming her genie sidekick had woken up when she got back. The woman had sleep down to an art form.

As she unlocked the door, amazed they'd remembered to lock it as they clung to each other in a frenzied embrace, Jo heard a distinct thud from upstairs, followed by a second: two feet being planted on the floor. Next came the creak of the bedroom door opening and a husky voice: 'Are you still there, Jo?'

Jo hesitated. Better to scarper now and meet up later? Then again, she had no reason to run away. She'd done nothing wrong, and the caffeine-starved inhabitants of Cranley could wait a bit longer for their daily fix. 'I'm still here!' she trilled, slinging her coat back on the hook. She squinted at the blotchy mirror on the coat stand. Eek! She looked like an extra from *Dawn of the Dead,* and with no means of repairing the damage.

'Are you OK?' Harvey reached the bottom step, dragging a hand across his face. 'I was going to make you some breakfast. Not being presumptuous or anything, but I got in eggs, bacon and black pudding.'

'Ah, that would have been lovely, but I've got to get back home, fix my face and open the café.'

'Your face looks perfect to me.' Harvey stepped forward, and Jo instinctively stepped back. Not only did she look a fright, but she hadn't brushed her teeth or put on deodorant. The last thing she needed was to floor Harvey with a hideous bad-breath-and-body-odour combo. 'At least join me for a cuppa?' His expression reminded Jo of a schoolboy who'd lost at conkers.

'OK, but better make it a quickie.' Jo's cheeks flamed as

Harvey's eyes widened in mock surprise. 'The tea, I mean, I don't have time to—'

Harvey closed the space between them and planted a soft kiss on Jo's forehead. 'I'd never want to rush with you, Jo. I hope I can see you again soon.'

'As you've seen more of me than anyone has in a very long time, I'm just delighted you're still interested,' she joked. 'Middle-aged jiggly bits and all.'

Harvey led her into the kitchen and chucked two tea bags in mugs before topping them up with the still-hot water. Jo noticed that he selected a specific mug for himself, the one he'd used before.'Your so-called jiggly bits are what I call womanly curves in all the right places. If I wanted to go to bed with something flat and shapeless, I'd get it on with an ironing board.'

* * *

STILL CHUCKLING at Harvey's comment, and basking in his lengthy goodbye kiss, Jo let herself into the house. Maybe she'd have time for a shower and damage repair before Aaliyah stuck her oar in…

'You dirty wee stop out! What time do you call this?' Aaliyah pointed at her WIFI. Not only did it grant wishes, it also acted as a clock and an alarm. An alarm that Aaliyah frequently slept through, although sadly she was now wide awake.

'I call it quarter to nine, and time for both of us to get to work.' Jo smiled sweetly, keen to head off the barrage of snide comments and double entendres gathering force behind Aaliyah's sardonic stare.

'Nice try, pet, but you're not getting off the hook that lightly. I need the skinny on you and horny Harvey. Did the earth move, or was it just the clatter of your chastity belt hitting the floor?' Aaliyah hooted with glee at her one-liner.

Jo fixed her with a glacial stare and tossed the café keys in her direction. 'My lips are sealed, as should yours be if you want to keep on living here. Go and open up, and I'll join you when I'm showered and ready.'

Leaving Aaliyah cackling and making revolting pseudo-sex noises, Jo thumped up the stairs. A minute later, the door banged.

Jo sat on the edge of her bed and allowed herself a moment to reflect on the previous night. She could count her lovers on the fingers of one hand, but none had made her feel the way Harvey did. Not even her fiancé — certainly not her fiancé — who'd regarded her body as a raunchier version of the children's board game Operation. Graham had poked and prodded, never quite hitting the mark. Luckily, Jo's nose never lit up during his inept fumbling.

Showered and dressed, Jo locked up and headed to the café. She felt light and carefree, enveloped in a little bubble of joy. Nothing, and no one, was going to burst it today.

CHAPTER 37

'Do you have this in other colours?' Jo held up the pretty moss-green top. Well, pretty on anyone else, but it didn't flatter her skin tone.

'I might have it in powder blue. Let me check.' Alison Gale disappeared behind the curtain at the back.

Jo continued rifling through the rail of tops and blouses, determined to find something new for tonight's date with Harvey. She'd already sorted out her best underwear — well, second best, as her finest still languished in the laundry basket after her night of passion.

'Sorry, give me a minute,' shouted Alison.

'No problem,' replied Jo, fingers alighting on a bodysuit in charcoal grey shot through with fine threads of silver. Too daring? It would eliminate the need for knickers, but those pesky poppers presented a challenge both to the wearer and any poor sod attempting to undo them.

Pushing the bodysuit aside, Jo reached for a simple but classy white blouse with mother-of-pearl buttons and a ruffled collar. A bit Lady Di, but teamed with her trusty black skirt, it might speak of starchy schoolmistress with an underlying hint of—

'What the heck?' Jo gasped as something wet tickled her ankles. For a ridiculous moment, she imagined Harvey on all fours, giving her legs an enthusiastic lick. The thought wasn't unpleasant, but extremely unlikely.

'Oh God, I'm so sorry! Hector, leave Jo alone.' Alison dashed to Jo's rescue, dumping an armful of tops on the counter. 'He shouldn't really be in here, but my dog sitter let me down again.'

Jo hunkered down, giving the pooch an affectionate ruffle around the ears. He responded with another slobbery lick, his tongue making contact with her ear. Again, Harvey sprang to mind.

'Here it is in blue. Darker than I thought, but it would look great with jeans.'

Jo slipped the top over her head. Sadly, it looked better draped over Alison's arm than on her. 'I think I'll try these on, but I'll need to use the changing room.'

Clutching the blouse and the clingy bodysuit, Jo slipped behind the curtain and tugged it into place. She removed her long-sleeved T-shirt and frowned at today's bra. Originally white, too many turns in the wash had given it the hue of well-trodden snow. Still, if she went with the charcoal bodysuit…

To her delight, it fitted perfectly. The elastic sucked her in at the middle, and the neckline plunged just enough to tease a hint of cleavage. The white blouse, in contrast, screamed frump.

Jo got dressed and returned to the counter, where Alison was feeding doggy treats to an ecstatic Hector. 'I'll take this one, please.'

'A good choice.' Alison smiled and Hector gave a half

woof/half whimper suggesting that he approved too. Or that he just wanted another handful of dog biscuits.

'He's a sweetheart.' Jo handed over her credit card and stroked Hector's silky ears. 'Is Janette still helping out with him?'

Alison finished wrapping Jo's purchase in tissue paper and swiped the card. 'When she can. I've signed up for puppy training classes. So far, Hector's chewed his way through my slippers, peed in virtually every corner of the house, and left a trail of poop outside my bedroom.'

Jo accepted the pretty floral bag proffered by Alison. 'But he'll settle down eventually, and he must be good company?'

'Hmm, I guess so.' Alison smiled as another customer entered the shop. 'He likes cuddles, but I doubt we'll ever snuggle up together getting the wrong answers on *Pointless*, or bicker over who empties the dishwasher.'

'It must be difficult without your husband. I've never been married or had a dog, but I still miss my parents, even though they died a long time ago.'

Alison nodded as the new customer left without a backward glance. 'Grief doesn't have an expiry date, in my experience. Some days I can barely prise myself out of bed, and others I remind myself how lucky I am to have a comfortable life and sons who don't see me as an interfering old bat.'

Jo wandered home, her feelings a mixture of melancholy and butterflies about seeing Harvey later. A drink might help, though she rarely imbibed during the day. Still, a small glass of wine wouldn't hurt, and she could avoid Aaliyah's incessant gibbering.

Entering The Jekyll and Hyde, Jo spotted Ken deep in conversation with his son, Ed. Judging by Ken's pained expression and Ed's gesticulating, the topic wasn't a cheery one. 'Hi, Jo,' said Ken. 'Sorry, just sorting something out. Jamie'll be over in a minute to take your order.'

Ken gave Jo a watery smile, and her heart squeezed at the memory of what might have been when they'd teetered on the brink of turning their friendship into something more. For the umpteenth time, Jo thanked the gods of common sense for raising the drawbridge before she and Ken had taken that fateful step.

'Hi, Jamie.' Jo greeted the young barman, whose dalliance with Aaliyah still caused her concern.

'What can I get you?' he replied, his manner gruff as always. What Aaliyah saw in him was anyone's guess, although single and passably attractive young men were scarce in Cranley. Single men — full stop — were a rarity.

'A small glass of Pinot Grigio, please.' Jo handed over a fiver and waited as Jamie counted out the change. 'How are things going?' She didn't dare to ask him directly about Aaliyah, but making polite chitchat seemed harmless.

To her surprise, Jamie leant across the bar, gesturing for Jo to move closer. 'Not good. Mags had an episode this morning and it's taken Ken hours to calm her down. He had to get the doctor out to give her something.'

'Oh, that's awful. Poor Mags, and poor Ken. I hope she feels better soon.'

Jo took her drink over to a corner table. The chances of Mags getting better were non-existent, as Alzheimer's tightened its grasp. The last time she'd seen Mags, a large food stain had marred her top and her once-immaculate hair was tangled and unwashed. She'd asked Jo the same question several times, and talked about Ed as if he were a teenager approaching exam time.

'Mind if I join you?'

Jo looked up in surprise at the familiar voice: Harvey, a twinkle in his eye as he clocked her untouched glass of wine. 'Don't tell me you needed some Dutch courage before seeing me again.'

Heat rose to Jo's cheeks, a combination of the effect Harvey had on her and being busted boozing in the afternoon. 'No, this is just a wee treat after a successful shopping mission.' She pointed at the bag next to her, and Harvey made to grab it. 'Paws off! A woman is entitled to her secrets, particularly when they pertain to clothing. If you play your cards right, all will be revealed later.'

'Jo, I only came in for a cheeky half pint. Now I might have to spend the rest of the day taking cold showers and picturing nuns in habits.'

'And how do you know this isn't a raunchy nun's outfit, hmm? How come you're here, anyway? You said you'd be working on your screenplay.'

Harvey hung his head in mock shame. 'I wrote a thousand words, deleted half, and felt the walls of Brae Cottage shrinking around me. I came here to escape. Finding you here beats a beer any day for raising a man's spirits.'

Jo raised her glass to Harvey just as a commotion at the door had the punters swivelling on their bar stools. Aaliyah flew across the room, breathless and dishevelled, and tugged furiously at Jo's arm. 'I need to talk to you. *Now!*'

Jo shrugged off Aaliyah's frantic tugging. 'I'm busy right now. And don't tell me you've left the café unstaffed.'

'Please, Jo. No, it's not. It's...' She pulled a face at Harvey, who made a show of checking his phone as if his life depended on it.

Outside, Jo squared up to Aaliyah, her temper rising to boiling point. 'What's so bloody important that you've come racing in here as if the hounds of hell are at your heels?'

Aaliyah, for the first time Jo could remember, looked repentant. 'I did something stupid.'

'Don't tell me you mixed up the salt and sugar again.' Hardly a hanging offence. 'What did you do, Aaliyah?'

'Well, when I said the café wasn't unstaffed, I meant that someone else is looking after it.'

'Who?'

'Dhassim.'

CHAPTER 38

'HOW DID HE GET OUT?' JO HUFFED AND PUFFED NEXT TO Aaliyah as they sprinted from the pub to the café.

'He … escaped.'

Of course he did. Jo knew little of the ways in which genies worked, but engineering a way out of a lamp Houdini-style didn't quite fit.

'You rubbed him— I mean, you rubbed the lamp, didn't you?' Jo halted, bending over, hands on thighs, breathing heavier than a X-rated hotline caller.

'I might have done. OK, I gave his lamp a bit of a polish, but only because … because I miss him.' Aaliyah let out an anguished wail.

'But I thought he drove you mad. And you've got Jamie now, haven't you?' Much as she'd doubted the wisdom of Aaliyah and Jamie hooking up, now Jo would happily fling confetti at their wedding and scrawl 'Just Married' on the boot of their car. Anything to avoid the terrifying reality of two genies invading her life. This could not be happening.

'Cooee!' The vision that greeted Jo reminded her of a

cartoon character from her childhood. She couldn't be sure which, but one that zinged with energy and looked capable of creating havoc in a heartbeat.

'Dhassim!' Aaliyah rushed into her erstwhile lover's arms. A bout of squelchy kissing ensued, prompting the café's only customers to harrumph and exit post-haste.

'Jo, this is Dhassim.'

Really? I thought it was Arnold Schwarzenegger. Jo folded her arms.

Dhassim folded his arms, too, then a moment later wrapped them around Jo in a sweaty and altogether too intimate embrace. 'Pumpkin, I've heard so much about you! Well, as much as one can hear when trapped in a metal prison, but now we've all the time in the world to get to know each other!'

No, no, no to the power of ... however many powers were available. Maths had never been Jo's strong suit.

'Isn't it wonderful? He's back, we're together again, and everything's just perfect.' Aaliyah nuzzled Dhassim's neck. Dhassim murmured something that might have been *Je t'aime*, but Jo couldn't have cared less.

'No, it isn't perfect. It's a million light years from perfect. What were you thinking? I can't have the two of you rattling around here. Get him back in that lamp, pronto, before I do something I'll regret.'

'Ma chérie.' Dhassim disentangled himself from Aaliyah. 'You need to take a chill pill, as they say in these modern times. I prefer a little hubble-bubble myself: very soothing for the soul. Please, we will find a way to work things out.'

Jo took in Dhassim's jogging bottoms and his pale chest, barely concealed by the A Bit of Crumpet apron. He gave her a lascivious wink and bared his pointy little teeth.

'Did you actually *serve* those people?' Jo asked incredulously. She hadn't recognised them, thank goodness, but lord knows what they had thought when greeted by Mr Semi-Naked.

'Of course. Am I not put on this earth to serve?' Dhassim gave a sweeping bow and the loosely tied apron fell away, revealing his baby-smooth torso in all its gleaming glory.

Jo took a step towards him and sniffed. 'Have you smeared yourself in my best extra-virgin olive oil?'

'I did not inspect the label, mon petit chou. Perhaps you can provide me with something more luxurious when we return to your abode.'

Before Jo could retort that there was no room at the inn, Janette bustled in, accompanied by Cranley's queen of bubble perms and blue rinses, Peggy. 'Whit are you for, Peggy?' asked Janette. 'Ooh, you've got chocolate éclairs, Jo. My absolute favourite.' Raising her head from the cake display, Janette spotted Dhassim and eyed him with even more enthusiasm than she'd given the éclairs. 'And who do we have here? A new recruit, Jo? Business must be booming if you need two assistants. And a rather tasty wee specimen, if I say so myself.'

'Enchanté. I am Dhassim. And you, beautiful lady, are…?'

Janette flushed to the roots of her newly shorn hair. 'Get away with you, you silver-tongued rascal. Janette's the name and this is my hairdresser extraordinaire, Peggy.'

'Nice to meet you,' said Peggy, shyly, as Aaliyah gripped Dhassim's arm possessively. 'Are you two related, by any chance?'

'Absolutely not.' Jo wished she had a crowbar to separate the lovebirds. Instead, she barked out an order to Aaliyah to grate some cheese. Aaliyah pouted, pecked Dhassim on the cheek, and retreated into the back.

'But they look so alike,' pressed Peggy. 'Exotic and — what's the word — unScottish.'

'Ah, that's because the lass is from down south or some

other far-flung place.' Janette smirked, proud of her knowledge, and hefted herself into a chair. 'You might want to
tighten up your apron, son. I'm no' sure my ticker can cope
with nipples at this time of day. Or any time of day, to be
frank.'

Peggy joined Janette at the table. Jo glowered at Dhassim,
who glowered back. Eventually, Dhassim covered up his
torso and shimmied over to the ladies. 'So, coffee, tea or me?'
he asked, with a seductive hip wiggle.

Janette fanned herself with a paper napkin. Peggy asked
for a tea — 'just dunk the bag for a second, pale and interesting is the way to go' — and Janette opted for a glass of
milk.

'The lass has fabulous hair,' commented Peggy. 'I used to
have hair like that back in the day.' She ran forlorn fingers
through the thinning strands clinging to her scalp.

'Aye, and I used to look like Sophia Loren.' Janette took a
slurp of milk, the residue adhering to her top lip. 'Any chance
of those éclairs, darlin'?'

Aaliyah sauntered back in, chewing on a chunk of cheese.
Should I make a run for it? thought Jo. Perhaps Harvey was still
in the pub. She could order another wine, squeeze his hand
till his knuckles blanched, and tell him about the insanity
whirling around her. Except she couldn't. Whatever cards
Harvey kept close to his chest, Jo's story of house-sharing
with one and now possibly two genies would trump them all.
And not in a good way.

'I've a special on at the salon now.' Peggy neatly chopped
her éclair into four even pieces. 'A tenner for a cut, nose and
ear-hair trimming included.'

Jo's head buzzed like a swarm of angry bees. A red mist
blurred her vision and she tried to claw her way back to
reality.

Aaliyah gave Peggy a withering stare. 'Are you suggesting I have hair growing out of my nostrils and ears?'

Peggy laughed and pointed at Dhassim. 'Not you, love. Your, erm, whoever he is.'

Now it was Dhassim's turn to look affronted. 'I am very happy with my hair, thank you. And like Aaliyah, I do not have extra hairs sprouting elsewhere. Unlike you' — he stabbed a finger at Peggy — 'with several sticking out of your—'

'Dhassim! That's enough!' Jo shrieked. Janette tipped half her milk down her front and poor Peggy fingered her chin with a wounded expression. 'Could you two please go through to the back and find something useful to do?'

Granted a few moments' respite from the dynamic duo, Jo stammered out an apology to Janette and Peggy. Janette dabbed at her soggy jumper and Peggy pulled out a compact mirror to scrutinise her chin.

'You didn't say who That's Him is.' Janette brandished her glass for a refill.

'Who *what*?' The buzzing in Jo's head had upgraded to men in hobnailed boots performing an exuberant rendition of Riverdance.

'That's Him. Strange name, mind. Is he on one of them government training schemes? I had a lad once come for work experience. Huh, the only thing he experienced was a clip round the ear when I caught him emptying the till into his backpack.'

'His name is Dhassim.' Jo enunciated the name carefully. 'And he's a friend of Aaliyah's. He's just passing through and helping out for a few days.' *If only that were true.*

'Right, Peggy.' Janette wrapped the remains of her éclair in a napkin and swigged her milk. 'Let's get a wiggle on and leave Jo in peace to deal with her wee team. You'll be wishing for a quiet life after having to keep tabs on those two!'

Jo slammed the door as soon as they left. Dammit, *wishes*! Did Dhassim's unexpected appearance mean that she had to come up with three more wishes, on top of the one still outstanding?

CHAPTER 39

If Harvey scratched his head (metaphorically) any harder, his nails would connect with his grey matter. What was the real story with Jo's assistant? The errant daughter of a friend, or … something else?

Everybody had secrets, not all of them earth-shattering or life-changing. Lindsey's biggest secret had been a fondness for cheesy songs from the seventies and eighties. She'd pretended to like the cool stuff, but her real passion lay with one-hit wonders and groups who bounced around on *Top Of The Tops* with mullet hairdos and dodgy outfits. Many before Lindsey's time, like 'Y Viva Espana' with its rattling maracas, and 'Shaddup You Face', which still brought Harvey out in a rash.

As for his own big secret… Being a gullible old fool who'd trusted a young woman with an agenda to advance her career. Innocent until proven guilty, but without any court case, the simmering accusations had left a permanent stain on Harvey's character. Abby had refused to confirm or deny her allegations to this day. *No smoke without fire.* She was currently starring in a six-part TV drama, playing the Xanaxaddicted wife of a controlling older man whose previous wife had died in suspicious circumstances. Against his better judgement, Harvey had watched the first episode. Abby played the victim very well. In fact, she had it down to a tee.

Harvey checked the time. Still two hours until Jo came round for dinner. She'd invited him to her place, but Harvey wanted to impress her with his cooking skills. Heating up ready meals and toasting Pop Tarts would hardly earn him the title of MasterChef.

He skimmed through the online folder of saved recipes he'd created by searching for key ingredients. Tinned tomatoes, feta cheese, red onions, butternut squash. By some miracle, Janette had a butternut squash — 'odd-shaped bugger, dinnae ken what it's for' — and quinoa, which she described as 'like fish food '. No fresh spinach, but Harvey reckoned frozen would do just as well.

Assembling the ingredients for the dish, he heard his phone ping. Praying it wasn't Jo cancelling on him, he hurried through to the lounge. He looked at the cracked screen and icy shards of horror stabbed at his gut.

Hi, Harley. Been a long time. Just wondered how you were and if we could meet up soon. I have something I want to talk to you about. Abby x

A torrent of thoughts flooded Harvey's brain. Hadn't he blocked her? He couldn't remember now. What with fielding calls from journalists and dealing with the crippling grief of losing Lindsey, he hadn't known his arse from his elbow. What could she possibly want to talk about? Unless … unless she felt guilty about the whole fiasco and wanted to set the record straight.

Harvey slammed the phone down on the table. He didn't want to talk to her. Instinct told him that whatever Abby had to say would not draw a line under the whole sorry saga.

More like exhume it and parade it around for her own personal gain.

Sod it, he needed a drink. He'd conjured up his nemesis by allowing her into his head. Harvey returned to the kitchen, chopped a red onion with serial-killer fervour, and poured himself a generous measure of whisky. Alcohol wasn't the answer, but right now it seared his insides with caustic precision.

Put that knife down before you add a couple of fingers to tonight's meal. Lindsey? No, just the voice he conjured up when life threw another pile of shit in his direction. He'd never forget her: she'd always occupy a special place in his heart. A heart the size of a large fist, but with an infinite capacity to expand and welcome newcomers. Like Jo. She'd already snuck in there and made herself at home. He hoped he'd earned a little space in her heart, too.

As he sautéed and soaked, Harvey wondered again whether he should have fought harder against Abby's false allegations. Arthur, his elusive agent, had advised him to lie low, not pursue legal action which could hamper his career. The last thing Harvey had wanted was to drag the whole sorry business through the courts. He'd adopted the ostrich approach, but his career had tanked anyway.

Bringing the quinoa to a boil, Harvey pondered the Aaliyah enigma. Something didn't add up, but he couldn't put his finger on it. Maybe she was Jo's estranged daughter, returned to the fold after years apart. Yet whatever secrets Jo might keep, a long-lost daughter didn't seem likely.

Focusing on the task ahead, Harvey scrutinised the squash. It was indeed a peculiar shape, with a skin that would have challenged the scalpel-wielding skills of Buffalo Bill in *The Silence Of The Lambs*. Harvey picked out a paring knife and began hacking away. A minute later, he conceded defeat and chopped the beast into chunks. Wasn't the skin good for you, anyway?

Another message arrived. Bloody Abby again. *I hope you're not ignoring me. You know I don't like that. It's in your interest to hear what I have to say.* No signing off or kiss this time: just an underlying essence of bunny boiler.

Harvey doused the squash chunks in olive oil, seasoned them liberally, and bunged them in the oven with the onions. He considered roasting his phone at the same time, watching it char and crisp until Abby's messages turned to ash.

Only an hour now till Jo arrived. Time to freshen up, make Brae Cottage look halfway decent and hope that the evening provided a distraction in the nicest possible way.

Lathering up in the shower, Harvey tried a little 'count your blessings' exercise. Lindsey had insisted on it, even when the cancer declared itself the outright winner in the duked-out battle.

'I met you.'

'And you are a very lucky woman to have done so.'

'Modest as ever. I had a lovely childhood, great parents, and only one person ever mocked me at school for having sticky-out ears.'

'And you decked them with an impressive right hook, if I recall correctly.'

'I did, and you always encouraged me to wear my hair up and show off those jug handles with pride.'

'Because your beauty eclipses your ears. I love you for all your faults— Ouch, that hurt!'

'And I love you because there is absolutely no reason not to love you. My darling, leaving you will be the hardest thing I've ever done. Apart from sitting maths exams. Why did I waste so much time on this earth stressing about algebra and trigonometry when I could have been living?'

At that point — so near the end of Lindsey's life —

Harvey had lost it. Sobbed till his body trembled and convulsed. Now… He held out a hand and pressed his thumb to his palm.

I met you.

Next finger. *You believed in me when my belief tank was running on empty.*

And another. *I always thought sex was just sex. Making love was for sappy books and slushy movies. You taught me that love is made when two people click like pieces of a puzzle. No gaps, no awkward edges, just a perfect fit.*

One more finger and a pinkie. Harvey crushed them into his palm, scouring the flesh with his nails. *I'm moving on, Lindsey. That doesn't feel much like a blessing. I'd give everything I have to bring you back. But I promise that my love for you will never wane.*

Harvey stepped out of the shower, his face damp from both the water and the tears that he couldn't contain. Yet he felt at peace with himself. Damn Abby and her stupid attempts to stir things up. Tonight he'd revel in Jo's company and thank his lucky stars for having a second chance at happiness.

CHAPTER 40

'OF COURSE YOU DON'T HAVE THREE MORE WISHES!' AALIYAH
pulled a face and giggled.

Dhassim retrieved his WIFI from the pocket of his
jogging bottoms and thrust it at Jo. 'Look. Nada, zilch, zero.
This baby is in sleep mode.'

'Genies don't grant wishes for other genies, duh.' Aaliyah
shook her head in disbelief.

'How was I supposed to know that? Nobody gave me an
Idiot's Guide to Genies.' Jo felt like a complete idiot. She was
supposed to be looking forward to a romantic night with
Harvey. Instead, she was flanked by two otherworldly beings
treating her like a halfwit. It was enough to drive a woman
round the bend and back again.

'Jo, Jo, Jo.' Dhassim draped an oily arm around her shoulders. She shrugged him off, not wanting greasy marks on her
brand-new bodysuit. 'It is difficult to understand, I know,
but only mortals can be granted wishes. You did not
summon me, therefore I am merely a visitor with no powers.'

'Apart from the power to enchant me,' purred Aaliyah.

Pass the sick bag, please. Jo left Cranley's answer to Rose and Jack adrift on their ocean of lurve, and went to check her appearance. No oil stains, and the stress of having two genies playing tonsil hockey downstairs hadn't caused too many worry lines.

'Are you, like, going to stay over with your man?' As per bloody usual, Aaliyah sauntered into Jo's bedroom without so much as a tap at the door.

'I don't know.' Jo spritzed herself with perfume and smoothed a stray strand of hair into place. 'Are you going to tell *your* other man that he's been dumped in favour of an oily creature who came out of a tin?'

'Dhassim's a genie, not a sardine,' huffed Aaliyah. 'And we live in lamps, not tins. There's no need to be so bitchy, Jo. It doesn't suit you.'

'Whereas you wear bitchy like a crown,' retorted Jo. 'And you still haven't answered my question.'

'You mean Jamie?' Aaliyah swiped Jo's perfume bottle and doused herself from head to toe. 'Nah, no need, pet: it was just a bit of fun while it lasted. You were right, for once. I'm better off sticking to my own kind. Advice you might want to follow, too.'

'What on earth do you mean?' Jo snatched back the bottle as an eardrum-piercing sound emanated from below.

Aaliyah swooped out into the hallway, screeched 'Turn the bloody racket down, Dhassim!' and returned to Jo. 'Thinks he's a rock star, bless him. Shame he sounds more like a cat with a firework up its bum.'

Although relieved that Dhassim's excruciating warbling had ceased, Jo's frustration with Aaliyah climbed another notch. 'What exactly do you mean, I should follow my own advice? Harvey's a human, and a very nice one.'

'If you say so. I have a sixth sense about people, and my instinct tells me that man is not to be trusted.' Aaliyah tapped her nose in a 'genie knows best' manner.

'Like Sam, you mean? You got all weird around him without any explanation.'

Before Aaliyah could respond, the bedroom door burst open and Dhassim bounded in. Jo glowered at them both. 'Give me strength! Do I need to install bloody traffic lights to get some privacy around here?'

'My little chickadee, do not get your knickers in a knot. We are here to help you. Aren't we, angel cakes?'

A larger sick bag, please. Jo checked her watch: fifteen minutes until she was due at Harvey's. 'Right, I'm out of here now. There's plenty of food in the fridge. Please, please don't leave the house.'

'Why would we go out when we can be total snuggle bunnies in your cosy love nest?' cooed Dhassim. 'And if you need any housework doing, I'm an absolute demon at dust-busting. Just say the word, and I'll buff and polish to absolute perfection.'

'You can buff and polish me instead.' Looking less than impressed at Dhassim's offer to whizz around with the vacuum cleaner, Aaliyah stuck her dainty pink tongue in his ear. That gave a whole new meaning to cleaning, and not one Jo wanted to witness.

'OK. I'm off. See you whenever.' Jo galloped downstairs, Dhassim and Aaliyah trailing behind. She'd wanted to ask Dhassim if he'd also detected something suspicious about Sam, but that could wait. She had an evening of good food, great company and hopefully, magical sex ahead. Leaving Aaliyah and Dhassim entwined on the sofa like a couple of horny octopuses, Jo slipped on her favourite mid-heel boots and headed out into the night.

* * *

HARVEY HELPED Jo out of her coat and hung it on a peg. 'Sorry I'm early,' she said.

'By approximately three minutes,' he teased, making a show of checking his watch. 'Either I'm irresistible, or you could smell my cooking and broke into a sprint.'

Jo sniffed the air; something did smell delicious. She took Harvey's outstretched hand and allowed him to draw her close. His body heat melted the chill she had felt in the short walk from her place to his. His lips sought hers and they kissed, gently at first, then with increasing intensity. Jo pressed herself closer, in no doubt of Harvey's state of arousal. Either that, or he was packing a kitchen utensil in his boxers.

An icy draught seeped through the letterbox and fluttered around Jo's exposed arms. 'Erm, do you think we could move out of the hallway?' She shivered and Harvey hugged her tighter.

'Of course. It's warmish in the lounge, thanks to the delightful two-bar electric fire and its ability to pump out the equivalent of a bee's fart in heat.'

'I didn't know bees farted, never mind that they produce heat at the same time.' Jo kept close to Harvey as they side-ways-shuffled into the lounge. 'What's cooking?' she asked. 'Should I inspect the kitchen bin for telltale takeaway boxes?'

Harvey shook his head. 'Oh, ye of little faith. Tonight's menu is one hundred per cent prepared by yours truly. Vege-tarian, in fact.'

'I'm impressed, but I only eat meat.' Harvey looked nonplussed, and Jo burst out laughing. 'I'm kidding. I'll eat pretty much anything apart from raw oysters and offal.'

'But oysters are an aphrodisiac,' said Harvey. 'As is cham-pagne, which I happen to have a bottle of.'

'Then what are we waiting for? Not that I think we need an aphrodisiac.' Jo took a seat as Harvey went to fetch the

bubbly. Without so much as a sip, she felt giddy and excited:
she could easily have skipped the food and gone straight for
dessert of the carnal kind. But there was no rush, and she
wanted to sample Harvey's home cooking.

'Here we go.' Harvey handed Jo a fizzing plastic flute. 'I
bought a pack of these at Janette's, otherwise we'd be supping
from mugs or wine glasses.'

'Tastes the same, whatever you drink it from. Cheers.'

They'd barely taken a sip when loud banging at the door
interrupted them. 'Are you expecting someone?'

Harvey shook his head. A distinct look of unease
distorted his features.

'Maybe it's the TV licence people. Or a couple of earnest
Mormons touting for new recruits.' Jo was aiming for levity,
but Harvey looked like a man facing a firing squad.

'Stay here. Don't move. I'll get rid of them.'

Jo froze, unsure what to do or think. Did Harvey owe a
ton of money, and now the debt collectors were on his
doorstep, prepared to snap a limb or two if he didn't pay up?
Or perhaps it was a dumped, vengeful ex, intent on ripping
her hair out by the roots.

'What are you doing here?' The closed lounge door
muffled Harvey's voice, but didn't disguise the note of panic.
So it was someone he knew, but who? 'This isn't the time or
the place. Wait a second.'

The front door banged and all was quiet apart from Jo's
heart, thudding as if it was fighting to escape her chest. She
fiddled with her plastic flute, unsure what to do. Should she
make her excuses and leave? But she didn't want to leave.
Instead, she went to check on Harvey's cooking, in case it
needed a stir or rescuing from the oven.

Whatever he'd prepared, it looked under control. Jo gave
the dish a desultory prod with a spoon and returned to the
lounge.

At that moment, the front door banged again and Harvey reappeared. 'I'm so sorry, Jo, I think we need to call it a night. Something's come up, and… Well, I'm truly sorry.' His face spoke of genuine regret, tinged with anxiety and something else. *Fear?*

'Where's your visitor?' Jo tried and failed to conceal the sharp stab of disappointment in her voice.

'At The Jekyll and Hyde. I'll meet them there in a few minutes.'

Them. More than one person, or a device to throw Jo off the scent? The scent of a woman: of that she had no doubt.

'Fine.' The one-word grenade every man feared. Hurting more than she wanted to admit, Jo gathered up her things and left, Harvey's apologies ringing in her ears.

CHAPTER 41

'HOW DID YOU FIND ME?'

Abby smirked. 'I have my sources.' Dressed in a caramel trench coat and sporting a felt fedora tilted at a jaunty angle, she exuded an air of sexy sleuth. A part she'd played well in *Chasing Shadows,* but that was fiction.

'To be honest, I don't give a flying fuck how you found me. Just spit out what you want and let me get on with the life you tried to destroy.' Harvey gripped his pint glass so hard that he feared it might shatter.

Abby took a delicate mouthful of her white wine and puckered up her perfectly lip-sticked mouth. 'Tastes like cat's piss,' she complained. 'Not that I expect much from a dive like this.' Her pert nose crinkled in disdain as she took in her surroundings. The usual crowd unwinding after a day at work, eating and chatting in a place Harvey had grown fond of.

'Sorry it's not a champagne and oyster bar' — he cringed at the memory — 'but this is home for me and I didn't ask you to come here.'

'But you ignored my messages, Harley, and I don't like being ignored.'

Jamie wandered into view, gathering up empties and wiping down tables. 'Excuse me, can you fetch me a gin and tonic? None of that cheap stuff and only branded tonic.'

'You need to order at the bar. Over there.' Jamie tilted his head in the direction of the bar and continued wiping.

'The peasants are indeed revolting,' sighed Abby. 'Could you be a sweetheart, Harley, and—'

'If you want another drink, get it yourself. You have precisely five minutes to say your piece before I'm out of here.'

Abby tutted and removed her hat, shaking her hair loose in a provocative manner. 'You really need to be nicer to me, you know. I'm doing you a favour coming here.'

Harvey almost spat his beer across the table. 'Doing me a favour? The biggest favour you can do me is to haul your arse out of here. No, scratch that. How about admitting in public that all that stalking and harassment stuff was a pack of lies?' His raised voice attracted a few curious stares. He pulled his chair closer to Abby, even though instinct screamed at him to leg it to Jo's. Not that he'd receive a warm welcome. She'd probably never speak to him again.

'But it wasn't a lie, was it?' Abby twisted a strand of hair around her finger, her slate-grey eyes cold as ice. 'You followed me around like a devoted puppy and sent me all those texts.'

'Because I thought we were friends!' Harvey banged his fist on the table, prompting more raised eyebrows.

Ken approached, a concerned frown creasing his face. 'Everything OK here?' He looked from Harvey to Abby, who treated Ken to her finest butter-wouldn't-melt expression.

'Everything's just fine. Except that your rude staff

member wouldn't fulfil a simple order. Perhaps you can have a word with him and rustle up a decent G&T for me.'

Ken shrugged and gave Harvey a sympathetic smile. 'If you tried saying please, you might get somewhere. Seeing as I know Harvey, I'll get your drink, but manners matter around here.'

Watching Ken's departing back, Harvey barked out a laugh. Abby, however, was unamused.

'I didn't come here to be insulted,' she hissed, eyes shooting invisible daggers in Ken's direction.

'I'm still waiting to discover why you came,' retorted Harvey. 'And for the record, I never followed you around like a puppy, devoted or otherwise. I thought you genuinely cared about what I'd been through with Lindsey. I never acted inappropriately towards you, and I still can't believe you made those terrible allegations.'

Abby exhaled with force. 'And your name's Harvey now? Change one letter, and assume a new identity? Haven't any of the yokels here twigged who you are, or don't they have TV in these parts?'

'For the love of God, enough with the cheap jibes. You tried to wreck my career, so are you actually here to apologise? Somehow, I don't think that's likely.'

Abby laughed, a fake tinkle that jarred Harvey's already fraught nerves. 'I didn't press charges, did I? It was only ever my word against yours, and the public sided with me. Sad old lech versus pretty young actress: no contest, really. Great publicity, but you know the old saying about today's news being tomorrow's fish and chip wrapper. And it was a while ago, so—'

'I've heard enough. Here comes your gin and tonic.' Harvey tossed a tenner on the table. 'Here's enough to pay for it, and I sincerely hope I never see you again.'

Harvey stood up to leave. Ken placed the gin and opened bottle of tonic in front of Abby and ignored the cash.

Abby grabbed Harvey's sleeve and tugged it hard. 'You're not going anywhere. Here's the deal. I've been offered a substantial sum to talk about my experience as a young woman dealing with sexual harassment in the workplace. I won't name *you*, of course. Isn't that nice of me?'

Nice? Harvey could think of several words to describe his former colleague, but nice wasn't one of them. Opportunist, brazen, and without an ounce of empathy summed her up better.

'And you expect what from me? A congratulatory hug? A round of applause?' Harvey gawped in disbelief at Abby. 'You do realise that people will put two and two together, and yours truly will be back in the firing line?'

Abby took her time pouring tonic into the gin. Harvey wondered what he could do to dissuade her, and quickly decided that the answer was nothing, short of clubbing her over the head and burying her in a shallow grave. Sadly, that wasn't really an option.

'I didn't *have* to tell you,' she said, stirring her drink rapidly. 'It's part of a documentary series on women in the public eye and their experiences at the hands of predatory men. Trust me, I've been on the receiving end of several unwanted advances.'

Harvey nodded reluctantly. He'd witnessed enough instances of women being touched inappropriately or subjected to lewd remarks to know the score. Sadly, the majority of the culprits got away with it, their victims too scared to rock the boat. It wasn't fair, but life rarely was. 'Listen, Abby. You do what you want to do; I can't stop you. But I *will* deny until the day I die that I did anything wrong. You know the truth, and your silence has done more damage than you'll ever know. Now, if you'll excuse me, I'm off home.'

A flutter of something, possibly guilt, glided across Abby's face. It vanished in an instant, replaced by a steely smile. 'Take care, *Harvey*. Hope you find some work soon. You were a good actor, if a bit intense at times.'

Without a backward glance, Harvey strode out of the pub, the cool night air hitting him with welcome force. Seeing Abby again and hearing her latest publicity-seeking scheme had filled him with fury, but he was powerless to act.

For a moment, he contemplated swinging by Jo's, to apologise and try to explain… But what was the point? He'd only end up digging a deeper hole than the one he currently inhabited. Maybe if he'd been honest in the first place and told Jo the whole sorry tale, she'd have believed him.

Trudging towards Brae Cottage, Harvey wondered if he could possibly feel any lower. When you thought you'd hit rock bottom, finding another level of misery below did little for a person's sense of self-worth.

CHAPTER 42

'You're back early!' Aaliyah regarded Jo with all the enthusiasm of a drug mule facing a cavity search.

'Things didn't quite go to plan,' said Jo. 'Sorry if I'm interrupting anything.' Judging by Aaliyah's rumpled appearance and Dhassim's back-to-front jogging pants, she'd narrowly avoided embarrassment. Taking her time opening the door and bellowing out a hearty 'Hello, are you decent?' had been a smart move.

'Aww, my downcast dumpling.' Dhassim rushed over and threw his arms around Jo. 'Your little face is filled with sadness. Are you going to cry? Please feel free to cry. Aaliyah, fetch some tissues.'

Throwing Dhassim a look of disgust, Aaliyah flounced into the kitchen.

Jo allowed Dhassim to squeeze her harder, like a past-its-best lemon. No juice, just a steady trickle of tears. Dhassim patted her back and murmured words which Jo didn't recognise but helped ease her heartache.

'Here you go, pet.' Aaliyah thrust an entire kitchen roll in

Jo's direction. 'Couldn't find tissues, but I thought this would do.'

Tearing off several sheets, Dhassim dabbed at Jo's face with great tenderness. She conjured up a watery smile before taking the paper and blowing her nose. 'Thank you.'

Dhassim guided Jo to the sofa and sat down next to her. Aaliyah sat on her other side, putting Jo in a veritable genie sandwich. Maybe now was the time to make her third wish: to banish Harvey from her life and accept that they were never meant to be. But that seemed a waste of a wish. She didn't need genie magic to put distance between them.

'So, did lover boy prove a flop?' Aaliyah arched an eyebrow. 'What you need is a younger man to spice up your life. Jamie's free, by the way—'

Jo stifled a snort of derision. 'I don't need a man, young or otherwise. To be honest, I'd be better off with a dog. At least they're loyal and reliable, and don't need more than feeding, walking and petting.'

'Ooh, can we get a chihuahua?' said Dhassim. 'I *adore* those little darlings, and you can pop them in your handbag. Not that I have a handbag, but I'm totally open to getting a cute across-the-body number. What do you think, angel cakes?'

Jo levered herself off the sofa, leaving chihuahua-loving Dhassim to snuggle up to Aaliyah. 'Absolutely not. It's hard enough giving houseroom to two genies, never mind chucking a pooch into the mix. I'm off to bed. Switch off the lights and keep your libidos on silent mode.'

Removing her make-up — what little remained after her bout of crying — Jo brushed her teeth and scrambled into her favourite fleecy pyjamas. Her phone remained downstairs, which was just as well. If Harvey had sent an apology, she didn't want to read it. If he hadn't…

To the faint thrum of the television downstairs, Jo sought

sleep, but found it as elusive as a winning lottery ticket. She pummelled a pillow, flung a leg outside the duvet, then hauled it back in when her toes turned icy. The bedside clock read 10.30. There were too many hours ahead to thrash around in frustration and ignorance. Better to get up, make a cup of tea, and…

Sod the tea. And whoever Harvey's mystery caller had been, Jo didn't need to know. What she wanted — *needed* to know was where they stood, and now seemed as good a time as any to find out.

'I'm off out,' she called to Dhassim and Aaliyah, who were engrossed in a chat show.

'Dressed like that?' Dhassim nudged Aaliyah, who gave Jo a scathing glance before turning up the volume.

'It's cold outside,' retorted Jo, zipping up the oversized coat she'd bought on a whim in Edinburgh several months ago. Admittedly, it resembled a giant sleeping bag with room to spare for another occupant. But it concealed the fact that she was still wearing her pyjamas.

'If you're hoping to ignite flames of passion with your fella, wearing *that* is a big mistake, ma chérie.'

'Yeah, it makes you look like a quilted hippopotamus,' added Aaliyah. 'Or a puffy elephant balloon.'

Dhassim erupted into a fit of giggles. 'If the flames get too strong, you can always use it as a fire blanket.'

Honestly, why I give those two houseroom… Jo grabbed her comfy boots and wrestled them on: no easy feat when cocooned in a feather-stuffed fat suit.

Waddling along the road to Harvey's place, Jo questioned her sanity. Not in terms of her sartorial selection, or having housemates who drove her round the bend, but because turning up unannounced, again, didn't rank highly on the smart-o-meter. But what did she have to lose?

Relieved to see the lights still on, Jo rapped on the door.

She unzipped her coat a fraction, aware that its generous padding had caused an outbreak of underarm sweat and an unbecoming facial flush.

'Jo.' Harvey stood in the doorway, puzzlement writ large on his face. 'What are you doing here?'

Oh, just channelling my inner idiot and clinging to the tiny hope that we had something special going on. Also wondering what possessed me to wear the most unflattering garment I own. 'It's called unfinished business, Harvey. One minute we were settling down to share a romantic meal, the next I was hustled out the door like an unwelcome virus.'

Harvey blushed. Now they resembled a pair of red traffic lights, appropriately, as neither moved an inch. Jo waited. Harvey hesitated. A car sped by, rap music emanating from inside. Probably not a local.

'Can I come in? I haven't eaten, and your food smelt delicious. Unless you scoffed it all with your unexpected visitor?'

'I didn't. It's still in the pot and likely past its best. A bit like me. Jo, come in. I can't believe you're here.'

Jo stepped in, pausing to shrug off the monstrosity of a coat. Harvey didn't comment, but his mouth twitched as he hung it on a peg which collapsed under its weight.

'Oops. Sorry about that.'

'Not a problem. Come on, let's see if the food is salvageable.'

A quick glance at Harvey's vegetarian delight revealed it to be well past its best. It was welded to the bottom of the pan and an unappetising sludge green.

'Not to worry, I'll settle for a cuppa and a biscuit.' Jo smiled, the tension between them easing. Following Harvey into the tiny kitchen, she pressed herself against a chipped cabinet, conscious of their close proximity.

Harvey opened a door and retrieved a beige canister with *Tea* emblazoned on the side. He flipped the silver clasp and delved inside. 'Janette's finest, and I use the word "finest" with a degree of sarcasm.' He bent down to the fridge, pulled out a carton of milk, and sniffed it. 'Not yet rancid. Miracle of miracles.'

Eager to help, Jo filled the kettle and switched it on. Harvey mumbled something about needing to charge his laptop, and disappeared.

Jo took an educated guess and reached for the cupboard directly above the kettle. Bingo! A handful of mugs sat on the lower shelf, the upper one empty apart from a small stack of side plates. None of the mugs matched, not that it bothered Jo. She loved her eclectic mix of tableware at A Bit of Crumpet, as did her customers.

Hearing Harvey clatter around in the lounge, Jo grabbed a pale-grey mug decorated with snowflakes. Another caught her eye: mauve and white, with a sepia photo of a couple on a bench, and the words, *The most wasted day of all is that on which we have not laughed. Well, today hasn't been totally wasted,* she mused, her fingertips touching the delicate handle.

An almighty crash from the other room startled Jo. The mug slipped from her grasp and shattered on the worktop, pieces cascading on to the floor.

'What the—' Harvey stood in the doorway, clutching a charger cable. His gaze swept from the worktop to the shards below, then alighted on Jo. His face contorted, a darkness descending that chilled Jo to the bone.

'I'm so, so sorry,' she stammered. 'I heard a crash and it startled me. It was an accident. Please, let me clean up and I'll pay for a replacement.'

'It can't be replaced.' Harvey pushed past Jo and unearthed a dustpan and brush from under the sink. 'Some things can never be replaced.'

Stunned at his reaction, Jo rushed into the lounge and grabbed her purse, then hurried back to the kitchen and slapped a ten-pound note on the worktop. 'If it's not enough, let me know. Again, I'm sorry. I'll let myself out.'

Minutes later she was home, still shaken by what had happened. Clearly the mug held significant value to Harvey, but emotional rather than monetary. Yet Jo couldn't comprehend the dramatic change in his demeanour, from amiable host to hostile witness of an innocent mishap. As it turned out, her first assessment had been correct. Harvey Quinn was a man to be avoided.

CHAPTER 43

'Yes, that's no problem. I can do a selection of savoury and sweet nibbles and a princess-themed cake for the birthday girl. Just email me details of any special requirements and any allergies.'

Jo ended the call, about her first catering job in a while. It brought back memories of Harvey helping out, and how her opinion of him had softened. But she had to face facts: the man had serious issues that she couldn't fix. And it was more than grief for his wife; he kept something else locked away beneath that taciturn exterior.

'Hey, Jo, you look like you lost a fiver and found a penny. Everything OK?'

Pocketing her phone, Jo looked up at Jinnie's concerned face. Next to her stood Sam, with Jinnie's gran Wilma bringing up the rear, wheeling her tartan trolley. 'I've had better weeks, but seeing you always helps.'

'Aye, I feel the same when Jinnie pops round for a wee cuppa and a tea-leaf reading,' interjected Wilma, adding a curse as one of the trolley's wheels snagged on a rogue tile.

'Mind you, since she snagged Mr Dreamboat her visits are nae as frequent.'

Jinnie tutted and Sam gave a wry smile. 'You know that's not true, Gran. I still see you most weeks, *and* we took you to The Edinburgh Dungeon for your birthday.'

'Interesting choice, Wilma,' said Jo, ushering them to a table. 'Wasn't it scary?'

Wilma parked her trolley in the corner and gave a witch-like cackle. 'Sweetie, when you've lived as long as me, not much scares you. I had a bigger fright the other day when Madge from next door dropped in for lunch. She got a fit of the hiccups and her teeth landed in the lentil soup.'

Howls of laughter followed, and Jo wiped away tears — this time happy ones — as she assembled their order on a tray. Both Aaliyah and Dhassim were tucked away in the back, tasked with washing Tupperware and tins and binning those past their prime. At least they *were*, until Dhassim strutted into the café flapping a tea towel like a demented matador.

'Jo, my delicate skin cannot cope with all this scrubbing and scraping. Look!' He proffered a hand with a pinkish hue.

A gasp from the corner distracted Jo from examining Dhassim's hand further. 'Oh my God!' Jinnie's face was chalk-white.

Sensing a scenario defying any logical explanation, Jo hustled Dhassim away with promises of soothing lotions and a break from scrubbing duties. She wasn't quite fast enough to stop Dhassim from blowing a kiss at Jinnie and winking at Sam, though.

'Isn't that your long-lost cousin?' Sam frowned at Jinnie, who was watching Dhassim's retreat with open-mouthed horror. 'David, the one who got jet lag flying from Jersey.'

Realising that Jinnie had lost the power of speech, Jo launched into damage limitation mode. 'No, no, that's Dhassim. He's a friend of Aaliyah's, just staying for a bit until his flat gets sorted out. It, erm, flooded when he left the bath running.'

'That happened to me once,' said Wilma. 'My late husband, bless him, fancied a bit of a splash around, if you catch my drift. The daft pillock went off to the shops to buy some bubble bath and left the taps on. And I didnae notice, because I was having a wee kip before we—'

'Gran, too much information!' Jinnie, thankfully back in the zone, cut Wilma off before she expanded on her bath-time frolics. 'Let's enjoy our drinks and cake and — Sam, didn't you have an appointment back at the shop?'

Sam shook his head. 'I don't think so, Jinnie. And I'm still puzzled about what's going on here. You looked really shocked when David — I mean, Dhassim — appeared.'

Poor Jinnie. Jo hurriedly doled out the food and drinks. Wilma took charge, pouring teas and slicing pastries and scones.

'I'm sure you had something to do or someone to see. Oh, I think I left the kettle on!' Jinnie clapped her hands together gleefully, while the others mirrored Sam's perplexed expression.

'Don't the electric ones switch themselves off, sweetie?' said Wilma, piling jam onto her scone. 'Or has Sam got one of thae hob ones that keeps boiling till the room turns into a sauna?'

'It's electric, but the switch is a bit dodgy so it doesn't always turn off. Sam, I think you'd better go and check.' Jinnie squeezed Sam's hand and gave him a beseeching look.

Sam, to his credit, stood up, giving his untouched pastry and coffee a wistful glance. 'I suspect something fishy is going on here, but we can chat later. Take care, Jo. Wilma, behave yourself.' Sam kissed Jinnie and Wilma in turn.

Wilma patted her other cheek, and Sam gave a good-natured sigh as he leant in for a second kiss.

'Right,' said Jo. 'Wilma, can you excuse us for a few minutes?'

'Aye, pet. I'll just chow down on the scones and give myself a wee tea-leaf reading. Maybe romance is on the horizon for me, too.'

Jo hustled Jinnie into the back room just in time to interrupt Aaliyah and Dhassim indulging in a squelchy smooch. They peeled apart, the sound reminiscent of a plunger extracting something nasty from a plughole.

'Jinnie!' Dhassim enveloped Jinnie in a bone-crushing hug. 'Oh, it is so good to see you. I have missed you, my little powder puff.'

'I've missed you too,' said Jinnie, extricating herself from the hug. 'Well, not everything, but I really never thought I'd see you again. Or you, Aaliyah.'

Aaliyah finished coating her lips in gloopy pink gloss and smacked them together. 'Well, today must be your lucky day. And perhaps you can give this one' — Aaliyah jabbed a finger in Jo's direction — 'a few pointers on making wishes. It's taken her an eternity to come up with two. A third soon would be nice.'

Again, Harvey tiptoed into Jo's mind through the mental door she'd attempted to bolt shut. *No, no and a thousand times no.* Whatever she wished for, that man had no place in her future.

'You don't sound at all Geordie now, Aaliyah,' said Jinnie. 'It did make me laugh, having a Geordie genie. You've definitely got an east-coast twang now. Hasn't she, Dhassim?'

Dhassim shrugged his slender shoulders. 'I do not know what a twang is. Unless it is the sound my heart makes when I gaze at the woman I love.' He pressed his hands against his chest, performing a pitter-patter movement that made Aaliyah giggle and Jo gag.

'People, we have a situation here.' Jo eyed the trio. 'I have two genies in my life, and one is absolutely more than enough.'

'Maybe it was like a BOGOF deal?' Jinnie giggled too. 'You know: buy one, get one free?'

'I didn't buy Aaliyah, and I certainly didn't want a second one. Jinnie, help me out here. Has Sam got something to do with all this, or not?'

The air of joviality dissipated immediately and all eyes turned to Jinnie. She flushed and fidgeted with her hair. 'Of course not! I mean, I did wonder before, but the idea's insane.'

'Is it?' Aaliyah stepped closer, her eyes narrowing in an accusing fashion. 'Your man ends up with both our lamps. And his name's downright suspicious. Right, Dhassim?'

'Well, I'm no expert, but I believe the name Sam is quite common among male mortals—'

'Not Sam, you eejit!' Aaliyah stamped her foot in frustration. 'His other names. Al Addin. I did some online research, and *that* dude hit the jackpot when he hooked up with a wish-granting genie.'

'That's a blinking fairytale!' Jinnie looked at Jo for support. 'You can't honestly believe that Sam — my lovely down-to-earth Sam — is some kind of genie thingie. He runs an antiques shop and writes crime thrillers, for goodness' sake.'

Jo wanted to lie down, preferably for a long time, and wake up genie and Harvey-free. 'I really don't know what to think any more. Jinnie, if you've any idea what I could wish for, let me know. In the meantime, let's get back to your gran.'

CHAPTER 44

'YOU IDIOT! YOU COMPLETE AND UTTER IDIOT!' HARVEY buried his head in his hands, having downed several whiskies in rapid succession. He groaned at the sudden stab of heartburn, but accepted the pain as penance for his stupidity.

The shattered pieces of the mug lay in front of him, next to a tube of glue. He had as much chance of sticking it back together as he had of salvaging his relationship with Jo.

'Accept it, your life is a shambles. You can't pin everything on losing Lindsey and being shafted by Abby.' Harvey raised the dregs of whisky to his lips and welcomed the extra stabbing sensation. 'You're a walking disaster zone, like King Midas in reverse. Everything you touch turns to shit.'

He'd composed a series of apologetic messages to send to Jo, then deleted every one. No trite words could compensate for his handling of the Abby situation, or his ridiculous overreaction to the mug breakage. It was an object, steeped in sentiment, but still just an object.

'Lindsey, why did you have to leave me? I was an idiot with you at times, but at least I was a functioning one with some redeeming qualities.'

Silence. No imagined comforting words or gentle rebukes. He couldn't even conjure those up anymore.

With an anguished howl, Harvey swept the mug shards onto the floor. They landed with a tinkling sound, some shattering further. He went to refill his whisky glass, then paused and peered at the floor, his booze-addled brain struggling to register what lay before him. A near-perfect heart, mosaic-like in its appearance.

'You're still here, aren't you?' Harvey swayed over to the mantelpiece and picked up the framed photo. 'I knew you wouldn't desert me. You'll always be in my heart, Lindsey, even if it's in pieces too.'

Did she just *wink* at him? Harvey rubbed his tired eyes and looked again. Of course she didn't bloody wink. This was real life, not a movie where inanimate objects did unexpected things.

'I like Jo, Lindsey. I really, really like Jo, but I screw things up with her over and over again. My acting career is finished, my so-called screenplay is dead in the water, and I have no one to talk to but you. Most people would find that a tad disturbing, not that I care what other people think. Apart from Jo, who's probably sticking pins in a voodoo effigy of me right now.'

Harvey returned the photo to the mantelpiece and weaved his way into the kitchen. Locating a tatty old brush and pan, he swept up the mug shards lest he tread on them barefoot in the morning. That seemed an eternity away, unless he drank himself into oblivion. Nope. No whisky remained, and the thought of facing Janette's puckered-up, judgemental face filled him with horror.

'Coffee. Make some coffee.' Harvey fished out his favourite ground beans and fixed himself a potent brew. He washed down a couple of antacid tablets with the first cup, wincing as the hot liquid scorched his throat. His brain fog clearing a little, he tipped the broken mug pieces into a plastic bag and dumped them in the bin. What next?

His closed laptop taunted him, untouched in days and a sorry reminder of his inertia. Harvey flipped it open, keyed in the password and up popped the work in progress. Or rather, the work in a state of limbo. He pulled up a chair, cracked his knuckles — a habit that had driven Lindsey up the wall — and began to write. Scattered words and random emotions tumbled from his frenetic fingers. A wash of tears blurred his vision, but he continued to type like a man possessed.

Two hours later, Harvey sat back. His eyes stung, and he'd lost sensation in his buttocks. The cheap chair did his rear no favours and he wriggled back and forth to ease the numbness. Five thousand words. Five thousand fricking words. As some comedian had once quipped, he'd hit all the right notes, although not necessarily in the right order.

Rubbing the stubble on his chin, Harvey realised his direction had changed dramatically. His earlier, doom-laden opus now resembled a cross between *Ghost* and *When Harry Met Sally*. Who knew that romance coursed through these veins? Well, he'd certainly known love with Lindsey. He'd hoped that, just maybe, he'd find love with Jo. *When Harvey Met Jo*. A love story of two opposites, sparring until they realise their differences make them a perfect match.

Oh, who was he kidding? He and Jo weren't about to skip off into the sunset, content in the knowledge that demanding dressing on the side didn't spell relationship disaster. His Harry had well and truly dumped on Sally, and a happily ever after was as likely as snowflakes in Fiji.

An ominous gurgling in his stomach suggested that whisky and strong coffee wouldn't win him any dietary plaudits. A scan of his cupboards and fridge revealed nothing edible, unless he scraped the mould off a doorstep of bread and covered it in wilted ham. 'Guess it's the pub, then.' Harvey checked he'd saved the document, shrugged on a coat, and stuffed his wallet in his trouser pocket.

Entering The Jekyll and Hyde, his foul mood lifted a little at the cosiness of the place. A couple of locals grinned at him, and landlord Ken gestured him over with a pint glass raised aloft. 'One of these, or do you need something stronger?'

Harvey's alcohol demons united in an effort to top up the residual effects of his earlier session. He eyed the pint glass and the optics before asking for a soda water and lime, then squinted at the blackboard. 'Anything good on the menu?' He'd forgotten his reading glasses and the words blurred before him.

'I'll try not to take offence at that,' said Ken, as his wife Mags sidled up. 'Everything we serve here is good. Isn't that right, my love?'

'Oh, yes, it is. Except I don't like those sweet peas that cook keeps adding to stuff. And that tattooed young man — what's his name again? — said I needed help with my make-up. Said he'd get his girlfriend to lend a hand. Cheek!'

Harvey knew about Mags' dementia. He smiled as she hurried away, muttering under her breath.

'My wife means chickpeas, and the tattooed man is our son, Ed.' Ken attempted to smile back, but his mouth rebelled, turning downward. 'The pesto chicken stew with dumplings is pretty amazing, as is the pork with gorgonzola and nduja sauce.'

'I have no idea what en-doo-ya is, but I'll give it a go.' Harvey flipped out his wallet and counted the notes. Enough to cover the food and drink, just. He rarely used his credit card these days: too risky. Harvey budgeted carefully, bottles of whisky notwithstanding. 'Has … erm … Jo been in today?'

Ken shook his head as he called out Harvey's order to

Jamie. 'Nope. You two are an item, right? Nothing much gets past the folks of Cranley.'

Harvey stared into his glass: fizzy water with a hint of sickly cordial. His stomach contorted and his appetite curled up into a defiant ball of refusal. 'No, we're not. Listen, cancel the food, mate. Here's the money for the drink. I've just remembered something important I have to do.'

Ken shrugged before beckoning Harvey closer. 'No worries. None of my beeswax, but you couldn't do better than Jo. A bloody amazing woman, with a heart of gold.'

Harvey left, Ken's words itching in his ears. Yes, Jo was bloody amazing, and he'd had her heart — or at least, a piece of it. Until he'd smashed it to smithereens.

CHAPTER 45

Not a dicky bird from Harvey. No call, no text, no apologetic visit where he arrived armed with flowers and explanations. Jo didn't know what she'd expected, but complete radio silence? Another nail in the coffin of a relationship that had never really stood a chance. Time to pull on her big-girl pants and face the fact that she'd likely stay single for the rest of her life. Not that being single was a bad thing, but Jo had dared to hope that she'd found someone to stroll with into the twilight years.

Striding into Janette's shop, Jo plastered on her brightest smile. Wallowing was for wallies, and Jo prided herself on being a glass-half-full sort of person — except when the glass contained nothing more than bitter sediment. 'Hi, Janette, how are you today?'

Janette, resplendent in a lurid green pinafore and unfeasibly tight leopard-print leggings, greeted Jo with uncharacteristic enthusiasm. 'Just the wummin I've been wanting to see! Hang on a mo while I sort out Peggy's bits and bobs.' Lobbing potatoes, carrots and several family size bars of chocolate into Peggy's string shopping bag, Janette snatched

the proffered tenner with indecent haste. Tossing the change
on the counter, she ushered a bewildered Peggy to the door
with flapping hands and incoherent mutterings.

Before she could ponder why Janette wanted to see her,
Jo felt steely fingers grab her arm and haul her into the
biscuit and dried goods aisle. 'I ken who it is!' Janette gave Jo
a jubilant grin, displaying the gap where a tooth had fallen
victim to a rock-hard pork pie past its sell-by date.

Jo smiled back, but her brain flipped through the possibilities. Could Janette somehow have figured out Aaliyah's true
identity? It seemed unlikely, but recent events suggested
anything was possible. Who'd have thought Jo would acquire
a genie as an assistant, with a sidekick thrown in for good
measure?

'Sorry, what are you talking about?' She grabbed a packet
of ginger nut biscuits and a packet of instant noodles, neither
of which she wanted. She couldn't even remember why she'd
come into the store. Perhaps for stamps, or a pack of plasters.
She'd nicked her thumb that morning dicing carrots for her
much-loved pasties. Distracted by thoughts of Harvey, her
attention had been a million miles away from the job in
hand, and as per usual, only one ridiculously small plaster
remained in her bathroom cabinet.

'Who our mystery man is! Mr Sour Puss, who widnae
crack a smile if you sprinkled glitter on his porridge. I'm
telling you, it's nae wonder he swapped the bright lights of
the city for our wee village. Mind you, he'd have been better
off takin' a hike to a remote island, considering what he did.'

Jo's heartbeat accelerated faster than a Formula One
driver. Whatever Janette meant, it didn't sound like good
news about Harvey — and that didn't sound like good news
for Jo, either. Damn it, she'd finally met a man she liked —
until it all went pear-shaped — and he was an axe murderer.
Or a serial killer who preyed on lonely middle-aged women.

Or a porn addict, his computer stuffed with unsavoury images. Except it didn't matter anymore, because—

'Look here!' Janette pulled out a dog-eared celebrity magazine from her pinafore pocket and thrust it under Jo's nose. Jo had little interest in the shenanigans of soap stars, overpaid footballers or so-called 'influencers'. Mind you, she did recognise the couple on the cover, the glamorous former host of a popular daytime quiz show and the lead singer with a well-known boy band. The caption under the photo read: 'When you find your soulmate, you just know your love will last forever.'

Jo snorted as Janette flicked through the pages. As far as she could recall, the soulmates had separated acrimoniously after six months, with their war of words splashed all over the tabloids. Allegations of infidelity were launched on both sides, and scathing comments about the size of the singer's tackle dominated the headlines for days.

'Take a gander at this.' Janette tapped a page spattered with what looked like bloodstains. 'Ignore the splatters. I like to read when I'm eating, and I'm an awfy messy eater.'

Jo put on her glasses, and the headline and accompanying image came into sharp focus.

'Star of primetime drama *Chasing Shadows* Harley Dempster accused of stalking and harassing his 23-year-old co-star, Abby Kinsella.' Below was a photo of Harvey (Harley) staring moodily into the camera, the image emphasising the scar on his cheek. Jo had never asked him about it, and doubted she ever would now.

'I'll give ye a wee recap so you don't have to read the whole thing,' said Janette. 'Turns out our not-so-nice neighbour had taken to following the lass home after work, sending her flirty notes and pestering her to go out with him. Eew, what 23-year-old would want to go out with an old creep like him?'

Jo's first random thought was: *He's only fifty-two, for good-ness' sake!* Her second thought knocked the first one side-ways: *He's old enough to be her father.* She shuddered, her eyes still drawn to the photo. Next to it was a picture of his accuser, Abby Kinsella. Another professional shot of a young woman with a geometric blonde bob, expertly made up, with lips that might well be surgically enhanced.

'Did it … was he… I mean, what happened?' Part of Jo wanted to snatch the magazine from Janette and sprint home to read the whole sordid story on her own. Or go round to Brae Cottage and whack Harvey repeatedly over the head with it.

'I'm no' sure, hen, but I think the lassie refused to press charges. Said she didnae want to ruin his career, although I'm pretty sure he left the show soon after. Never watched it myself. Can't be doin' with those moody things that look like they've been filmed with a 60-watt lightbulb. And all that foul language and gratuitous sex, no thank you. Give me a good old-fashioned romance or an episode of *Countryfile* any day.'

Jo flicked back to the front cover and scanned it for the date. Just over six months ago. Harvey had arrived in Cranley two months ago. What had happened in the interim? She'd heard of *Chasing Shadows,* but like Janette, had never watched it. Obviously, or she'd have known immediately who he was.

'Erm, I'll just pay for these.' Jo gestured to the biscuits and noodles. 'And these, too.' She added a pack of plasters and counted out the right change as Janette rang up the items on the till.

'Who'd have thought, eh? A famous person living in our wee village, even if he is a sleazy old pervert.' Janette bundled Jo's meagre shopping into a flimsy plastic bag and handed it over. 'Can't believe it took me so long tae put two and two together.'

Jo headed for the door, and Janette called after her, 'Far be it from me to gossip, but a little bird told me she'd seen him round at yours on more than one occasion. None of my business, but I hope you'll proceed with caution from now on.' She tapped her nose, adding a wink for good measure.

'But if she didn't press charges, he wasn't convicted of anything.' Jo fumbled with the stubborn door handle, desperate to get home and switch on her laptop. Whatever the truth about Harvey, she'd find some answers on the internet.

'Aye, but you know how the old saying goes,' said Janette. 'There's no smoke without fire.'

CHAPTER 46

'WHAT HAVE YOU GOT TO LOSE, MAN?' HARVEY SCOURED HIS shower-warm skin with a towel more suited to sanding down floorboards.

He'd slept fitfully last night, his mouth drier than the Sahara and his empty stomach emitting rumbles of self-pity. After checking the clock every hour on the hour from two am, he surrendered and shuffled out of bed at six.

Now, his inner dialogue was switching between reasons to visit Jo and reasons why that would be an act of award-winning stupidity.

'The worst that can happen is that she refuses to see you. Or makes derogatory comments about your sexual prowess. No, that wasn't the problem. You being a major dickhead was the problem.'

Back and forth his thoughts scurried, Alka-Seltzer and paracetamol barely scratching the surface of his stomach problems and thumping headache. Still, he deserved the pain. At least he felt something, instead of the numbness that had followed Lindsey's death. Meeting Jo had taken an ice pick to his frozen heart and chiselled away until he felt something again. Something that felt a lot like love...

'Ach, you daft old sap, it's too soon to be thinking of the L word. Which is probably *loathing*, as far as Jo's concerned.' Harvey slapped on the dregs of a bottle of aftershave, a brand Lindsey had bought him every birthday and Christmas. Once this one ran out, he'd try something different.

Just after eight. Jo would be at the café, unless she'd handed over the reins to her young assistant. A strange girl, but if she helped lighten Jo's workload, who was he to criticise?

Dressed in a favourite shirt and dark jeans, Harvey paced around the cottage. To go or not to go, that was the question.

Are you waiting for a thumbs up from me? Or a middle finger, seeing as you're moving on?

Lindsey again, but somehow different. Not her beautiful, melodic voice, but a version that jarred his ears. Harvey's own voice, in fact. No whisperings from the grave, just his thoughts seeking airspace.

'You were never really here, were you?' Harvey choked back a sob as he stood in front of Lindsey's photo. 'Our conversations were all in my head. Of course they were, because however much I yearn to talk to you again, it will never happen. I can't keep chasing ghosts or shadows. I need to move on, Lindsey, and I know you'd give me your blessing.'

Before he could change his mind, Harvey removed the photo and took it upstairs. He slid it into the drawer of his bedside cabinet, next to a box containing Lindsey's engage-ment and wedding rings and the bundle of birthday, Christmas and Valentine's cards she'd given him over the years. Always quirky, often downright rude, but so very, very Lindsey.

'Sleep tight, my love. Out of sight, but never out of mind.

If I'm going to have any chance of fixing things with Jo, I need a clean slate. I'll tell her everything — about Abby, my career collapse, and my propensity for opening my mouth before engaging my brain. If she gives me another chance, I'll snatch it like a drowning man tossed a lifejacket. She's ... well, she's a good 'un.'

Eulogy over, Harvey grabbed his coat, put on his shoes, and gathered up his phone, wallet and keys. His cold heart defrosted another degree or two at the thought of seeing Jo and begging her to listen, to understand, and to accept that, damaged though he was, he believed in them. Two lonely people, colliding in a world mired in misery, who'd found a mutual attraction. Harvey had found true love before; was it too much to hope for a second chance?

* * *

PEERING through the window of A Bit of Crumpet, Harvey spied a handful of customers tucking into their drinks and snacks. There was no sign of Jo, just Aaliyah, stomping around with a sour face and a damp cloth.

Harvey greeted Aaliyah with a cheery smile. 'Is Jo not around?'

She responded by wiping a table occupied by two pensioners picking sultanas out of their fruit scones. 'Oy! Mind what you're doing, love. We might be saving those for later.' The man chuckled, moving a handful of discarded sultanas to one side.

'No, she is not.' Aaliyah glared at Harvey, venom shooting from her eyes. 'She went to check something on the internet.'

'Ah, online shopping, I suppose.' Lindsey had loved browsing for books and clothes online, although why Jo needed to dash off when she could easily have used her phone—

'Imbecile!' Aaliyah sank her nails into Harvey's arm and manhandled him into the back room, which was currently occupied by a swarthy young man he'd never seen before. He too regarded Harvey as if he'd risen from the bowels of Hell sporting horns and a pointy tail.

'What's your problem?' Harvey rubbed his arm, convinced he'd have puncture wounds.

'The problem is that you've upset Jo — again — and we're not happy about it. Are we, Dhassim?'

Swarthy Boy clicked his tongue to indicate his agreement. 'No, we are not. Jo is a special lady and we think you are taking the Mickey. Whoever Mickey is. I'm not sure what that actually means; I just heard it on a TV show.'

'Look, I know I upset Jo the other night, and I want to apologise. But you said I'd upset Jo again. I'm not sure what else I've done.' Harvey gave his head a metaphorical scratch. OK, he hadn't got in touch with Jo, but he was here now. Although she wasn't.

Aaliyah tutted loudly. 'You've been keeping secrets, but now the cat is out of the bag. Not an *actual* cat, Dhassim,' she added, as her companion scanned the floor. 'Jo's found out, and she's gone to read exactly what you did.'

Fear coursed through Harvey's veins. She could only be referring to one thing. If Jo now knew his dirty little secret, any chance of a reconciliation had just shattered like his precious memento of Lindsey. 'I have to go. Listen, I'm not a bad person, just a supremely stupid one. And I'm going to try to fix this.'

'Any chance of some service around here?' boomed an irate voice from the café, and Dhassim scuttled off. Aaliyah stayed put, disdain oozing from every pore.

'Good luck with that. Jo is my friend — well, kind of — and I don't take kindly to friends being lied to. She didn't say much before she left: just enough to suggest that you're not who you claim to be.'

Harvey considered an explanation, then realised that the only person he needed to explain anything to was Jo. Visions of her scrolling through the whole sordid Abby story brought bile to his mouth.

Haring along the road, Harvey sent up a silent prayer to a god he had no faith in. *Please let Jo believe my side of the story. Please let it not be too late...*

CHAPTER 47

Jo stared at the computer screen. Multiple tabs were open, all with one thing in common. They each contained articles about the fall from grace of actor Harley Dempster, former star of hit TV drama *Chasing Shadows*. She'd looked at countless photos of the man she'd grown close to, those distinctive blue eyes so familiar. Only a couple of the images showed the scar on his left cheek and the faint traces of youthful acne, no doubt covered with make-up for professional shots and filming. Even his hair looked different: much lighter, with a gelled spikiness.

An actor through and through, thought Jo, rereading the lurid details about his harassment of young co-star Abby Kinsella and the subsequent collapse of his career. 'You had me fooled for a while, Mr Whatever Your Bloody Name Is,' she muttered. 'Even Aaliyah got it right. Lucky I got your measure before I made a total fool of myself.'

She swiped at a rogue tear as she recalled their time together, both good and bad. On balance, the bad probably outweighed the good, so why was she crying? She knew he still grieved for his wife, in itself a reason to steer well clear.

What she hadn't known was that he'd stalked a young woman who still struggled with the fallout of being the object of someone's unwanted desires. Another, more recent article mentioned that Abby was taking part in a TV series focusing on women dealing with sexual harassment in the workplace.

'In this day and age it seems unimaginable that women like me still need to fight our corner over stuff like that.' A pretty girl — woman — but something about her jarred Jo. And something about the whole sorry situation niggled at her, like a wobbly tooth you had to keep prodding.

Innocent until proven guilty. Abby had never pressed charges against Harley/Harvey. Why not? Because she couldn't face the inevitable media circus? Or perhaps he'd threatened her, or had something on her that he could use to his own advantage if needed.

Jo massaged her temples, her fingertips trying to quell the tsunami of emotions pummelling her brain. Harvey had obviously run away to Cranley seeking anonymity. And he'd achieved it, until the village's version of Miss Marple uncovered his real identity.

'If he had nothing to be ashamed of, why didn't he tell me the truth?' Jo stared at a photo of Harvey taken at some showbiz event, a striking, dark-haired woman beside him. Lindsey, of course. Whatever else he'd lied about or omitted to mention, his love for his late wife shone like a beacon. Could Jo ever compete with a dead woman? Did she even want to?

Abby Kinsella's participation in the new TV show struck Jo as odd. Her allegations against Harvey had never been tested in a court of law, yet she was prepared to speak out about something that people were bound to connect with him. It brought to mind the downfall of a TV presenter many years ago, whose career had nosedived after sexual assault allegations provided endless tabloid fodder.

'I don't know what to think any more.' Jo closed all the tabs except one, a shot of Harvey from early in his career. Youthful optimism leapt from the image, his face an unlined canvas of hope. The scar stood out, but only added to his attractiveness. 'Oh, Harvey. I wish I could change things, but dishonesty is a deal-breaker for me. Even if I have been hiding the truth about Aaliyah and Dhassim—'

She jumped at a loud hammering at the front door. Oh God, had something awful happened at the café? Had Dhassim run amok with the cook's blowtorch, or had Aaliyah assaulted a customer?

Imagining a stern-faced firefighter or police officer ready to break bad news, Jo stumbled to the door and wrenched it open. Harvey stood there, fist raised to give the door another battering. At least, Jo hoped that was the reason for his clenched hand.

'I have a doorbell, you know.'

'Sorry. I just wanted to be sure you heard me.'

Jo felt sure that the entire street had heard him. 'You'd better come in, I guess.' She kept her tone neutral, determined to maintain the upper hand.

'I went to the café but you weren't there. Well, obviously, as you're here. And I got hauled over the coals by Aaliyah and some young guy, so I thought I'd better come and see you.'

'So you know your cover's been blown, Harvey. Or should I say Harley? Not terribly creative on the name-changing front, are you?' Jo headed for the lounge, Harvey trailing in her wake.

'Jo, you probably hate me right now, although I doubt you could hate me more than I hate myself. I never meant to hurt you: I just didn't want to drag you into the shitshow of my previous life.'

Before Jo could reply, Harvey approached the open laptop. He faced his younger self, beaming at the camera, and his shoulders drooped. 'Seems like an eternity ago,' he mumbled. 'How easy it is to lose everything you cherished and worked hard for. Gone, just like that' — he snapped his fingers — 'with no chance of getting it back.'

Jo sat down and gestured to the chair opposite. Weariness shrouded Harvey's entire being, his face a crumpled mockery of the image on the screen.

'Did you do it?' Whatever Jo had meant to say next, her directness took her by surprise.

'Did I stalk and sexually harass Abby? No, I didn't. I thought she was a friend, nothing more, but she twisted things. She saw it as a way to get her name in the press and amp up her profile.' Harvey gave Jo a crooked smile. 'I loved my job in *Chasing Shadows*, but grief still occupied my every waking thought. Abby was so kind at first, and I didn't have anyone else I could confide in. A real Billy No-Mates.'

Jo laughed, torn between wanting to slap him and give him a hug. 'Why didn't you stand up for yourself and tell the world the truth? If you did nothing wrong, why sit back and let her spread malicious lies?'

Harvey slumped down further in the chair, hands draped limply over his knees. 'Because I'd felt like a dead person masquerading as a living one for so long. When Abby took the time to talk to me — listen to me — I felt a glimmer of hope. That turned to despair when she turned against me, and I just didn't have the energy or strength to fight back.'

Jo reached out and squeezed Harvey's hand. She wished she could say or do something to ease Harvey's pain, but the right words eluded her. His touch stirred up a vortex of emotions. Compassion was in the lead, laced with a hint of lust. Totally incompatible, like herself and Harvey.

She withdrew her hand and tucked a strand of hair

behind her ear. 'I understand, I think. It's hard to fight back when you feel the world's against you, but there must be a way forward. If I can help in any way—'

Harvey bit his lower lip. A wash of red swept over his face, the silvery scar more pronounced than usual. Some scars were more visible than others, but the ones kept hidden inflicted the most pain. 'Jo, meeting you has been the best thing to happen to me in a very long time. I came to apologise, but I don't expect you to fall into my arms again. Friendship would do, if you'll have me.'

Aaliyah's nagging voice scratched at Jo's ear: *You have one wish left.* One chance to do something good, to make a difference.

'Harvey, of course I'll be your friend. And friends do nice things for each other, don't they?'

CHAPTER 48

'Let me get this clear. Lover boy repeatedly lied to you, pines for his dead wife, and freaks out when a mug gets broken. And you want to waste your last wish on him?'

Aaliyah smoothed a layer of caramel over the millionaire's shortbread she'd prepped earlier, while Dhassim stirred chunks of chocolate over a double boiler. Two genies, working in perfect culinary harmony. It would have been a camera-worthy moment, if Jo hadn't left her phone at home when she'd legged it back to the café.

'It's not a wasted wish: I really want to do something for him. My other wishes were about pleasing me, but now I can make a real difference to someone else's life.'

'And how exactly do you propose we do that? Wish for a personality transplant, or whisk him off to a remote island where no one gives a stuff about his dodgy past?' Aaliyah poured the molten chocolate over the calorie-laden shortbread and spread it evenly with a spatula.

'I don't know.' Jo slapped Dhassim's hand as he swirled a finger through the remnants in the bowl. 'I've given it some thought, but my head's in a guddle.'

Dhassim licked his finger in a manner befitting Nigella Lawson at her minxiest. 'Hmm. I am not sure what "guddle" means, but I guess you are confused. Do you love this man, Jo?'

Did she? If you looked up 'loveable' in a dictionary, Harvey's often-grouchy face and prickly demeanour wouldn't command the top of the page. And yet he'd got under her skin and reached a part of her that she hadn't known needed reaching. 'I don't know. I like him when he's not being a miserable sod. Maybe, given time, love might grow.'

'Jo, love isn't a pot plant. When it's right, it hits you like a thunderbolt. Like it did for us, ma petite saucisse.' Dhassim waggled his chocolatey finger at Aaliyah.

Aaliyah sniffed and pulled a face. 'Being called a sausage isn't exactly romantic, Dhassim, and we both know I needed a little persuasion.'

'You were putty in my hands from the moment you set eyes on me,' retorted Dhassim, going in for another swipe of congealing chocolate.

Jo resisted the urge to bang their heads together. She needed genie wisdom, not the pair of them arguing over whom Cupid's arrow had struck first. 'If we could focus for a minute on Harvey, that would be great—'

'Jo, are you there?' Jinnie's familiar voice echoed through the café, followed by a louder voice recognisable as her gran, Wilma.

'Sorry, love, I was just having a chat with the team. How are you both?' Jo greeted Jinnie and Wilma with a smile and the tray of gooey millionaire's shortbread.

'All the better for seeing that,' said Wilma, parking her trademark trolley and hefting herself into a chair. 'Two slices, please, and a pot of tea. Or would you rather a coffee, sweetie?'

Jinnie shook her head, shuddering. 'I don't know why, but lately the smell of coffee makes me heave. Sam gets through gallons a day and I usually join him, but now... I'll share the tea, thanks. And do you have one of your fab tuna rolls, Jo?'

Jo dealt with the order. She was still no further forward with Operation Harvey, as she'd mentally dubbed it moments before. That sounded exciting and covert, like something that might feature in *Chasing Shadows*. A show she intended to watch at some point, regardless of what happened with Harvey.

'You're a bit pale, Jinnie,' said Wilma. 'And that chocolate's no' set properly, Jo, not that it bothers me.' She used her teaspoon to scoop up a mouthful and sighed contentedly.

'I'm fine, Gran,' replied Jinnie. 'Have you any gherkins to go with the tuna, Jo?'

Unsure, Jo headed through to the back, where Aaliyah and Dhassim were huddled together, whispering furiously. 'Do we have any pickles?' she asked, rummaging in the fridge.

Dhassim gave a sheepish grin and pointed to a doorstep cheese sandwich surrounded by a mound of gherkins. 'I was famished, Jo, and I have acquired a taste for these little beauties. Mustard is a foul creation with no place anywhere, except for the bin.' He mimed retching as Aaliyah nonchalantly spread a thick layer of the vivid yellow condiment over her own ham sandwich.

'Well, Jinnie wants pickles, so if you don't mind...' Jo scooped several off Dhassim's plate and back into the jar. 'What are you two whispering about, anyway?'

Aaliyah grinned like a winded baby after a bout of colic. 'We've come up with a solution for your last wish. It came to me when I recalled watching a strange film about a musician who was the only person on earth to remember a famous group.'

'*Yesterday,*' replied Jo.

'It doesn't matter which day of the week I watched it,' huffed Aaliyah. 'The point is, we can undo things. Make things disappear, so that only one person remembers them. And that person would be you.'

'Eh?' Jo absent-mindedly nibbled on a gherkin, then made a face and spat it into her hand. She loathed the evil little things, all vinegary sourness.

'We can erase everything you want us to erase. Wipe the slate clean, so your man starts afresh. Although he always looks like he could do with a good wash. No offence meant.'

'None taken.' Jo grabbed a napkin and deposited the semi-chewed gherkin in it. 'Are you saying that I can wish for the whole Abby episode never to have happened? For a terrible moment, Jo wondered if Aaliyah meant that they could resurrect Harvey's wife. She cherished the extra time she'd had with her parents, but bringing someone back to life was something else entirely.

'Your wish, your choice,' said Aaliyah. 'Personally, I'd wish for a hunk of burning love to carry me off to a petal-strewn bed and stun me with his enormous—'

'Personality?' Jo took in Dhassim's dejected little face and tutted at Aaliyah. 'Sometimes, Aaliyah, you make puddles look shallow. I'm off to take these pickles to Jinnie. We can talk more later.'

Jo placed the jar of gherkins next to a delighted Jinnie, who speared a few onto her half-eaten tuna roll. There was no sign of Wilma, just a smattering of crumbs and a drained tea cup as evidence of her presence.

'Gran's popped out for a vape,' said Jinnie. 'So, what's new? I need a distraction from all the weirdness in my life. Sam's still acting peculiar — I've no idea what's going on — and I can't get my usual caffeine fix.'

Watching Jinnie scoff her roll with indecent haste, Jo batted away a thought. She needed to focus on the job in hand: what to do about Harvey. 'There's just the small matter of my final wish to deal with,' she said, keeping a watchful eye out for Wilma's return. 'It's a bit off the wall — something Aaliyah and Dhassim came up with — but it might change someone's life.'

Jinnie dabbed at her lips with a napkin. 'I'd be wary of anything those two dreamt up, but if you're OK with it…'

Wilma stomped back into the café, followed by Alison Gale. 'This wee lass needs a sugar fix, pronto.' She hustled Alison into a chair and Jo went to fetch a piece of the shortbread.

'What's up, Alison?' she asked, when she returned.

'Oh, just me being an idiot. I ordered a consignment of clothes from a company that turned out to be dodgier than Del Boy. Lesson learned.' Alison gratefully accepted the shortbread and a herbal tea.

'Ach, I've made mistakes in the past ordering on the internet,' said Wilma. 'I bought a pair of suck-it-all-in knickers once. They didnae so much suck in as shove my bits up to my chin. My belly and bosom were like neck warmers.'

Jinnie and Jo laughed. Alison looked bemused, but forced an awkward smile.

'I need to crack on, ladies.' Jo made her excuses and headed through to the back. *No more procrastinating. Time to put some genie magic into action...*

CHAPTER 49

A STEADY STREAM OF CUSTOMERS KEPT JO ON HER TOES FOR the rest of the day. Angie and Ed, oozing lovey-doveyness from every pore. Ken, looking exhausted, but still able to conjure up a wan smile. Janette and Peggy, the former sporting a white-blonde pixie cut courtesy of the latter. And finally, Sam, sent by Jinnie to pick up another tuna roll and a Danish pastry. There was no opportunity to put together a plan for Harvey's redemption. That would have to wait until the evening.

'How are things, Sam?' As Jo bagged up the goodies for Jinnie, she realised he looked almost as tired as Ken. Dark rings circled his eyes.

As if on cue, Sam gave a tonsil-revealing yawn. 'Knackered, to be honest,' he replied. 'Jinnie's been waking me up during the night...' A deep flush spread across his face. 'Sorry, not for — you know. Not that I'd mind, but, erm...'

Jo patted his hand, outstretched to take the bag. 'The thought never crossed my mind,' she fibbed. 'I spoke to Jinnie earlier and she seemed worried about you. Is everything OK?'

Sam nodded, then shook his head. 'I don't know, Jo. Apart from Jinnie being super restless and not sleeping, when I do drift off I get these crazy dreams. Mainly about lamps like those.' He eyed Aaliyah and Dhassim's lamps and shuddered. 'It's nuts, but I also hear voices telling me I'm the chosen one. Chosen for what? Damned if I know.'

Reassuring Sam that wacky dreams were completely normal — 'I recently dreamt of being marooned on a desert island with Hugh Jackman in full *Wolverine* mode!' — Jo said goodbye.

Once Sam had left, she flipped the café sign to closed and crumpled to the floor. Drawing her knees up to her chin, she practised a relaxation exercise she'd downloaded to help with anxiety. *Say the word 'relax' four times. Relax. Relax. Relax, Ree...laaaax.*

'Pet, are you asleep or unconscious?' Aaliyah nudged Jo hard with her toe.

Jo started, scrambling to her feet. She'd drifted off, this time with Harvey spoon-feeding her strawberries marinated in something alcoholic and delicious. 'I'm awake now. Thanks for the kick.' She dusted down the seat of her trousers.

'You've closed early,' said Aaliyah. 'Are you feeling sick?'

'You do look a bit pale,' added Dhassim. 'I overheard Sam talking about our lamps and being the chosen one. I think our suspicions are correct and he is connected to us, although he doesn't look like an all-powerful Djinn.'

'More like a librarian,' scoffed Aaliyah.

Before Jo could question a genie's familiarity with librarians, a pounding on the door interrupted her. She went to answer it.

'Jo.' It was Harvey, soaking wet from a sudden downpour that had turned the sky inky black.

'You really need to stop hammering on doors, you know.'

Jo stood aside to let him in. A puddle of water formed at his feet and he shook his head vigorously, droplets spraying Jo's face.

'Sorry. I just wanted to see you one last time.' Harvey removed a cloth handkerchief from his pocket and gently wiped away the rain splatters. Jo relished his touch, tiny jolts of electricity sparking through her body.

'What do you mean, one last time?' The sparks fluttered and died as she took in his grim expression. 'Harvey, you're scaring me.'

Muffled giggles behind her reminded Jo that genie ears were flapping. 'Can you two tidy up in the back and be ready to leave in ten minutes?' Jo locked the door and waited until the giggles subsided.

'I just can't stay here any longer.' Harvey returned the hankie to his pocket. 'Messing you around, knowing that word will soon spread about who I am and what I'm supposed to have done.'

'But you *didn't* do it!' Jo curled her hands into fists. 'You ran away before. Running away again isn't the answer.'

'I don't know what else to do, Jo.' Harvey closed his eyes and exhaled, swaying slightly. Moving closer, Jo detected a whiff of alcohol on his breath. Now wasn't the time to be judgemental, though. The man had already been unfairly judged. 'Sit down, please.' Jo pulled out a chair.

Harvey shook his head. 'I need to go and pack my things. I've booked a bed and breakfast in Edinburgh for a couple of nights till I figure out what to do next.'

'So what was all that about us being friends?' Jo's voice grew louder as irritation competed with sympathy. 'I said I'd help you and I meant it. Don't you trust me?'

Harvey shook his head again, looking down at the floor. 'I don't trust myself. I've anger issues, grief issues and a talent for hurting people. It's better I move away and leave you in peace, Jo.'

Frustration flooded every fibre of Jo's being. She was so, so close to making that last wish: the one that would put Harvey's life back on track and allow her to lead a genie-free existence. But if he left, where would that leave her?

'Harvey, please don't go. Stay. Or we can meet up later and—'

'Let him go, Jo.' Aaliyah stepped between them, hands on hips, nostrils flaring like an irate donkey. 'He does not deserve you. There are plenty more fish in the sea.'

'Poissons dans la mer,' added Dhassim, sidling up to Aaliyah. 'It sounds much better in French.'

'Can you two go home and fix some dinner? There's fish fingers and chips in the freezer.' Jo's mouth twisted at the irony of eating something fishy after their comments.

'As long as there's tartare sauce,' said Aaliyah.

'Ketchup for me,' said Dhassim.

'Just *go!*' Jo slammed the door behind them and faced Harvey. His face was full of sorrow and regret. Something twanged inside her, and she wrapped her arms around him. At first he resisted, then buckled in her embrace.

'Don't leave.' Jo pressed her lips against his stubbly cheek, maintaining her grip as he rocked back and forth.

'I can't stay,' mumbled Harvey, stroking the back of Jo's head with exquisite tenderness. 'A beautiful, generous woman like you deserves much better than me. I'm just glad I had a little time with you, even though I made a pig's ear of everything.'

'You don't get to decide what I deserve.' Jo clung to Harvey, a chasm of despair opening up between them. 'Only I can do that.'

Harvey fingered his scar. 'If I could turn back time and be

the kind of man worthy of someone like you, then maybe...'
His hands dropped to his sides and he let out a groan.

'Harvey, I can't force you to stay. But I can ask you to do one thing for me.'

He frowned as Jo took a step closer. 'What's that?'

Jo took a deep breath. 'Kiss me.'

Harvey hesitated, then complied. A butterfly touch at first, growing in intensity. Jo responded, closing her eyes and losing herself in the moment. A moment that ended almost as quickly as it began.

'I could kiss you forever, Jo.' Harvey breathed heavily, his words weighted with regret. 'Meeting you was magical, but we both know magic isn't real.'

Isn't it? Jo reluctantly stepped aside as Harvey headed for the door.

'Take care of yourself, Jo. I know you'll meet someone wonderful, and... Well, I wish things could have been different.'

Jo didn't watch as Harvey walked out of her life. If all went to plan, he'd soon be back in it. If he wanted to be...

CHAPTER 50

'YOU REALLY WANT TO DO THIS?' AALIYAH DUNKED A FISH finger into a pool of tartare sauce. Her sparkly WIFI emitted a series of jingles and beeps as it vibrated on the kitchen table.

'Use your wish wisely,' intoned Dhassim, shovelling a handful of chips into his mouth.

'With all due respect, you two, I've thought long and hard about it.' Jo pushed away her plate, nerves clawing at her insides. OK, long and hard might be a stretch, but it felt the right thing to do. Jo didn't know if flipping the reverse switch on Harvey's life would make *her* happy, but that wasn't the point.

'If you don't want yours...' Dhassim pulled Jo's plate towards him, his eyes alight with glee at the cooling leftovers.

Jo marvelled again at how ridiculous her life had become. Host to two genies, smitten with a man she'd disliked at first sight, and now planning to defy the laws of the universe. Could it really work? 'Let's do it. If you've finished shoving food down your necks, that is.'

Her patience dwindled further when Dhassim raided the biscuit barrel for Jaffa Cakes and Aaliyah flounced upstairs, muttering something about needing to retouch her lip gloss.

As they waited for Aaliyah, Jo wondered what Harvey was doing. She pictured him packing a small suitcase, tossing in a handful of toiletries, probably nursing a large glass of whisky. She wondered if he'd already given notice on Brae Cottage, and her stomach tightened.

'Right, pet, let's get this over and done with.' Aaliyah smacked her freshly lacquered lips and reached for her WIFI.

'Wait!' Jo snatched away the WIFI. It felt warm to the touch and gave out a steady hum, like a bee flitting from flower to flower. 'If I make my last wish, will you both disappear?'

'Don't sound so enthusiastic about us leaving.' Dhassim pouted. 'I was heartbroken when I left Jinnie, and I'm sure she felt the same.'

I doubt it. Yet Jo felt a pang of guilt at her desire to see the pair of them slither back into their lamps. They'd stuck around like reliable old knickers. Useful at times, but now they definitely needed to go.

'We still have unfinished business,' said Aaliyah. 'Sam, and his plans for us. We will not leave until we know our fate.'

Jo envisioned cramming them back into their lamps and delivering them to Sam, leaving Jinnie to explain the unorthodox contents. That probably wasn't an option.

'You need to say the wish out loud, in case you've forgotten.' Aaliyah clicked her fingers impatiently and Jo passed over the WIFI.

'I'm not sure how to phrase it exactly. Should I wish for things to go back to how they were for Harvey?'

'Before when, ma chérie?' Dhassim licked the chocolate off his last Jaffa Cake. 'You said some woman had told lies about him. Ooh, what is that funny way you have of saying lies? Porky pies! You know, Jo, I am still a little hungry.'

Aaliyah drummed her fingernails on the table. 'Right, you want to wipe out everything she said or did, so his life returns to the point before that?'

'Yes, I think so. Oh heck, I don't know! My other wishes were a piece of cake compared to this. And no, Dhassim, I don't have any bloody cake.' Jo ground her knuckles against her forehead, as if doing so would extract the correct wording to get the wish up and running. *Think, Jo, think.*

Then, as if a cartoon light bulb had lit up above her head, she had it. 'OK. Here goes. I wish… I wish for Harvey to be happy.'

Total silence. Even Aaliyah's WIFI went quiet, after a small string of squeaks that sounded suspiciously like farts.

Aaliyah gave an incredulous snort. 'That's it?'

'Jo, you must think a little longer.' Dhassim draped an arm around Jo's shoulder and gave her an encouraging squeeze.

'I don't have to.' Jo swallowed a hard lump of worry at what she might be doing. She had the chance to wipe the slate clean for Harvey, but it didn't feel right. He'd struggled — was still struggling — with the fallout from Abby's self-serving claims, but she knew he'd get through it. 'Harvey needs to get back in the work saddle. If I wish for him to be happy, he'll find a way forward. With or without me.'

A wave of tears gathered force and stormed Jo's cheeks. She snatched up a wad of tissues, remembering Harvey's old-school cloth hankie, and mopped her face.

'You humans are so weird. You've got a chance to make a real difference, but you go for happy. What even is that?'

Jo looked at Aaliyah through a haze of tears. 'It's when you feel good about yourself. Despite all the bad stuff, you find a way to put one foot in front of the other. You wake up with hope and go to sleep with it, too. It's simple, really.' A picture of her parents and the second-chance time she'd had with them flashed into her mind, a brief but glorious bubble of happiness that still buoyed her spirits.

Aaliyah didn't look convinced. 'Seems a waste to me, but it's your wish. Let's get on with it.'

They huddled around the WIFI. Its bout of flatulence over, it returned to beeps, jingles and flashing lights.

'If you wish for Harvey to be happy, that doesn't mean he'll stay in Cranley.' Dhassim gave Jo a sad smile.

'I know, but at least he'll be able to move forward. I read somewhere that happiness is letting go of what you think your life is supposed to look like.' Before she could change her mind, Jo intoned: 'I wish for Harvey to be happy.'

Aaliyah peered at her WIFI and gave a thumbs up. 'Your wish is granted. I guess your man will be doing cartwheels round his living room right now.'

If he hasn't already left, thought Jo. *There's only one way to find out...*

CHAPTER 51

Jo stood on the doorstep of Brae Cottage, listening to loud music blaring from inside. Its poky windows rattled in time to Pharrell Williams singing about ... being happy.

After another futile attempt at ringing the doorbell, Jo whipped out her phone and fired off a WhatsApp message. She stared at the screen, willing the double tick to appear. A minute later it did, and Pharrell ceased his warbling.

'Jo!' Harvey flung open the door, grinning like a cross between the Cheshire Cat and the Joker. It was slightly unnerving, and in sharp contrast to his usual dour expression. 'Come in, come in.'

Jo stepped into the hallway and gulped at the sight of a small holdall and a laptop bag propped up in the corner. So he was leaving after all.

'Dance with me.' Harvey seized Jo's hand and twirled her around, which was no mean feat in a narrow hallway. Jo's elbow collided with the wood chip wallpaper and she yelped.

'Sorry, sorry.' In a bizarre pastiche of the Gay Gordons, Harvey led Jo through to the living room, twisting her this way and that until she feared he'd strangle her.

'Harvey...' Jo wriggled free and flopped into a chair. 'I need a breather.' She scanned the room: nothing had changed since her last visit. Nothing, except ... the mantelpiece was bare.

'You seem a little different.' Jo eyed Harvey warily. Had her wish turned him into someone in need of medication to dampen his Tigger-like enthusiasm?

'I am, Jo.' Harvey's smile dialled down a notch or two. 'I can't explain, but something weird happened when I left you. Not right away, but when I started packing to leave.'

'Are you still going to leave?' Jo squirmed in the chair as a wayward spring poked her bum.

Harvey did a hop-skip jig. He appeared to be possessed by the ghosts of ceilidhs past, with long-dead pipers whirling and skirling for his ears only. 'Not right away, no.'

In an attempt to find comfort, Jo swung her legs over the arm of the chair. *Better.* She waited for Harvey to continue.

'I felt dizzy scrambling under the bed for shoes and stuff, so I had a wee lie down for a minute or two. Then I carried on packing my stuff and plonked the bags by the door, but something inside me had changed. All the bitterness and anger had evaporated, as if by magic.'

'But you don't believe in magic,' said Jo, raising an eyebrow.

Harvey continued jigging on the spot, as if the threadbare carpet were electrified. He looked so ridiculous that Jo started laughing. A genteel giggle at first, turning into a full-blown bout of hysteria. *What have I done?*

'I'll, erm, sit down now.' Harvey ceased his jigging and sat down opposite Jo. Beads of sweat trickled from his brow, and his hands continued to beat a tattoo on his thighs.

'Can I get you a drink? Water, or something stronger?' Jo needed water herself. Her laughing fit threatened to induce hiccups, and the situation was mad enough without adding that into the mix.

In the kitchen, Jo found two glasses and went to fill them at the sink, which was itself full of empty whisky and wine bottles. She stacked them on the draining board and returned with the water. 'Did you go on a bender before your epiphany?' she asked, handing Harvey his glass.

He shook his head, his demeanour thankfully more relaxed. 'When the weird feeling hit me, I went to have a drink. The smell made my stomach heave, so I tipped the lot away.' His eyes twinkled, and he knocked back his water in one gulp.

Jo sipped hers, the desire to hiccup abating. She watched Harvey warily, unsure what to say next.

Luckily, Harvey's newfound happiness had also given him the gift of the gab. 'I feel like a new man, Jo. It's incredible, as if an enormous cloud's been lifted and I can see sunshine instead of rain. I'm not going to break into song, I promise.' Harvey beamed at Jo. 'All this time I've dwelt on the negatives. I festered in a pool of resentment towards Abby and everyone who'd turned their back on me. Yes, I was grieving for Lindsey, but she'd kick my pathetic butt for being such a loser. In fact…' He hesitated, then dragged his chair next to Jo's. The smile stayed on his face, but a hint of apprehension lowered its corners.

'What is it?' Jo edged closer, ignoring the chair spring's fresh assault on her rear.

'For a while now, I've heard Lindsey talking to me. I told you that before, didn't I? Anyway, obviously it wasn't *actually* Lindsey, although at times I felt it was. And it helped, because she always knew the right things to say. Crazy, I know.'

Harvey paused for breath and Jo's heart contorted at the look of love his late wife's name invoked. No man had ever looked at her like that, and she doubted one ever would. Except… They'd had *something* together, hadn't they? A smattering of moments, a handful of, well, happiness. Was there a collective noun for the sparks when two people come together and hit it off? A glitter of goodness, perhaps.

'I don't think it's crazy at all.' Jo thought again of the comfort she drew from her memories of her parents. The expressions they used; how they always backed her up, even when she messed up. 'We all have voices in our heads: hopefully good ones.'

Harvey nodded. 'Yep. Ones telling us to commit murder wouldn't be very appealing.'

Jo laughed, and Harvey joined in. No hysteria this time, just normal, comforting chuckles.

'So, Mr Happy Pants, what's your next move?' He'd said he wouldn't leave just yet, but surely, if he wanted to resuscitate his acting career…

Harvey gave Jo's knee a gentle squeeze. Her pulse increased, and pleasurable tingles flooded her body. She hoped he'd move in for a more intimate squeeze, but— Damn it, he galloped off to the dining table and flipped open his laptop. 'I'm going to finish this. My screenplay.' He swept a hand in front of the screen. 'It took rather a dramatic turn recently. It might end up never seeing the light of day, but I'm going to finish it.'

'That's fantastic,' said Jo, wishing he'd hurry back. Then she reminded herself that she'd wished for Harvey to be happy, and that didn't guarantee he'd be happy with *her*.

'And I've emailed my so-called agent, Arthur, to end our contract. He slithered under a stone when the whole Abby saga unfolded, and now he can stay there. I'll find a new agent and get my career up and running again. I'll start from the bottom if I have to, but right now I feel positive. As if anything is possible.'

'It is.' Despite her fear of losing him, Jo couldn't help being caught up in his enthusiasm. 'Everything's there for the taking, Harvey. If you believe in yourself, magic really can happen.'

Jo got up to leave. Harvey needed time to deal with his newfound joie de vivre, and there was still the small matter of two genies lurking at home.

Harvey bounded over and stood in front of Jo. 'Where are you going?'

'I need to, erm, talk to Dhassim and Aaliyah. I think they might be leaving soon, too.' The words snagged in Jo's throat, the thought of everyone departing bringing tears to her eyes.

'Jo, I'm not leaving soon.' Harvey took her hands, his gaze questioning. 'Unless you want me to, of course.'

Jo shook her head. 'Of course I don't, you daft man! But you've a lot to sort out. I don't want to get in your way.'

Harvey pulled her into his arms, and Jo snuggled into his chest. It felt like a safe place, his heartbeat soothing and synching with her own. After a moment, he loosened his grip and tilted Jo's chin to look into her face. 'Jo, I might be speaking out of turn, but I think I'm falling in love with you. Maybe you don't feel the same way, but I hope—'

Jo silenced him with a kiss. A long, luscious kiss that told him all he needed to know.

CHAPTER 52

'YOU CANNOT BE SERIOUS!' SAM LOOKED FROM JINNIE TO JO and back again. He blinked rapidly and ran a hand through his already ruffled hair.

'It's true, Sam. Don't ask me to explain, but somehow you're the link to Aaliyah and Dhassim. I think the right terminology is a Djinn.'

Jo had locked up the cafe and ordered Aaliyah and Dhassim to stay in the back room until she gave them the all-clear. Now, she and Jinnie faced Sam, who wore the expression of someone who'd learned that Santa Claus was real, the Tooth Fairy existed, and as for the Easter Bunny...

'This is nuts! I got the lamps from a house clearance ages ago. OK, the lady who sold them seemed a bit jittery, but that doesn't mean I'm some kind of genie master.'

Jinnie grabbed Sam's hand and squeezed it.

'Can you squeeze harder, or pinch me, because this really cannot be happening?' Sam shook his head so hard that his glasses tumbled off his head and clattered to the floor. Jinnie bent down to retrieve them at the same time as Sam, and they clunked heads on the way up.

'Ouch!'

'Double ouch!'

Jo smiled wryly as the couple rubbed each other's bruised bonces. That was how it had all begun, really. A rub of an innocuous object, bringing forth beings who defied rational explanation. Beings currently squabbling in the back room, judging by their raised voices.

'Jinnie. I knew there was something strange going on, but this is entering the realm of stark raving bonkers. Why didn't you say anything before?'

'Because you'd have thought I was stark raving bonkers and run a mile.' Jinnie looked at Jo for affirmation.

Jo shrugged and smiled at Sam. 'I had three wishes. To spend time with my parents again, and to win a TV baking show. As for my third...'

'Yours are so much worthier than mine!' Jinnie flipped her immaculate locks away from her face. 'I got perfect hair, a fancy-schmancy TV, incredible cocktail-making skills and a magic-carpet ride. Oh, and something else.' Jinnie halted, colour flaming in her cheeks. 'A wish I didn't need because it had already come true.'

'To meet the love of your life and live happily ever after?' Sam's tight features softened. 'You didn't need magic to make me fall in love with you. Not that I'm suggesting that's what you wished for, but— Hang on, doesn't that make five wishes?'

Enter Dhassim stage left, closely followed by Aaliyah. He gave a dramatic bow, while Aaliyah chomped on a piece of gum and glowered at the cafe's occupants. 'Ah, Sam the man! My beautiful lady and I disagree on the wish-giving front. It all comes down to our WIFIs—'

'Wish Instigating Finder Instruments, in case you're not up to speed with genie parlance,' added Aaliyah, blowing an extravagant bubble.

'Jinnie had some bonus wishes, that is all. Jo had three, but I will let her explain.'

Jo blushed, and Jinnie nudged her with a broad grin. Jo had already filled her in about Harvey, who was currently battering away at his screenplay with glee.

'Sam is the ultimate master of our fates. He dictates when we return to our lamps and who will be the next lucky recipients. We thought—' Dhassim glanced at Aaliyah, who made a 'get on with it' gesture. 'We thought Sam might be the embodiment of evil, but we now know he's a pussycat. With awesome powers.'

'OK, Dhassim,' said Sam. 'I get the picture, though it's beyond mind-boggling. And pardon my scant knowledge of genie mythology, but aren't Djinns usually evil, or in animal form?'

'Ooh, I can just imagine you as a wily old fox, you silver-streaked rascal!' Dhassim slapped his thigh like an excitable pantomime hero. 'Of course you're not evil. Is he, my saucy soulmate?'

Aaliyah picked at a corner of chipped nail polish. 'We had our doubts for a while, but by pairing our WIFIs and tuning into the FBI—'

'I assume you don't mean the Federal Bureau of Investigation?' Sam raised a bemused eyebrow. 'Don't tell me I'm on the Most Wanted list for crimes against lamp dwellers.'

'No, silly. It stands for the Federation of Benign Intelligent Beings.' Dhassim slapped his thigh again. Jo prayed for the bell to signal the arrival of a customer.

'Erm, that's FBIB,' said Jinnie. 'Not to be nit-picky or anything.'

'Whatever.' Aaliyah yawned, revealing a well-masticated wad of gum. 'Anyway, the FBI*B*' — she put extra emphasis on the final 'B' — 'confirmed that your man is totes legit, pet. A proper, bona fide Djinn, even if he looks like an accountant with starch in his knickers.'

'I'll try not to take offence at that,' said Sam. 'Jinnie, how exactly did you discover that I was a Djinn? I'm assuming Laurel and Hardy here didn't enlighten you right away.'

Bang on cue, Dhassim scratched his head and Aaliyah huffed out an irritated breath. 'For your information, we had you sussed for a while, even if we didn't know if you were a goodie or a baddie.'

'Oh, he's definitely a goodie,' cooed Jinnie. 'I can vouch for that.'

The look of exquisite tenderness that Sam gave Jinnie made Jo's insides skitter around. Once upon a time, she could only have dreamt of a man looking at her like that. Now… She wrapped her arms around herself, imagining Harvey's warm embrace and kisses that transported her to heaven.

'Jo, stop fondling yourself and get with the programme!' Aaliyah pointed at the two lamps, now resting on a table.

'So, what happens next?' Jinnie asked Sam, who shrugged, blank-faced.

Dhassim stepped forward. 'In order for us to return to our vessels, Sam must incant the ancient words as laid down in the Charter For Harmonious Upstanding Genies. CHUG, for short.'

Everyone looked at Sam, whose expression remained baffled with a side order of bewilderment. 'Forgive me for not incanting right away, but I have absolutely no idea what I'm supposed to say.'

'Close your eyes and focus, and the words will come,' urged Dhassim.

'Get on with it!' grouched Aaliyah. 'If I have to sift any more flour or assemble another sodding Battenberg cake, I'll scream my head off.'

'You'll miss me, really,' said Jo.

'Ha! As if! Well, maybe a teeny tiny bit.' Aaliyah stared at Jo, and Jo stared back. To her amazement, something that might just be a tear glistened in Aaliyah's eye. She swiped at it, mumbling something about a stray eyelash.

'I will miss you, Jo,' said Dhassim, who looked on the verge of a full-blown howling session. 'And you, Jinnie. I only hope our new masters will be as kind as you have been, and that we will meet again. I cannot say where, or when—'

'Jeez, cut the Vera Lynn impression, and let me get on with it!'

An irate Sam bowed his head, and everyone around him followed suit. Silence reigned, barring the thrum of the coffee machine going through its cleaning cycle.

'OK, here goes.'

Sam, Jinnie, Aaliyah, Dhassim and Jo grasped each other's hands, forming a séance-like group. The silence stretched thin, then— 'Erm, can you two pop back into your lamps, please?'

'Sam, that is the most rubbish all-powerful Djinn thing I've ever heard. Not that I've heard one before, but…' Jinnie doubled up with laughter. Jo laughed too, while Dhassim and Aaliyah exchanged frustrated frowns.

'Sam, mon ami, delve deeper into your Djinn consciousness,' pleaded Dhassim. 'The words are there: you just need to … excavate them.'

'Is this an archaeological dig, or what?' Exasperation flooded Sam's face.

Jinnie giggled again, then let out a loud burp. 'Oops, sorry. Heartburn.'

'Right. I'm digging deep. I could do with a script but … here goes.' Sam inhaled, and everyone else held their breath. 'By the power vested in me as an almighty Djinn, supreme being and protector of genies, Dhassim and

Aaliyah, I command you to return to your lamps. Now, please.'

The café plunged into darkness. The windows rattled, and the temperature plummeted. A strange wailing sound reverberated around the room, followed by a loud bang, then … silence.

'Is it over?' whispered Jo, blinking as the lights came back on.

The trio looked at the two lamps, tipped on their sides, a faint mist hovering above them.

'I believe it is,' said Sam. 'For now.'

CHAPTER 53

ONE MONTH LATER

'RIGHT A BIT. Left a bit. Just a little higher. Nearly there. Ooh, that's perfect!' Jo squirmed with delight as Harvey kneaded a particularly hard knot of tension in her right shoulder.

'You need to get another assistant, my love,' said Harvey, applying firmer pressure to the troublesome spot. 'I love coming in to help, but with me heading off to London soon...'

Jo reached back and squeezed his hand. 'I know, I know. I've asked Angela if she can help, and Jinnie's mucked in a couple of times, but...'

Harvey kissed the top of Jo's head. 'You think she's unwell, don't you? Have you suggested that she sees a doctor?'

Jo reluctantly got to her feet from her cosy position wedged between Harvey's muscular thighs. 'Not unwell, exactly.' Jinnie's last shift at the café had ended abruptly when she heaved the contents of her stomach into the food-waste bin. Jo didn't need a medical degree to guess why, but it wasn't her place to make a diagnosis. Jinnie and Sam — Sam, in particular — were still reeling after the whole Djinn thing. Both lamps now lived at their home. Where they ended up next was anyone's guess.

'It's a shame Aaliyah and Dhassim disappeared so abruptly,' said Harvey, fetching a chilled glass of Coke for Jo and an alcohol-free beer for himself. 'Was it something you said?' He laughed, already knowing the 'truth,' and tipped a packet of mature Cheddar and red onion crisps into a bowl.

Jo had invented a story about Aaliyah, Carole's 'daughter', rushing back to Wales to assist with Carole's wedding to the divine Austin. As for Dhassim... She'd simply said he was a friend of Aaliyah's who'd had to rush off for an urgent appointment with a gastroenterologist following a severe bout of stomach pain. The lad was certainly full of wind at times.

'I'll miss you.' Jo ran a finger round the condensation clinging to the glass.

'I'll miss you, too.' Harvey proffered the bowl of crisps. Jo declined and sipped her drink. 'It's only for a few days, and it might come to nothing, but... The world's waiting for my ugly mug to appear on screen again, right?'

By some miracle, Harvey's agent, Arthur Petch, had pulled an audition out of the bag. Shocked into action by Harvey's threat of binning him, he'd found a role as a late-to-fatherhood dad dealing with the harsh realities of nappies, sleepless nights, and juggling work with his failing marriage.

'You'll be a shoo-in,' said Jo. 'I can feel it in my bones. My achy old bones.'

Harvey's progress on his screenplay kept him occupied when he wasn't with Jo at A Bit of Crumpet. After much begging from Jo, he'd allowed her to read a few scenes, which she declared 'genius'.

'There is nothing old about you, beautiful lady. Heck, you're still in your forties, while I'm galloping towards the big 6-0. Well, maybe not galloping: more lolloping with extreme trepidation.'

Jo put down her glass and planted a Coke-chilled kiss on Harvey's lips. 'Silly man, you're miles away from sixty! Anyway, you're only as old as the woman you feel. But don't go feeling any younger ones...' Her voice tailed off as she realised what she'd said. They'd agreed not to mention Abby, focusing on positives and Harvey's newfound happiness. Now she'd put her size five feet right in it.

'Hey, why the long face?' Harvey shook his head and enveloped Jo in a bear hug. 'You don't need to censor everything you say, Jo. It was a joke, and I'm much better at taking those these days. And hell will freeze over before I risk losing you.'

* * *

An hour later, they entered A Bit of Crumpet. Jo had stayed closed for the morning, determined to devote more time to herself and Harvey. She couldn't bring herself to call him Harley yet. Let folks grumble: there were more important things in life than keeping Cranley's residents filled with pastries and pies.

'Right, boss, what needs doing?' Harvey donned his apron, emblazoned with 'An Apron Is Just A Cape On Backwards.' It was a gift from Jo, and it still made her smile.

'If you could rustle up some chocolate-chip cookies, I'll get on with the Cornish pasties,' said Jo.

'I don't like chocolate, remember?' Harvey twirled his apron around and adopted a superhero stance. 'But for the woman of my dreams, I'll do anything.'

Laughing, Jo went through to the back to find the chocolate chips. *Mice droppings*, as Aaliyah had dubbed them. Where would she and Dhassim pop up next, and was it really in Sam's hands? The whole Djinn thing still baffled Jo, but trying to make sense of it all was like attempting to climb Kilimanjaro in ballet slippers.

'Kiss me quick before I get down to business.' Harvey pulled Jo close and she surrendered to a long and delicious smooch, which was sadly interrupted by the not-so-dulcet tones of Janette.

'Thought you'd run off with your new man,' she huffed, when Jo appeared. 'I passed by earlier and you were shut. And I'd promised myself a wee steak bake and a cappuccino.'

Jo apologised, saw to Janette's order, and grinned at Harvey crooning 'That's Amore' from the kitchen, with more pizazz than Dean Martin at his peak. 'He's a good man, Janette,' she said, not for the first time. Since Janette's uncovering of Harvey's past, Jo had tried to explain how he'd been wrongly accused, but she suspected the words fell on deaf ears.

'Hello, Janette.' Harvey emerged, stirring a bowl of cookie dough and treating Janette to his meanest, moodiest stare. Janette shuddered, grabbed her order and left as quickly as she'd arrived.

'Not my Number One fan,' commented Harvey wryly. 'Although the only fan-club member that counts is you.'

Jo ushered him back into the kitchen, ready to crack on with the pasties. She hesitated, her gaze drawn to the shelf where the lamps had once sat. It all seemed unreal: a dream she'd woken from, an episode in her life never to be repeated.

'Wherever you are, and wherever you go next, I wish you well,' Jo whispered. 'Thank you for the wishes you granted me. And maybe we *will* meet again, one day.'

ACKNOWLEDGMENTS

My fifth book! It took far longer to complete than I'd hoped, but now it's out there in all its mad glory…

A huge thanks again to the talented Lisa Firth at Fully Booked for the stunning cover. Lisa has designed all my covers, and nails it every time.

Editing is vital to ensure a book emerges into the world in the best possible shape. Liz Hedgecock took on board my rough manuscript and kicked it into shape, in the nicest possible way. Any errors that remain are entirely down to me.

I'd like to thank so many Facebook groups and Twitter friends for supporting and helping me along the way. When you're wallowing in doubt, a little word of encouragement means so much. Social media gets a bad press, but I've generally found it a kind and friendly place.

Finally (are you still awake)? can I just say thank you for reading this. When it's five o'clock in the morning and I'm clattering away at the keyboard, staring at the screen through tired eyes, it's you who keeps me going. Knowing that someone enjoys these stories I make up is a wonderful feeling, and I appreciate it more than you know.

If you have just a moment more, I really need your help. Today's blockbuster authors have publishers who don't mind spending millions promoting their books, but I have something better. I have you! If you enjoy what I write, you can play a huge part in keeping these stories flowing, simply by sharing.

Readers trust other readers. Would you please leave a review on Amazon? (Reviews are the lifeblood of today's authors). After that, if you're a social media user, please help to spread the word. Tell your friends, share your review, mention me over a cup of coffee. Whether it's Facebook, Twitter, Pinterest, Instagram or down the pub, I'd be eternally grateful if you'd be part of my team and help get the word out.

Thank you! ♥♥ Audrey

ABOUT THE AUTHOR

Audrey Davis published her first romantic comedy novel *A Clean Sweep* in 2017, followed by a short prequel, *A Clean Break*. She originally released her second book *The Haunting of Hattie Hastings* as a novella trilogy, before combining it into a standalone novel. Her third — *A Wish For Jinnie* — released in June 2020, followed by *Lost In Translation* in January 2021.

Audrey lives in Switzerland with her husband and enjoys shopping, cooking, eating and drinking red wine. And — of course — reading and writing. She is a social media addict, so please get in touch through FB, Twitter or Instagram. Or, you can sign up to her newsletter where she babbles on about books, hair and other exciting subjects. www.getrevue.co/profile/audrey_cowie

For a **free** short prequel to *The Haunting of Hattie Hastings*, just pop over to to sign up for your copy of *When Hattie Met Gary*. www.audreydavisauthor.com

Finally, authors love to be followed on Bookbub, as it helps raise our profile and offers us more promo opportunities. Plus, you'll hear from them when the next book is out!

ALSO BY AUDREY DAVIS

A Clean Sweep

The Haunting of Hattie Hastings

A Wish For Jinnie

Lost In Translation

Printed in Great Britain
by Amazon